Finding Southern Comfort

by

Barbara Lohr

Purple Egret Press

Purple Egret Press
Savannah, Georgia 31411

This book is a work of fiction. The characters, events and places in the book are products of the author's imagination and are either fictitious or used fictitiously. Any similarity of real persons, living or dead, is purely coincidental and not intended by the author.

Cover Art: Kim Killion – The Killion Group
Editing: Nicole Zoltack

Print ISBN: 978-0-9908642-1-9
Digital ISBN: 978-0-9908642-0-2

for

Gianna

Chapter 1

Harper Kirkpatrick shoved her Catwoman mask into place and rang the doorbell. Hard to look casual with a whip under her arm. A late evening breeze ruffled the Spanish moss overhead. Didn't matter. She was sweating big time under the black spandex costume. Savannah in February was a lot warmer than Chicago.

An older woman answered the door. "Yes?"

"I'm the entertainment for the party."

She stood aside. "Right this way, please. I'm Connie."

The heels of Harper's black boots clicked on the white marble floor as she followed Connie inside. Pink tulips drooped in a crystal vase on a long hall table. Harper sure hoped they were fake. Holding her breath, she scurried past.

Bypassing a parlor stuffed with antiques, Connie led her around the wide staircase where etchings of the Savannah squares hung above the wainscoting. She'd studied those squares as a design student and knew them well. A wide archway opened into a library and beyond that she glimpsed a dimly lit dining room with a long shiny table.

Pretty snazzy, as her mom would say. These sprawling southern mansions felt so elegant compared to the solid brick houses in Oak Park, the Chicago suburb where Harper grew up. Still, why was this house so quiet? Where were the birthday party decorations, the cake and the kids? The back of her neck prickled. In the three months she'd worked for Party Perfect, this was a first. Something wasn't right.

The note from Rizzo was tucked under the spandex so she couldn't check.

Good grief, had she goofed up again?

"Here you go, miss." Connie yanked open a door under the staircase. Raucous male laughter shot up a narrow stairway.

"Thanks, Connie." Harper reached for the handrail. These suckers looked steep. The door closed behind her, and she was left in the darkness. Maybe the children had brought their parents? She started down. Her wired tail flailed the steps, almost keeping time to the music.

"Keep 'em in line," Rizzo had told her with one of his sleazy grins.

Sure. Right. She'd thought he was talking about rambunctious first graders, not the howling group below.

A man waited at the foot of the stairs. The low lighting glinted off blond hair when he glanced at his Rolex. "You're late."

"Sorry, I had trouble finding the—"

"I'm Cameron Bennett and you're thirty minutes late."

Her cheeks stung. "I'm Harper Kirkpatrick and I said I was sorry." She'd had trouble with the zippers. Probably not the time to share. His blue eyes iced her. Stumbling on the last step, Harper pitched forward.

"Good God." He broke her fall with both hands.

"Sorry. So sorry." *Cripes.* She pushed away from a chest that had seen a gym or two.

"You okay?" Cameron Bennett looked more annoyed than worried.

"I'm fine. It's dark in here, in case you hadn't noticed."

Squaring her shoulders, she peered into the room. "Where are the kids?"

"What kids?"

A chill shot down her spine. Guys with flushed faces lounged in leather chairs. The low-ceilinged room held a hint of Cuban cigars smoked long ago. Her lungs squeezed tight. She had rules and Rizzo had broken them.

But her rent was way past overdue.

"Nothing. Forget it." Her arrival time of ten o'clock didn't seem too crazy when Rizzo gave her the details. She'd worked a sleepover birthday party two weeks earlier for a bunch of cute second graders. She handed Baby Blues the CD Rizzo had given her. "My music."

"Good, because you're late."

"You said that already."

His lips pressed into a thin line. Anxiety chattered in her stomach.

"Cameron, ole buddy! Now, don't keep that sweet thang all to yourself," called out a guy who looked like a former lineman. He made a feeble attempt to stand before collapsing back in the club chair. They all roared. Felt like she'd stumbled into a locker room.

"Doesn't look like a sweet thing to me," said a guy with a pencil moustache. Her stomach flopped over.

3

"Gentleman—and we are gentlemen, in case some of you may have forgotten—y'all be on your best behavior now." Baby Blues pushed her forward.

Show time. Harper stretched a smile across dry teeth.

They began to clap in a steady rhythm —like this was a rock concert and the main act was late. Holding the black whip tight against her chest, Harper shimmied through the closely packed tables. A hip here, a hip there. Open bottles sporting expensive gold labels gleamed on the tables. Definitely not a beer crowd and they weren't on their first drink. A banner hung over the long bar. "Congratulations, Beau! Another Man Down!"

A blasted bachelor party. Her steps faltered. Grabby lap dances and straying hands. She needed chain mail, not spandex. Harper tightened her hold on the whip. She'd like to wind it around Rizzo's neck. Beau must be the one grinning at the end of the bar, a ball and chain cuffing one ankle and a mourning band on his arm. Head down, he looked close to passed out. Still, he shot her a sweet, wobbly smile.

She threw back her head. No going back now. Not unless she wanted to be out on the street. Swinging her hips, she smiled her way to the bar. When one heel caught in the berber carpet, she caught herself and glanced back. Leaning against the wall, Baby Blues raised his eyebrows.

Fine. She'd show him.

How? This wasn't exactly a hokey pokey group. That much she knew.

Breathe. Breathe. Just one foot in front of the other.

When she reached the bar, two men hoisted her up. Planting her feet wide, she nodded to Baby Blues. Sweat tickled along her hairline under the spandex hood. He pressed a button on the sound system.

"What's New Pussycat" blasted, and she shrank. *Really, Rizzo?* The guys loved it.

"Come on, Sugga!"

"Dance for us, you pretty thang."

Her chin came up. What would McKenna do? Time to channel her older sister back in Chicago. This was just a group of southern boys goofy with booze. Drunk, but harmless. Harper began to strut. Keeping her balance was tricky. Wings, pretzels, and pork ribs sat in bowls along the bar.

"Dance for us, darlin'."

"Yeah, give us a show!"

Her stomach plummeted into her boots. Maybe a few kicks. Bright smile. Hands on hips. Toes to the ceiling, as Mrs. VanderPool, their cheerleading coach used to say.

The bouncing sure didn't help her breathing. So hard to keep her eye on everything. She froze when her right foot connected with a bowl of pretzels that sailed through the air like a missile. Baby Blues jerked when the snacks took out some shiny statues on a shelf. Pretzels flew and awards crashed to the floor.

A roar went up. Baby Blues closed his eyes. Harper kept kicking.

"That's okay, sugga." Propping his head up, Beau threw her a goofy grin.

She smiled back. Piece of cake.

But boy, it was hot in here. With every bump and grind, the spandex tugged on her skin. Were the black whiskers melting off her face?

When Baby Blues turned down the lights, it threw her off. Then he hit her with a spotlight. This was getting serious.

A pleased rumble rolled through the room.

"Whatcha got on under there?" A meaty hand slapped onto her calf.

"Play nice, now." She tapped his head with the fluffy end of her tail. The guy looked like he could play for the Chicago Black Hawks but he pulled back with an embarrassed smile. Harper's confidence grew. Mother of mercy, maybe this would be better than waitressing. At least she wouldn't get carpal tunnel. Maybe she'd be able to keep a roof over her head after all.

With renewed confidence, she threw herself into the rhythm. The guys clapped. Yeah, this was more like it. She kicked. She strutted. She smiled.

Then they started to chant, "Take it off! Take it off!"

Holy moly. Really?

Just… bump … *shoot* … bump … *me* … bump … *now.* She pictured the horrified look on Sister Gabrielle's face. Her sweet fifth grade teacher often sent her to the office with messages for the principal.

"You're so dependable, Harper," Sister Gabrielle had told her. "Such potential."

If Sister Gabrielle could see her now.

The room closed in around her.

But she wasn't going down. Not like this.

Her airway felt like two thumbs were jammed against it. Harper just couldn't do the fainting thing again. She could hurt herself falling from up here but these boys wanted something. With a quick jerk, she yanked back the hood. Her hair fell to her shoulders. Chin up, she threw her head up and sucked in a deep breath. What a relief.

Applause ruptured the close, warm air. Baby Blues was fooling around with the thermostat. Wheeling around, he saw her and settled back against the dark paneling. Cool air blasted her from a vent right above. She drank it in.

"More! Give us more!"

"We want more, Pussycat!"

Pussycat? *Didn't* ... bump ... *they* ... bump ... *recognize* ... bump ... *Catwoman?*

Now, if this were a children's birthday party, they'd know. Kids loved all the super heroes—Catwoman, Batman, the Hulk, and Iron Man. She'd worn those costumes for recent gigs, and the children loved it. The parties had been fun and she'd made good money.

Six year olds never expected her to take off anything.

The chubby guy with bleary eyes staggered to his feet and began to jiggle his hips. Not a pretty sight but he was having fun. She smiled at him and his friends wrestled him back into the chair. "Bubba, no. You're going to break something again."

Bubba sank back into the chair. The men cheered. Bubba

smiled. And Tom Jones wouldn't quit. Up on the bar, breathing became a marathon event.

She never had to dance for the kids, just sing and clap. This group had definitely come for a show. Prancing along the bar, she tossed the whip lightly from one side to the other. Hands reached for the leather strips.

"More! We want more, Pussycat!"

What was she wearing under this suit?

Underwear hadn't been a consideration when she got dressed.

Slowly she unzipped her left sleeve. Angry pink tracks throbbed from when she'd snagged herself getting dressed. With every click of the zipper, the applause grew louder. Chest heaving, she stopped under an air vent. Cool air rushing over her, she closed her eyes. Big mistake.

"Gotcha." Fingers tightened around one booted ankle and she glanced down at Pencil Moustache Man.

"Stop that!" Harper jerked and the whip hit his cheek. Her heart stopped when an angry red line zipped across his skin.

"Bitch." He reared back.

"Oh, I'm so sorry, sir. I didn't mean…" When she bent over, she got dizzy.

His buddies found the whole thing hilarious.

"Randy, way to go!"

"Got what you deserve, buddy!" They thumped on the tabletops.

"Hands off, Randy. Let her dance." The host's voice sliced the darkness.

Randy fell back.

Baby Blues caught her eyes and tilted his head, like he was just waiting for the next mistake.

Fine, she'd show him. Forget the sleeve teasing. Her hands moved to the front of her costume. Wrestling with the zipper, she didn't see the wet patch on the bar. Before she could even think "white cotton," she was sprawled on her behind. Hurt like heck.

Baby Blues was there in a heartbeat. His nostrils flared and she could hear him breathing.

"I'm all right." She struggled to stand.

"Well, I'm not."

"You okay, darlin'?" Beau lifted his head from the bar.

"Cameron, ya tryin' to kill my party?"

A muscle twitched in Cameron's jaw. "Sorry, Beau, but it appears our entertainment for the evening is a little under the weather."

"I am not," she hissed, heaving herself upright.

"You damn well are."

Beau's eyes flagged. "You did great, Pussy…cat."

"Catwoman," she squeaked.

"No! She can't go." Bubba tried to stand again.

"We haven't seen anything yet!" The others joined the rowdy protest.

Ignoring them, Cameron helped Harper down and steered her through the disappointed men. His grip would probably leave a bruise on her arm. She fought back tears.

My rent. She wrenched her arm away. "I can…finish."

"The hell you can. You can barely breathe." He marched her along.

"I'm okay." Twisting, she saw Bubba trying to climb onto the bar while Beau gave him a shove. She couldn't help her giggle. But when she turned, Cameron's steely blue eyes lanced her. "If you're an exotic dancer, then I'm a...."

They'd reached the stairs. He pushed a button, grabbed the ejected CD and jabbed it in her direction. Anger flamed in her cheeks. The night was not going to end like this. Not one more man rejecting her. Harper grabbed his belt and pulled. "You have to give me another chance."

His eyebrows rose and he glanced down. "No second chances."

"Geez." She shoved him away and snatched the CD.

How long would it take for Charlie Roden, her landlord, to evict her?

Wails followed her up the stairs, Baby Blues right behind her, eyes about butt level. She was furious and heartsick. Rizzo had been asking if she wanted to earn better money. Maybe she misunderstood him. She thought he meant more gigs. Didn't matter. She was finished.

Upstairs, Cameron led Harper to the front door and yanked it open. "Thank you for your time but I asked Rizzo for a professional."

"I *am* a professional." She got a glimpse of herself in a huge gilded hall mirror. Melting makeup, crooked mask and tangled curls. Harper swallowed hard.

Cameron nudged her outside. The night air clung like cotton

candy.

"You could've let me finish."

"Trust me. You were finished."

Her lips quivered. "Well, aren't you so… lah dee dah."

That was all she could manage? Harper clamped her lips shut. On the street, gaslights glowed. Leaves whispered overhead and she breathed deep. Felt so good when her chest loosened.

Baby Blues' lips tweaked up. "Lah dee dah, huh? Good thing the guys were too tanked to complain. Much."

"They weren't complaining." Leering but not complaining. "I wasn't that bad."

"Yes, you were." The ghost of a smile softened his frown. Baby Blues was really handsome when he smiled. Handsome and hot. Jamming one hand into a pocket, he sighed and dug out a roll of cash she wished she could refuse. "Here, take this."

"Thank you."

"You're welcome."

A wail came from deep inside the house. "Good night," he said, nodding politely—the perfect southern gentleman.

"Okay, fine. Good night." Turning on her heel, she limped down the stone steps. A cool shower waited for her at home unless Charlie had turned off the water.

Her footsteps echoed on the pavement as Harper walked toward the car at the end of the side street. She hoped to heck it started. When her ex-boyfriend Billy had taken off for California, he'd left her with this heap of junk. Two years out of college and all her friends were pairing up like fruit flies.

All except Harper.

The beige sedan with the bumper held on with duct tape looked ridiculous on the elegant street. She slid inside. Even though the sun had set hours ago, the front seat heated her back and thighs. Thank God she'd never see any of those men again. Savannah was small, but she sure didn't travel in their circles.

The smell of money hit her when she fanned out the bills Baby Blues had given her. Generous but not generous enough. Reaching under the seat, she pulled out her beat up Coach bag and dug around for her inhaler. The first breaths were almost painfully blissful. Lungs expanding, she slumped back and tucked the money into her purse. What was she going to do? She'd think about that later. Right now she needed a shower and some sleep.

But first one quick call. She whipped out her phone.

"How'd it go?" Rizzo answered right away, like he'd been waiting.

"You're a rat, you know that?"

She could hear him take a drag on his cigarette. "You were lucky to get a shot at this group. Elite customer and I hope you didn't screw up with Mr. Bennett. Stop by on your way home with the cash."

"Oh, I don't think so, Rizzo."

"Hey, Chicago girl, don't get all uppity on me. Didn't you say you were interested in career development?"

He really was a trip. "What happened to the kids' birthday parties? This was a bachelor party, for Pete's sake. I am not a stripper."

His laugh was more of a bark. "They all say that. You dames are all alike."

The words hit her like darts. Harper blinked back tears, glad he couldn't see her. "I quit."

"No, you're fired. And you better get that money to me or you're toast, little lady."

She ended the call. What a creep. Jamming the key into the ignition, she turned it. The click was like taking another dart. Resting her forehead on the steering wheel, she squeezed her eyes shut. If she started to cry, her chest would tighten up. She forced herself to take deep breaths. When the swelling in her throat subsided, she grabbed her phone again. Maybe Adam, her neighbor, would be home.

But it was Saturday and Adam usually partied on Saturday nights. The phone rang and rang until his voicemail picked up. She didn't leave a message.

Cameron watched the taillights of the limousine pull away. Limo service was the only safe way home after a bachelor party, an unwritten rule in their group. But he'd never offer to host one of these parties again. Just not his thing. Unbuttoning his shirt, he welcomed the cool breeze. He didn't know whether to laugh or put his fist through a wall.

Stripper, my ass. Not that she didn't look hot in the Catwoman costume. And the hair? Definitely a turn-on. But something felt off. Any minute he'd expected to have to give her mouth-to-mouth resuscitation.

Cameron fought the mental picture that brought a warm rush.

Turning back to the house, he yanked his shirt tails out of his slacks. Was she one of the local college girls? Something admirable about that. He'd put himself through school washing dishes, valeting cars, bartending, and just about everything in between.

Gutsy girl who drew the line at stripping. At least she had principles.

The beat up car parked at the corner caught his eye. Really? Irritation made his head throb. People were always leaving their junkers on the street. Looked like this one had a license plate.

"Daddy?"

He swiveled. Inside, Bella gripped the banister at the foot of the stairs, a small pale figure in her yellow Tinkerbell nightgown.

Smiling at his four-year-old daughter, he stepped back inside. "Why aren't you asleep, sugar?"

"Too much noise, Daddy." She rubbed a small fist into her eyes.

"Yeah, I'm sorry about that." When he scooped her up, Bella felt so frail. His heart turned over. "You should stay in the air conditioning. Too much pollen out here."

Batteries of tests and the doctors still didn't know what made his daughter wheeze and turn pale. Scared the hell out of him.

At the end of the hall, Connie appeared in the doorway of the kitchen.

"Connie, can you take her back to bed? I have a situation outside."

"You bet. Come here, you little munchkin." Connie opened her arms and he handed Bella off. The dark rings beneath his daughter's eyes wrapped around his heart and squeezed.

"Night, Daddy." Bella leaned over for a kiss, her wiry dark hair smelling of baby shampoo.

"See you tomorrow, darlin'." He watched them mount the stairs before stepping back outside and pulling the door closed behind him. The car was still there. His loafers scuffed the warm pavement as he walked down the middle of the road. When he got closer, a head of thick sherry-colored hair eased its way up. Mardi Gras beads dangled from the mirror.

Perfect. Just perfect.

"Why are you still here?" he asked when he reached the open window. "You can't park on this street overnight."

Her back was toward him. Was she slipping the damn mask back on? When she turned, those green eyes sparked. "My car wouldn't start."

What a surprise. "Have you called a service station? AAA?"

"I've left messages for a friend. Somebody will call back." Her hands white-knuckled the steering wheel. "Any minute now."

Jamming one hand through his hair, Cameron stared down the dark, empty street. Thank God his neighbors were well asleep by this time. A clunker was a red light for everyone, and he didn't want them calling the police about his stripper.

Well, the girl who wasn't a stripper.

Maybe he should just let the police handle it. Wasn't she loitering or doing something illegal?

Then he saw the inhaler on the seat.

Damn. But not a total surprise.

"Give me a minute." He headed back to the house.

"Look, you don't have to do anything."

Like hell he didn't. He broke into a jog.

Two minutes later, he pulled his Porsche up next to her beat-up piece of crap. Leaning over, he pushed open the passenger side door. "Get in."

Mumbling something under her breath, she got out of the car and slammed the door behind her. As she slid into the Porsche, she gave him the name of her street. Then she folded her hands into her lap like a school girl, a Coach bag plopped at her feet. Must be a knockoff.

He pulled away. For a while, all he could hear was the sweet, low rumble of the car. Time for some music and he punched buttons until Billy Holiday filled the small car with "The Very Thought of You."

"Oh, I love this song." When she leaned forward a little, her reddish brown hair fell over one shoulder. The curls looked soft, like Bella's. She started to hum along.

"So, do you do this often?" he finally asked.

"Have a broken down car? Not if I can help it."

"No, I mean do you work for Party Perfect often?"

What he could see of her face turned sad. "Just worked some children's parties for him."

"Worked? As in the past?"

The soft hollow at the base of her throat pulsed. "Right. I just quit."

"Sorry. You didn't really do anything wrong. I mean, your kicks were good."

He caught her eye. They both burst out laughing, probably thinking of that bowl of pretzels.

"I am so sorry about your trophies." Her luscious chuckle hit him right in the gut.

"Not the first time they'd been knocked off that shelf." Damn, he needed to laugh. His latest restoration deal had fallen through that afternoon. He hated the thought of the wrecking ball taking that house down. For him every old structure in Savannah carried a precious piece of history. The stripper who didn't strip was just a bad end to a bad week. "Trophies only matter the day you win them. Besides, the football only broke off one of them. It's been glued before."

"Well, I won't be dancing on bars anytime soon." The sadness in her voice tugged at him.

She must have unzipped her costume to get some air. When she leaned forward and peered out the front windshield, he tried not to stare at the dusky valley between her breasts.

"Stop. Right there."

He jerked his eyes away. "Look, I didn't mean anything." What was wrong with him, ogling her like that?

But she wasn't looking at him. She was stabbing one blue-tipped finger at an older home with a serious lean. The building was like so many in this district of Savannah. Rundown. Probably cut into four different apartments. He pulled to the curb. She cracked open the car door. "Thanks so much for the ride. I hope I didn't ruin your party, Mr. Bennett," she added softly.

"You did fine."

"Yeah. Right."

What was he saying? She was terrible. But damn, that pinched look around her nose, the trembling of her soft lips—she was killing him.

She reached for her handbag and make-up spilled out. They both grabbed for it and their heads bumped. Her hair brushed his cheek, unleashing a crazy warmth that took him by surprise. Totally inappropriate for so many reasons.

"Sorry. I am so clumsy tonight. Thank you."

When he handed her a lipstick and a comb, their fingers touched and sparked. Damn. She sucked in a quick breath. He sat back. She stepped out until all he could see were those long legs.

"Well, thanks." One hand on the top of the car, she leaned forward.

"No problem." He trained his eyes on the empty bucket seat. It was hard.

"Good night, then." She pushed off and began to walk away.

Something purple on the floor caught his eyes. "Wait. You forgot your inhaler." Scooping it up, he handed the device through the open window.

"Thank you." She curled it tightly into her fist, backing onto the curb. "Aren't you going to take off?"

"Just waiting to see you in." This wasn't the safest neighborhood.

"Right. That's nice." As she turned, her boots crunched on the gravel. She looked absurd and hot as she took the stairs with that tail swinging behind her, whip tucked under one arm. Took her a little time to work her key. The front door stuck but finally gave way to a hip. After she banged it shut behind her and the porch light was turned off, he eased away from the curb. The feeling that dogged him all the way home was ridiculous. Why did he care if the girl needed help? He had enough on his plate.

But Cameron knew what it felt like to have no place to turn.

Chapter 2

Harper circled the block for the third time. Why go through an interview bound to be humiliating? *Overdue rent.* And she'd be giving up. Despite what her former boyfriend Billy said, she was not a quitter. She pulled over and parked. At least this time she wasn't wearing a black Catwoman suit.

"Just come back with the job," Adam had told her when he handed her the keys to his red Ford Focus. "Hey, girl, you can do this."

Sure. Right. In the morning sunlight, the pale brickwork of Cameron Bennett's mansion glowed. But the black trim and shutters gave a no-nonsense touch. The house had an edge, just like its owner. Her stomach knotted. What if he recognized her and laughed when she walked in?

But he wouldn't. Cameron seemed like the perfect southern gentleman.

Hadn't he taken her home when her car wouldn't start? He'd paid her something even though she hadn't delivered. Cripes. She drummed her fingers on the steering wheel. How could she face him again? Chest tight, she dug in her pink peony purse, found her inhaler and breathed in. After her lungs expanded, her stomach settled. She could do this.

Once out of the car, she marched toward the steps leading up to the house. The wrought iron railing felt warm under her hand. Harper hesitated on the bottom step, heart galloping.

Still time to turn back but she'd run out of options. She wouldn't be surprised to find everything she owned piled at the curb when she returned, her Frida Kahlo posters sandwiched between the drafting board and a box of dishes.

On the way over in the car, she'd practiced a different voice so Baby Blues wouldn't recognize her. Mary Ann Lacey, a classmate in college, had been from Charleston. How she teased Harper about the broad, Chicago vowels and her constant use of "yah."

Yah, today Harper would become Mary Ann Lacey.

She pushed off from the bottom step.

The eye-popping salary in the online ad for a nanny made her former jobs look like volunteer work. Harper had set her mug down so hard, the coffee slopped over the lip. Was she qualified? Her list of employers over the past two years was pretty pathetic. The Kirkpatrick clan had all chipped in for her education at the elite Savannah design school and she was working at Maisy's Resale Shop? She owed her family more than a series of part time jobs, but she'd hated her New York internship. Her career plans needed a serious readjustment.

Maybe this job could give her some breathing room—a chance to figure out her future. Only one child to take care of, or so the ad said. How hard could this be? She was blown away when a request for an interview came back two hours after she'd pushed the send button. Stretched out on her futon, she was watching *The Notebook* for like the fiftieth time. Even soaking wet, Ryan Gosling still sizzled. Her sobs were interrupted by the ping. She had mail.

One casual glance and she sat bolt upright. Gulping and pausing dear Ryan, she started typing. Sure, ten o'clock Wednesday would be fine. But when she did an Internet search for the address, hot and cold flashes danced across her skin.

The mansion on Victory Drive. Cameron Bennett. Holy cripes. She closed the laptop, only to reopen it fifteen minutes later. The pay was too good to pass up. Time to put on her big girl pants.

Now she squinted up at the building. "Here goes nothing."

Harper took the brick steps slowly so she wouldn't get all sweaty. Her stockings felt like sausage casings. Her older sister's words kept her climbing the dang stairs. "You only have one chance to make a good impression, Harper. Make it count."

She might not even have one chance if Cameron recognized her.

Her flounced skirt swung around her thighs and her hair was coiled into a demure bun at the nape of her neck. Just a touch of lip gloss and some mascara this morning. One more deep breath from her inhaler before she tucked it in her bag. The tortoise shell bracelets she'd scored at Maisy's shop jangled on her wrists when she punched the doorbell.

A couple beats and Connie opened one of the heavy black doors.

"I have an appointment at ten o'clock. Harper Kirkpatrick," she said, as if she'd never seen Connie before in her life. With some effort, she lifted the end of each sentence, just like Mary Ann had told her. "Just a tad, Harper, darlin'. Like you're lifting the edge of a flapjack?"

No hint of recognition when Connie stepped back. "Please come in."

"What a lovely foyer." Diving into a southern accent that clung like syrup to every word, Harper babbled about the marble floor, Oriental rugs and priceless antiques like she'd never seen them before. The same pink tulips flopped from the crystal vase.

Hah, so they were artificial.

Well, so was she. Thinking maybe she'd overdone her Scarlett O'Hara imitation, she zipped her lips.

"Won't you sit down, Harper?" Connie motioned to an ornately carved bench that sat under a watercolor of the marshes. The library pocket door slid open while Harper tried to get comfortable on the hard surface.

"Thank you so much for coming, Miss Daniels. Connie will get back to you. We expect to make a decision soon." Immaculate in gray pinstripe slacks and an alabaster shirt, Baby Blues stood in the doorway, his mauve tie a jaunty splash of color. The man had style.

"Then I'll wait to hear from you." The gorgeous Miss Daniels smiled with the confidence of a candidate who knew she'd aced her interview. The classic lines of her suit screamed designer and the sand color accented her blonde bob. Mile-long legs ended in nude peep-toe heels.

Harper smoothed one hand over the ruffles of her tiered skirt patterned with purple flowers. Suddenly, her pink jacket seemed too bright, the skirt too girly. She'd drawn the line at wearing the navy "interview suit" her mother had given her as a graduation gift. Navy wasn't in Harper's color palette. Now she wondered.

Cameron gave Harper a brief nod before sliding the door closed. Thank God for the mask she'd worn that night.

"I'll just tell him you're here," Connie murmured after she'd shown the girl out.

Right. Like he hadn't seen her sitting there. Harper expelled a tight breath as the library door slid closed behind Connie. Reaching into her bag, she fingered her inhaler. Touching the plastic ridges eased her anxiety.

While Connie was gone, Harper rehearsed her new inflection, giggling quietly at her whispered, "Yes sir, that is so very sweet of you." Air circulated in the white marble foyer, so much cooler than the party room downstairs that night. Memories of her performance sent butterflies skittering through her tummy. Studying the Savannah etchings hung along the stairway, she tried to identify each square. Took her mind off how desperately she needed this job.

The library door slid open, the dry sound of wood on wood. Connie padded toward her. "You can go in now." Bless her heart, the housekeeper shot her an encouraging smile.

Cameron lounged in a wing chair in front of a massive fireplace at the end of the library. He rose with a languid elegance that contrasted with his broad shoulders and a strong nose that spoke of power. She'd seen a lot of that silver spoon entitlement here in Savannah. He was the real deal.

But today he looked just plain tired. "Hello, I'm Cameron

Bennett."

She extended one hand. "Good morning. I'm Harper
Kirkpatrick."

He shook her hand, fingers long and cool. "Thank you for
coming. Won't you have a seat?" Cameron indicated the wing chair
facing him and grabbed a folder as he sat down.

Whew. No sign of recognition.

Connie peeked in. "Pardon me, but would you care for coffee,
Harper? Tea perhaps?"

She shook her head. "Thank you, no." Her stomach was having
enough trouble while she watched Cameron scan her resume. The
only sound in the room was the ticking of the impressive gold
clock on the mantel. Sunlight beamed through the heavy burgundy
drapes, and she studied the dust motes floating in the ray of light.
One shank of blonde hair fell over his forehead and he pushed it
back slowly as he read the sad facts of her life and career. Most of
them were true.

"You graduated from the design school here in town?"
Cameron looked up.

"Yes…probably like every candidate in the city."

"And your major was…"

"Fashion design."

His eyebrows peaked. "You didn't want to continue on that
path?"

What he really meant was, why are you here?

How could she explain the grueling internship in New York, a
city hopelessly crowded with cut-throat people clawing for work?

"Fashion design wasn't what I pictured."

"My word, life rarely is." Was he laughing at her? Tossing her resume onto the table, Cameron fixed her with intense blue eyes. The Inquisition had nothing on this guy. "Why are you interested in this position? Seems like a reach for a fashion major."

Mentioning money would probably be a bad idea. "I've always found children to be fascinating. I come from a large family."

His eyes brightened. "Lucky girl. So, why didn't you try primary education?"

"Too many kids at one time?"

Cameron burst into a surprised laugh that made her chuckle too. The tightness loosened in her throat. Then he seemed to remember why she was here and picked up her resume again. His fingertips flicked the edges of the top sheet.

Looking at those fingers with nails cut cleanly across, she tried to quiet the rogue chill chasing up her spine. Harper had a thing about a man's hands. "How do you deal with responsibilities? Dependable?"

That twinkle in his eyes made her wary.

"Yah, I would say I'm responsible." *Yah?* So much for hiding her Midwest accent.

"Always come through?"

Good grief, maybe he did recognize her. Mouth dry, she nodded. "Yah, er, yes, I do." Her hands tightened on the handles of her peony purse.

"Hmm." His cheeks sucked in. "Your references would attest to that, of course?"

"Of course." Thank goodness her legs were already crossed at the ankles.

With a rustle of paper, he flipped to the second page.

A jet of cool air blasted from somewhere, and Harper tilted her chin to lap it up. Why had she worn this hot pink jacket? Oh, right. The rip under the arm of her white blouse.

Baby Blues was back to the first page. "You've held several positions since graduation. Most of them waitressing and one as a …" A grin tweaked one corner of his mouth. "Party planner?"

Oh, Lord save her.

"What exactly is that?"

The first time she opened her mouth, nothing came out. Moistening her lips, Harper took another stab at it. "I help families with their birthday parties. Children, mostly."

Cameron seemed to study the slow burn working its way up Harper's neck. A cool drop of perspiration skidded down her spine. Her excitement about this job fizzled like pop left in the hot sun.

Dropping the resume onto the side table again, Cameron tented his fingers in front of his lips. How long had she been here, a year? Was the next candidate waiting in the hall? Harper edged forward, ready to be dismissed.

Puffing out his cheeks, Cameron leaned forward and rested his elbows on his knees. "Here's the thing, I have a four year old who won't eat." His voice faltered, and he cleared his throat, studying the pattern of the red and blue Oriental rug under his tasseled loafers. "Bella is four years old, and she still eats mostly baby cereal."

How was this possible? "So, she's never eaten stuff like applesauce or cinnamon chex?" Some of Harper's personal favorites.

He shifted his attention to the shelves of books like they might hold some answers. Pain flashed over his face like a lightning strike and disappeared. When he swung his focus back to her, his eyes were shuttered. Cameron Bennett probably never let his guard down.

"And Bella has asthma. At least, the doctors think it's asthma. She's on medication, but, well, we have to take every precaution."

"You have a lot on your plate," Harper murmured. This position screamed train wreck. As she shifted, the leather chair squeaked. "Aren't some of these normal issues for growing kids?" She'd have to ask Mark and Malcolm, her brothers. They had children.

"I have no idea." He blew out a breath. "Would you like to meet her?"

"Sure. Love to." She wanted to run from the room. The heavy burgundy drapes, dark antique furnishings, and portraits of men with drooping moustaches pressed in on her. This felt all wrong and she wanted out.

But she stayed.

Stepping out into the hall, Cameron called for Connie. "Is Bella home yet?"

"Jack just arrived with her."

"Would you ask her to join us, please?"

Harper checked the time on the mantel clock. Maybe she could cut this short by mentioning a non-existent dental appointment.

The little girl that tromped in behind Cameron two minutes later kept Harper riveted to her chair. Long dark hair framed enormous blue eyes that wandered the room before settling on Harper. One delicate hand plucked at the fussy flowered dress that probably came from a shop on Bull Street. The fingers of her other hand were tucked in her mouth.

"Bella, I'd like you to meet Miss Kirkpatrick."

Glowering, Bella sucked harder.

"Be polite and say hello now, darlin'. And take those fingers out of your mouth. Please…" Cameron added almost as an afterthought.

Brushing wet fingers down her dress, she inched forward. "Hello." She studied Harper's hot pink slings.

"Hey, Bella. What a pretty dress." *Pretty awful.*

Cameron touched his daughter's back, just one finger.

"Thank you." The words fell like a brick her dad had pried loose.

Easing himself back into the wing chair, Cameron pulled Bella onto his lap. Her eyes and frown never left Harper. "Why don't you tell Harper about *Sesame Street.* Don't you watch that show every day?"

"Daddy, I like Batman, not Big Bird." Who knew kids this age could do an eye roll?

But she had a point. "Me too. One Halloween I wore a Batman costume."

"You did?" The frown had been dislodged.

"Sure did." Harper smiled, remembering her mother's horror. Her mom had wanted her to be Cinderella. McKenna helped Harper lobby for a Batman costume, insisting she'd be Robin. Her older sister always came through.

A grin tipped one corner of Cameron's lips. Bella had his full lips, but that cute, snub tilt to her nose? Must be from her mother. Was Cameron widowed or divorced?

But Harper didn't want to know any more. Every cell in her body was screaming at her to leave.

"Bet you got lotsa candy." A nasal whisper, Bella's voice kept her there. "You know, wearing that Batman costume and all."

"Yep, lots of candy."

"Did people like your costume?"

"*I* liked it. That was all that counted."

Bella flashed a shy smile and then it was gone. Harper could have cut the tension in this room with a swizzle stick. Her neck ached, and she'd only been here thirty minutes. Something was seriously screwed up. She felt both appalled and drawn to the tyke with adult eyes.

"Any questions for Harper?" Cameron asked.

"Oh, no need. Really I…" Harper began.

Mouth puckering, Bella dropped her eyes, like she knew she was being kicked to the curb. Without a mother to show her the way and Baby Blues for a father, this kid didn't stand a chance.

Harper's stubborn Irish nature kicked in. Bella had "hopeless case" stamped all over her. And darn it, Harper couldn't resist.

"Okay then, why don't you say goodbye and I'll get Connie?" Cameron was on his feet and pressing a button on the desk.

Harper almost felt lightheaded. Five minutes ago, she'd been ready to sprint from the room to a dentist appointment she didn't have. Now she was rooted to the spot by a moody little girl. When the door slid open, Harper could see another candidate in a navy suit sitting in the foyer. The girl looked up expectantly.

Cameron whispered something in Connie's ear and she nodded. Taking Bella's hand, Connie stepped out into the hall, closing the door behind her. Cameron settled back, looking pleased.

"Your daughter is very…interesting," Harper offered cautiously.

"She misses having a mother, I'm afraid."

No kidding. "Must be hard." She couldn't even imagine.

"I'm looking for someone who can live in." Cameron's fingers tapped the arms of his chair.

She gulped. Was he offering her the job?

"You can alternate Sundays off with Connie," Cameron was saying. "And I can certainly handle Saturday."

She seriously doubted that. Harper wanted to thump the man over the head with one of his red Chinese vases. Looking off in the distance, Cameron seemed to be dictating. He probably did that a lot. "I work long hours, and we have plenty of room."

Obviously he didn't expect a refusal. Harper's fingers were destroying her peony purse.

He turned back to her. "Have I missed anything?"

Yes, a heart. Cameron Bennett needed a little time with Dorothy and the Tin Man.

"Not at all." A million reasons why she shouldn't take this job knotted in her throat. She swallowed them in one painful gulp when Cameron threw out a figure that was more than she'd ever made in her life. Live here in this mansion on Victory Drive? She could handle that. The vivid mental picture of her earthly belongings heaped at the curb began to fade. Relief left her light-headed.

Ten minutes later, she was out on the sidewalk. The sun beat down and birds sang from the trees. Taking out her phone, she called Adam to tell him the news.

As Cameron closed the door behind Harper Kirkpatrick, the gloom that had dogged his steps lately lifted. After interviewing five women who obviously couldn't handle his daughter, he'd found a keeper.

Harper's tough Chicago edge might be just what Bella needed. And he liked Harper's flamboyant style, pink plastic hoops swinging in her ears and bracelets clanking from her arms. Where on earth had she found that pink and purple skirt and those pink heels? No matter. Bella needed some perking up. He had no clue how to go about it. Poor Connie tried but she was getting on, and the last two nannies hadn't even lasted a week.

"So, what did you think?" he asked Connie when he found her in the kitchen. A yeasty scent filled the air as his housekeeper kneaded a lump of dough. He did so love her homemade bread. Grabbing a grape from the basket on the kitchen table, he bit down.

"I like her. I liked her Saturday night."

They shared a smile.

"That's one of the reasons I hired her. The girl has spirit. Bella needs some fun in her life."

A familiar sadness seeped through him. He grabbed another red grape. Not quite ripe but he ate it anyway, swallowing the tart taste. In the next room, the TV blared. Bella spent way too much time watching her shows. And as she'd set him straight this morning, she preferred super heroes to *Sesame Street*. Might be too violent for a little girl but what did he know?

"Harper's young." Connie gave the dough one more thump.

"So she is." Was there a double meaning in Connie's words? He glanced out the kitchen window into the secluded garden that always needed care. "Would you tell Jack that one of the trellises needs attention? The rain made a mess of them."

"I get him right on it." Connie gave the dough another punch. "I think Bella will like Harper."

"I hope so."

He liked these short talks with Connie. When it came to his daughter, he wanted to do the best thing. The right thing. It helped to talk things over with someone else, and Kimmy, well, he hesitated to bring Bella up with his girlfriend. Kimmy was so busy with her TV show.

"See you, Connie. I'll probably be late."

"I'll be here." Connie shaped the dough into a bread pan with firm pats.

Taking the steps two at a time on his way upstairs, Cameron decided to shower. He was sweating bullets. A southern gentleman never attended a meeting in a wrinkled shirt. Once in his gray marble shower, he blasted the cold water over his body in a punishing flow. Hiring Harper as Bella's nanny unfortunately did nothing to dispel the memory of her in the Catwoman suit.

He adjusted the water until it was ice cold.

Chapter 3

Harper studied Cameron Bennett's mansion Monday morning. This could be a big mistake. Adam put his black pickup in park. "Girl, when you move up, you do it in style."

"Unbelievable, isn't it?"

In the back of Adam's truck, her drafting table was sandwiched between boxes of clothes and art supplies. Her grandfather's rocker stood upright, covered with a faded blue quilted bedspread. In Harper's favorite poster, Frida Kahlo viewed the scene with mild distaste.

Frida wasn't the only one having second thoughts.

Adam turned off the motor. "Charlie let you out of your lease? How amazing is that?"

"Almost embarrassing how happy he looked. You can't blame the guy for wanting to be paid on a regular basis. That wasn't happening since Billy skipped town."

"Harper, don't get me wrong. I'm going to miss you. But that apartment wasn't helping you move on."

"You think he's really not coming back, huh?" She gnawed her thumbnail.

"Is a blue bird blue? And good riddance, girl." Adam snorted. Her boyfriend and her male friend never got along. Adam had a point. Leaving the old neighborhood might help her put Billy in the past. Staring up at her new home, Harper wished she felt better about this whole thing.

"Someday maybe we'll see Billy Colton's name in the credits for some outrageous indie film." Adam made a sweeping motion across the dashboard. "But he'll still be an idiot."

"Right. The butthead, as one of my nephews would say. With his luck, my ex-boyfriend will probably win an Oscar."

"Will he thank you in his acceptance speech for supporting him through his formative years?"

Her laugh sounded more like a bark. After four years of living together, Billy had dumped her. Still felt like that had happened to another girl.

"Earth to Harper." Adam snapped his fingers in front of her face.

"Sorry, Adam." Her hand jerked on the door handle.

Climbing out of the truck, she fought the memories of the bachelor party. She had to put that night out of her mind.

Adam lowered the back of the truck and they each grabbed a box. Connie had given her directions to the back door. Harper took the lead and they trekked around the corner to a gate left open in the high brick wall. Inside the courtyard, the perennials were bagged and tied neatly, just like Harper's mom did each year.

Adam's eyes widened as they traipsed through the yard. Long two-story porches overlooked a fountain where a mermaid frolicked, water spouting from her open lips. "Definitely good party material here."

"Let's remember, I'm hired help." Maybe Harper could sit out here with Bella and read books or play games. She pushed a button next to the back door and a bell rang inside.

The door opened immediately and the smell of fresh coffee wafted onto the morning air. "Come on in." Connie stepped back. When Harper introduced Adam to the housekeeper, Connie merely nodded. All business, she turned toward the front of the house. "Now, let's get you settled."

On the way down the hall, Adam mouthed, "Oh. My. God." Her box grew heavier as they trudged behind Connie to the second floor. Good thing she was wearing her running shoes. The lush Oriental rugs Cameron seemed to favor didn't look flip-flop friendly.

"One more floor." Connie pulled open a tall door in the center of the second floor landing. They kept climbing. Harper felt relieved that she wouldn't be sleeping on the same floor with Cameron. That would really have freaked her out.

Would help if he were a lot older.

Not so hot.

Didn't have those baby blue eyes.

How ridiculous. He was her employer, for Pete's sake. Finally they reached the third level. The heat up here felt alarmingly airless. Resting the box on one knee, Harper swept one hand across her damp brow. Thank goodness she'd put her hair in pigtails. In her denim cutoffs and pink T-shirt, she still felt the heat.

Connie bustled over to a thermostat. "I'll turn the air on. We don't use it unless we need it."

No kidding. Harper could barely breathe.

"The stairs will keep you in shape, not that you need it." Connie's soft stomach rolls suggested she spent more time in the kitchen than laboring up the steps.

Harper's shoes sank into the dated deep pink carpet. Cabbage roses patterned the faded wallpaper. Four doors opened from a spacious landing and Harper got a glimpse of a clawfoot tub in a bathroom at the end of the hall. She hoped a shower went with it.

"The nannies have all used this room." Connie pushed a door open.

Nannies? How many had there been?

Stepping into the room larger than her parents' living room, Harper took in the queen-size bed, antique white dressing table and matching dresser. Light filtered in through filmy sheer curtains at the dormer windows. At least, she would not have to deal with dusty brocade drapes. The pale mint green walls needed a little pep, but she could handle that. She'd painted the last apartment jewel purple for inspiration, with a bright spring green kitchen. Charlie had withheld their deposit, calling her beautiful paint job vandalism.

"This is just fine," she breathed. From the window she could look down into the huge live oak towering over the garden. The sudden urge to sketch took her by surprise. She hadn't felt that in a long time.

"Guess I'll put this right here." Adam set his box down on a captain's chest at the foot of the bed and Harper put hers right next to it. Later she'd unpack. This whole floor was hers and she loved it. Sure, the room looked like something from a bygone era, but it was a relief after her sad apartment with uneven floors and windows painted shut.

And minus one boyfriend.

Connie pushed back the sheers. "Myra comes at least once a week to help me clean, so no problem there. Your main responsibility is Bella. Trust me, she's a full-time job. Poor thing." Then she stopped, like she'd said too much. Stepping over to the dresser, she began opening drawers. Third drawer down, she dug out what looked like a pair of pink panties.

Face coloring, she crammed the wisp into one pocket of her khaki slacks. "Sorry. Thought I'd cleaned this out after the last one."

Adam and Harper exchanged a look. So the last nanny had left in a hurry? Harper sucked in a deep breath. The money was good and she was out of options. And this time she'd follow through.

"You never finish anything, Harper," had been Billy's parting words in the final phone call. Truth was, he was right. Why had she helped him finish his projects when she never got around to completing her own?

Connie clasped her hands together. "Washer and dryer on the lower level." The housekeeper spewed information with the ease of a well-practiced speech. Poor woman. Harper's ears perked up when she heard "car at her disposal" and "let me know about any special menu choices."

The benefits weren't shabby. Almost like a gift dropped into her lap.

Later, she would remember this and howl.

Two more trips to the pickup and she was moved in. Sweat coated her skin and she was reaching for her inhaler, but she was here. Adam helped set up her drafting table next to the window.

"Great place to work." He snapped the final leg into place.

Casting a glance into the secluded garden, Harper smiled. "Might be too many distractions."

"Time to focus. Work." Adam wagged a finger at her.

She straightened, remembering the promise she'd made to herself. No matter what, she was going to make this work. "I intend to but I'm sure going to miss having you next door. You know, to borrow that cup of sugar."

Chuckling, she hugged Adam goodbye. They both knew she never baked.

"Trust me. You don't want my sugar, sugga."

Yep, sure going to miss him.

Pulling back, he frowned. "Sure you're okay with this?"

"Absolutely." She pushed him away. "Look, I know I've been a mess, but it's time for me to get on with my life."

"Forget that boy. He's history."

"Got it." She socked him playfully in the arm. This new job would keep her too busy to wallow in the past. "Come on, I'll walk you down."

Ten minutes later, Harper watched Adam drive away from the row of mansions that could have harbored Scarlett O'Hara. So hoity toity, as her mother would say. Longing squeezed her heart. For just a second, she yearned for the trees of Oak Park, not these live oaks draped with moss.

Late the night before, she'd talked to her sister.

"Sounds like a great opportunity for you. Step into it. Own it."
McKenna always bolstered her spirits.

Harper lifted her head. Even the sun felt new that morning as
she crossed the back garden and sprinted up the stairs.

Connie was loading the dishwasher in the kitchen. "Bella's in
the TV room."

"Thanks, Connie." Harper found her new charge flopped on
the sage green sofa watching an animated cartoon. Figures in
intimidating black and brown wielded huge swords. Body parts
flew. In a fluffy pink dress, Bella looked dressed for a party. One
tiny patent leather shoe lolled over the edge of the sofa, beating
time to the sound effects.

"Hey, Bella."

She didn't look up.

"What are you watching?" Harper plopped down on the sofa.

Sighing, Bella twisted a length of her hair, eyes still on the
screen. No wonder that dark mass looked knotted. "Stuff. Ninja
warriors."

One more screech from the screen and another head flew off.
Bella didn't flinch. Did anyone supervise the kid's TV viewing?
Harper didn't see a TV Guide anywhere, and the basket of remote
controls looked intimidating. With plantation shutters closed
against the sunny day, the room felt like an elegant dungeon.
"Want to show me your room?"

"I'm watching TV."

"You can watch it later, okay?"

Bad enough that Billy had gotten the best of her. A four year-old? No way. Harper started clicking the remotes until she hit the jackpot and the screen darkened.

After a dark glance, Bella rolled off the couch and stomped from the room. Harper followed her indignant march up the stairs. A lemony smell that tickled the back of her throat pervaded the house. Did Myra realize that scent-free cleaning products came in a spray instead of aerosol? A shopping list formed in Harper's mind.

Bella kicked open a door at the top of the stairs. "Here." Myra must get tired of cleaning the scuff marks off this door.

Harper stepped into the room. "You sure have a lot of toys." The bedroom had the look of a toy store and the feel of a cave. A wide pink net strung across one corner sagged beneath the weight of stuffed animals. The high-canopied bed reminded Harper of the little girl's clothes—all ruffles and doodads. A white dust ruffle peeked out from a tufted pink comforter festooned with a gazillion tiny bows. At one corner of the bed stood a huge panda, with a giant giraffe in another. "These guys look big enough to be in a zoo."

Harper eyed the little girl cautiously. When she was a little girl, she'd always been afraid that there was a bear in her closet. Although her brothers had teased her, McKenna insisted Harper's door stay open at night.

"Yeah," Bella murmured, as if she'd read Harper's mind. "Kinda scary."

Harper's mental list grew. She'd have a talk with Cameron

about toys that could loom dangerously in the dark. She also wondered about all the stuffed toys that could harbor dust. Shelves of colorful toys lined the walls and a fully tricked out dollhouse stood in the corner. Was there anything this little girl *didn't* have?

A set of French doors opened out onto the upper porch.

"Wanna go outside?" Bella asked, pushing open one of the doors.

Harper nodded. Imagine having a room that looked out onto that garden, so secluded and magical. The height was dizzying, and she glanced at Bella running her hand over the wrought-iron railing. Was she really allowed out here alone?

Rattan furniture with green cushions patterned with palm trees was arranged along the porch that stretched all the way to what must be Cameron's room. Did he spend time out here?

She pulled her attention to the tree. "Will you just look at the birds," she murmured, eyes glued to the cardinals having a heyday in the tall live oak.

"We gots lots of birds." Clutching two of the porch spindles, Bella leaned back.

"Oh, be careful." When Harper pulled her charge's hands from the railing, the little girl thrust out her lower lip. "I just want you to be safe."

"My dad doesn't let me come out here very much," Bella admitted, releasing her hold.

Good to know. "Of course not but I'm with you now."

Wheeling away, Bella stalked back into her room with Harper close on her heels.

"Want to see my clothes?" Not waiting for a reply, Bella threw a door open. Talk about over-kill. The ruffles, bows, and artificial flowers seemed oppressive. Did little girls wear straw hats? Four or five were arranged on an upper shelf. Growing up, Harper probably had tennis shoes and dress shoes for the holidays. This kid had about ten pairs of shoes neatly arranged on a floor rack. Maybe they matched the linen dresses that looked about as comfortable as metal armor.

"Where did you get all these dresses?"

Bella's mouth pinched. "Kimmy."

Hmm. A new name. "Who is Kimmy?"

"Daddy's girlfriend. She always brings me presents."

Okay. Not a total surprise that Cameron was seeing someone. But Bella's expression made Harper sad. Never had a little girl looked less excited about presents, for Pete's sake.

"They're very pretty. Where are your play clothes?" Harper quietly shut the closet door.

"Play clothes," Bella repeated slowly, as if learning a new term.

"You know, when you want to go outside."

"You mean, when I go to school?"

"You go to school?" She'd check with Connie.

"I'm a big girl, and I gots to wear dresses to school." The sigh told Harper just what Bella thought of that. Walking out of her bedroom, Bella stared down at the other end of the hall. "Want to see my dad's room? He works a lot up here."

"No," Harper said so quickly that Bella's eyes widened. "I mean, maybe you could show me the downstairs. I've never really seen that." But as she started down the stairs, Harper glanced toward the far end of the hall. Could Cameron hear Bella if she woke up in the night?

Downstairs, Harper followed Bella through an archway into the front parlor.

In the living room, heavy sage colored draperies were drawn back, letting in the late morning sun. An elaborate chandelier glistened overhead with complementing sconces at either side of the fireplace. Unlike the comfortable TV room, the furniture in this room felt stiff and formal, from the Edwardian chairs to the Victorian loveseats. From what she'd studied, in these families furnishings were handed down, not purchased like her father's Barcalounger, his favorite Christmas gift.

"You use this room often?" Harper asked Bella, taking in the porcelain figures of the Three Graces on the mantel.

"No." She wrinkled up her face. "It's boring."

Okay then.

Trailing behind the four-year-old, Harper followed her into an enormous dining room. As a college student, she'd gone on plenty of house tours, including the Mercer House. In most southern mansions, the rooms were enclosed, isolating each family activity. Cameron's house had a nice, easy flow that suggested renovation had been done. An elaborate chandelier hung over a long cherry table. Silver pieces gleamed on the marble top of the side credenza.

"So, do you eat dinner in here?"

"Sometimes." Bella's voice became muffled after she tucked two fingers into her mouth. "Daddy and me."

Too late, Harper remembered Cameron's comments about

Bella's eating. The dining room might not be the little girl's favorite place.

"Time for lunch." Connie poked her head in the door.

"Bella mentioned that she goes to school," Harper commented as they walked into the kitchen. She wanted to keep the expectations clear.

"Mr. Bennett didn't tell you that?" Connie looked surprised.

"Not yet. I'm hoping to meet with him soon."

Muttering under her breath, Connie gave a shake of her short curls. "Always so much on his mind. Bella goes to school on Tuesdays, Wednesdays, and Thursdays. You can use the silver BMW for transportation. Keys are over there." She nodded to the wall with a row of brass hooks holding key fobs.

The BMW? Not too shabby.

The kitchen sparkled, from the copper pots over the spacious work island to the brushed chrome of the double-door refrigerator. Obviously Connie was proud of her domain.

"We usually have lunch in here." The housekeeper motioned to a cozy circular table and began pulling containers from the refrigerator.

"Can I help?" Harper didn't want the older woman waiting on her.

Bella climbed into her booster seat. Propping her head up with one hand, she gave the two women a speculative glance, as if biding her time. Sometimes she seemed much older than four.

"I'm just making some turkey sandwiches, but you could mix together Bella's lunch." Pulling out a box from one of the cupboards, Connie quirked one finger at Harper and began to pour what looked like baby cereal into a bowl.

"That looks sickening," she whispered to Connie.

"Only thing she'll eat," the housekeeper managed to say without moving her lips.

After the pleasant tour where she felt she'd made some headway with Bella, Harper's mood plummeted. Opening the refrigerator, Connie took out a carton of soy milk and poured some into a sippy cup and then into the bowl of dry cereal. Harper's stomach quivered as Connie stirred. Then the housekeeper plopped the bowl in front of Bella along with the sippy cup.

While the three of them ate, Harper tried to block out the image of Bella shoveling mush into her mouth. "Does that taste good, Bella?"

"Guess so." She shrugged.

Although Bella cleaned her bowl, Harper was alarmed by how thin she was. Didn't her father see this? But this was, after all, her first day. Not the best time for comments that could be taken as criticism. She was determined to like this job.

That afternoon while Bella took a nap, she made up a shopping list. "I don't know who buys the groceries," she said, handing Connie the list in the kitchen, "but could we add these to the list?"

Connie glanced over the paper. "Applesauce? Animal crackers? Don't think I haven't tried this. The eating issues just plumb tucker me out."

"Well, let's try. What about dinner? Does Cameron… I mean, does Mr. Bennett eat with her?"

Connie smoothed her hands over her apron. "Oh, no."

"Well, tonight, we'll eat together." My, she could almost hear her older brothers complaining that she was so bossy. Her hand went up when Connie began to protest. "You said it yourself, Connie. Bella is my responsibility, and I say we eat together. I mean, Bella and her father." She blushed. The last thing she wanted was to eat dinner with Cameron Bennett, but Bella needed a routine. Dinner at the Kirkpatrick house had been the highlight of their day.

That night, Bella sat across from Harper at the long dining room table. Connie hadn't said another word since their discussion earlier that day. She'd set the table with placemats and silverware. Connie said Cameron usually came home at six o'clock so Harper mixed a snack of cereal for Bella around four. The little girl gave her a mystified glance as she ate. Harper wondered if her strange diet accounted for Bella's moods.

"It's good to talk about all the things that happened to you during the day while you eat dinner," she told Bella. That had been the rule in the small red brick house in Oak Park. All seven kids had crowded around the table, jostling for room and their parents' attention as they passed around her mother's heavy platters.

Tonight, Connie had cooked a turkey breast and mashed sweet potatoes, with green beans on the side. Maybe Harper could convince Bella to eat the creamy potatoes. Her chest puffed with premature pride when she imagined Cameron's pleased look when his stubborn daughter was finally enticed to eat something besides cereal.

But the sweet potatoes cooled and congealed as time passed. Bella put her head down on her arms on the table. When had Harper ever felt so darned helpless... and sad? It was almost as if the little girl was being punished and she sure didn't want Bella to think of dinner that way.

Her stubborn Kirkpatrick streak kicked in.

Chapter 4

Seven o'clock and still no Cameron. "Let's eat," Harper told Bella.
The little girl shrugged a slim shoulder. Connie had left for the day
so Harper went out to the kitchen and mixed up more cereal.
While she stirred, anger brewed inside.

How could he blow off dinner with his little girl?

The two of them ate in silence. Bella's shoulders slumped and
Harper thought she heard a sniffle. "I'm not mad at you, Bella,
okay?"

"Okay." Yes, she was definitely crying.

Harper wanted to strangle Cameron. Instead she stabbed a
piece of turkey, her hand aching from gripping the fork so tight.
But she had no appetite. Neither did Bella and Harper called it
quits, cleaning up the kitchen and stowing the ample leftovers in
the refrigerator. They could be nuked in the microwave if Cameron
ever showed up. The classic animated movies had always been her
favorite, so Harper popped one about a puppet boy into the DVD
player in the TV room.

"Stupid," Harper heard Bella mutter. A lot of things were stupid
to her. Although Harper wanted to stretch out on the sofa, she sat
up and left space for Bella. But the little girl curled up on the floor.

Throughout the movie, Harper listened for the sound of the

back door. At nine o'clock she put Bella to bed. When she slipped the voile dress over Bella's head, her stomach twisted at the sight of Bella's spine marching down her back like a row of pearls.

"Did you like the movie?" Harper asked Bella as she tucked her into bed.

"It was sad." Bella's voice quivered.

"Sad?" The word stabbed Harper's heart.

Bella's eyes were distant. "All those little boys without their mom."

"It was just a movie," she offered, trying to ease the hurt darkening Bella's eyes. "He finds his dad in the end."

"I don't care. It was sad," Bella insisted as Harper pulled the sheet up under her chin.

Lordy. And here the kid was all alone in this huge bed. "Bella, I'll be right downstairs until your father gets home. And I'll always leave my door upstairs open. A night light is on in the hallway, in case you need me."

"I know." Bella turned to the side, tucking her hands up under one cheek.

"Night, Bella."

No answer.

Harper cast one final look behind her before leaving the room. Had she ever seen such a lonely sight? Her disgust brewed as she walked downstairs. Grabbing a magazine from the pile Connie kept in the kitchen, she stationed herself in the library. If it hadn't been for Bella, Harper would've packed her bag, called Adam, and waited on the curb for him to pick her up. She was that upset.

Heck with that stupid promise she'd made to herself about finishing projects.

Taking the same chair Cameron had sat in the day of her interview, Harper grabbed what looked like a business magazine and tried to read. Boring. Tossing it aside, she checked the hallway. No sign of Cameron. Time to explore that silver-framed history on the shelves. One of the photos pictured a boyish Cameron in a football jersey with a raven-haired cheerleader clinging to his arm. She was beautiful, with Bella's delicate features.

In another shot, the same girl held a tiny baby with a shock of dark hair. Although the young mother smiled, she looked tired. Any pictures of an older Bella did not have the mother. Sadness lodged in Harper's throat.

Pulling out her phone, she curled up in the wing chair and called her sister.

McKenna answered on the second ring. "Hey, how's it going?"

"I'm moved in."

"Terrific. You feeling good about this?"

"Not really." Pulling her feet up under her, Harper told McKenna about her move-in day. Sitting in the huge, quiet library, she felt so alone.

"Wow, you've got your work cut out for you," McKenna said when she'd wrapped it up and was feeling guilty for complaining.

Time to pull herself up by her bootstraps. "Nothing I can't handle."

"That little girl needs you, Harper."

Her sister was right. Made her furious to think that earlier nannies had left Bella at the mercy of a father who had no time for her. By the time she'd said good-bye to McKenna, Harper felt better. The clock on the mantel chimed, and she jumped. Eleven o'clock and this had been one long day. She needed some sleep. But not before she'd straightened out a few things.

About ten minutes later, she heard the back door open. Taking some deep breaths, so she didn't go off half-cocked, she listened for Cameron's footsteps on the marble floor. He was leafing through his pile of mail when she came to the library door.

Cameron's tie hung loose around his neck, and his shirt looked rumpled, like it had barely survived the day. A suit coat hung over one arm, and his dark blonde hair was in disarray.

This was clearly a man at the end of one busy day.

Didn't matter. She cleared her throat.

He glanced up from the sheaf of envelopes in his hand. "Harper." Said almost as if he were reminding himself that she existed. "You still up?"

"I have to talk to you."

Chucking the mail back onto the table, he heaved a sigh. "Sure. All right."

Should she rethink this? Harper hated feeling like one more problem. She'd only had this job for one day and she could blow it right here. Maybe that would be for the best.

But then there was Bella. Her sister's words came back to her. Dammit, he could just deal with it.

Heart quaking, she turned on one heel and marched back into the library, hoping he'd follow. She perched on the arm of a wing chair but when it began to tip, she stood. Cameron strolled in after her, head down and expression unreadable. When he stripped the tie from his neck and opened another button on his shirt, the scent of working man rolled over her. Her father had always come home looking and smelling like this.

But she'd never had this physical reaction to her father. Reminding herself that she was furious, Harper knotted her hands behind her back.

"Good God, Harper," Cameron sighed as he sank into the wing chair, probably still warm from her body. The soft leather settled around him. Seemed weird to be staring down at her employer so she took the chair across from him. "I hope you're not giving up on Bella. Not yet."

Yep, that's what did it.

"Of course not," she spit out, ashamed that the thought had even crossed her mind. "We waited up for you." My oh my. Didn't she sound just like a bitchy wife?

"You waited up for me?" He seemed at a total loss.

"Of course, we did. Bella needs a family dinner." Impatience gave her words a sharp edge.

Cameron narrowed his eyes. "Goodness sakes alive. One day here and you decided this?" The southern cadence fried her mind.

"Aren't suggestions allowed?"

His jaw shifted. "Most certainly but this sounds more like an accusation, not a suggestion. Believe I told you my schedule is busy."

"I understand that but Bella has an eating disorder."

The words had come out of nowhere and Harper felt as surprised as Cameron looked. The "disorder" part seared the air like a brand and misgivings tumbled in Harper's chest. Her brothers always said she called a spade a spade. But this was tiny Bella. Lordy, she gagged thinking of the baby cereal she'd watched the girl chuck down that day. "So, doesn't it make a lot of sense to make mealtime a family time? Most families do that."

Cameron's eyes emptied. Was she fanning some distant fire? His eyes skimmed down her crossed legs and she stilled her bobbing foot. By that time, a flush had burned its way up his cheeks. His fingers tapped the arms of the chair. "You may have a point."

May have?

"Didn't take you long to get a read on this, did it? My daughter is seeing a child psychologist." He closed his eyes and pressed long fingers against them. "I can rearrange some things. What time do you want me here?"

How could she ever have found this man attractive? Like dry ice, his cool detachment burned that earlier impression from her mind.

"Six o'clock. Bella goes to bed at eight. It would be nice if she had some time with you." My, she *was* getting bossy. Harper could almost hear her brothers heckling her.

A muscle twitched in his jaw. "How about two nights a week."

Was this a poker game? "Three."

He gave a short nod. "Done." As if they'd wrapped up a business deal. She hated him.

"Then there's the matter of her clothes." Why not? She had his complete attention. Granted, his eyes had turned to stone.

Cameron slumped back in the chair. "Darlin', I don't think you could fit one more dress into that closet."

Darlin'? How condescending. Harper wanted to stamp her foot. Instead she sucked in a tight breath and plowed ahead. "And that's the point. A little girl needs play clothes. Or doesn't Bella go out and play?" What a scary thought.

"Bella goes to preschool. You know that don't you?" He seemed to be searching his mind. Probably hard to recall what he'd told the procession of nannies.

"Connie mentioned school. Tuesdays through Thursdays?"

With a weary sigh, he pushed up from the chair. Obviously this meeting was over. Had she pushed him too far? "I believe that's the schedule. Car keys are hanging from a kitchen hook. All the cars are equipped with a carseat. Well, except for the Porsche."

She didn't intend to drive that car any time soon.

"Fine, I can handle that. I mean, I can take her to school."

He raised his eyebrows. Yep, she *had* overstepped her bounds. Her brain fogged. She had to remind herself that she was doing this for Bella. This was the longest first day on a job she'd ever had. She followed him to the door, eyes drilling into that broad back that tapered to such slim hips.

But back to business.

"Do her allergies prevent Bella from going outside?" Harper better get this straight, or she could make a dangerous mistake.

His narrow, aristocratic features tensed. "The truth is, we really don't know. The allergy tests all came back negative."

"Then she could play in the park?"

Mild curiosity softened his frown. "Well now, I'm sure Bella would like that. Very kind of you. I don't think a nanny has ever asked me so many questions," he added with surprise.

"I'm sorry. I just don't want to goof up."

"Goof up?" She thought she saw a grin but by this time they were in the dimly lit foyer. "I appreciate your concern, Harper. Really I do. I'm sure Bella will too."

Harper doubted that Bella appreciated anything. She was a spoiled brat, but the deck was stacked against her. Just thinking about that closet crammed with uncomfortable clothes and the cereal bowl full of mush made Harper's heart ache.

Darkness had settled over the mansion. Only one light glowed out in the kitchen. There was something very cozy about the two of them discussing Bella at the foot of the stairs. Might have been her exhaustion, but Harper's mind slid sideways into his blond hair and the blue eyes studying her. If he weren't the Tin Man, she might mistake the feelings rampaging though her body for attraction.

But that was stupid.

And that would be a real mistake.

"As for the clothes, Connie has a family credit card for any purchases."

Early in the game but Harper knew what Bella needed could not be bought with a credit card.

Cameron set the security system. "There. Done. Are we done as well?"

"Yes sir."

They were halfway to the staircase when he pivoted. "*Sir?* Please. Call me Cameron."

He looked totally puzzled, like she'd just reminded him that he was old.

Well, he was a lot older, right?

"Okay then. Cameron. We're, ah, done."

Dragging herself up the Oriental runner behind her new employer, Harper knew they weren't finished.

Not by a long shot.

Chapter 5

They left for school early on Tuesday since punctuality had never been Harper's strong point. She didn't want to get Bella in trouble and actually found Country Day without too much trouble. An impressive collection of Mercedes and BMWs lined up to drop off their precious cargo. As Harper edged the BMW up to the front door, she chuckled. Easy to tell the mothers from the nannies. The mothers were decked out in designer duds, while the nannies looked more like Goodwill. And that would be Harper.

"See you later," she told Bella after she'd helped her out of the car.

"See ya," Bella shot back, making Harper smile. But her charge seemed to drag her feet. Was Bella shy? A teacher stood in the doorway, welcoming the students. Still, Harper's heart squeezed when Bella disappeared inside. She just seemed so lost.

School lasted until two o'clock. Connie had given Harper the family credit card that morning and after picking Bella up from school, Harper drove straight to Belk's at the Oglethorpe Mall. Sure, she'd been in the store plenty of times but the children's department was a totally new experience. New and fun. Bella seemed unfamiliar with the mall and the store. Eyes wandering, she tripped as they stepped off the escalator.

Harper grabbed her hand. "Watch your step, Pipsqueak."

"Hey, I'm not a Pipsqueak." But Bella looked pleased.

Funny how that name had rolled off Harper's tongue.

"Pipsqueak" had been her own nickname when she was growing up. She glanced down at Bella trudging along, hand tucked securely in Harper's with such faith. At that age Harper had felt so loved. But Bella didn't have six siblings to cushion growing pains. And she certainly didn't have Big Mike, as her father was called, and Maureen. Maureen Kirkpatrick spent her days in a frenzy of cooking and cleaning, her laughter and scolding filling the small house.

That certainly wasn't the case at the mansion on Victory Drive.

"Here we go, Bella. Now you tell me what looks good."

They started with the first rack of play clothes and worked their way through.

One hour later Harper tossed bulging shopping bags into the back of the SUV. They'd picked out enough outfits to clothe a small village, all in colorful soft cotton. The sparkly pink headband was an add-on.

"I want a scarf like yours," Bella said when they were ready to leave the department.

Looking at Bella's wiry hair that never stayed put, Harper fingered the orange and citrus green scarf holding her own hair back. Nothing special but apparently in Bella's eyes, it was. "Oh, I don't know if they have long scarves for little girls."

"How about a headband?" The young salesclerk snatched something pink and sparkly from a display.

"Perfect." Harper fixed the plastic band on Bella's head. "Look in the mirror, sweetie."

The smile stayed on Bella's face all the way home.

The large green sticky note on his desk reminded him about dinner Thursday. Come hell or high water, he was getting home on time. When he left the office for his project in the historical section, he slapped the note right on his briefcase. No way was he going to tangle with the new nanny again. Monday night, Harper had ambushed him like a disapproving parent. He'd had enough of that to last a lifetime. He supposed her nose was still out of joint because they couldn't begin the Family Hour, as he called it, on Tuesday. But he already had a meeting on the calendar for that evening. No way was he canceling a meeting with Darcy Livingsworth, whose support he desperately needed for a project in the Victorian District.

Promptly at six o'clock he pulled into the garage. When Connie served the tomato bisque at six fifteen, he was snapping a napkin onto his lap. Bella sat in her booster chair to his right.

"Now, don't you look nice tonight, Bella." He detected a pleased glow. "What's that on your head, sweetheart?"

Bella's hand went to the sparkly thing that didn't seem to match her red shirt. "We got it at the mall."

"Harper took Bella shopping," Connie supplied.

"Well, that's wonderful. Where is Harper?"

"In the kitchen."

That's not how this was going down. "Connie, would you

please ask Ms. Kirkpatrick to join us?"

Eyebrows lifting, Connie trotted out to the kitchen.

When Harper appeared in the doorway, she looked ready for the St. Patrick's Day parade in her bright green top. The scarf running through her hair matched the flaming orange pants. And she was in charge of Bella's wardrobe? His lips twitched and he pressed them tight before asking, "Would you please join us?"

"Well, I…thought this would be just family." She toed one of her orange flats against the other.

He pinned her with his eyes while she squirmed. And Harper was good at squirming. He'd seen that at the bachelor party. "Well, you are part of the family now, aren't you?" But he knew the danger in that and flicked his eyes to Bella while Harper took a seat. Family members didn't just up and leave and that had been the case with so many of his nannies. Connie bustled out with another placemat and silverware.

"Connie, you are most welcome to join us as well." But she liked to have dinner with Jack. His comment was for Harper's benefit.

"If you don't mind…"

"Not at all. I know Jack is waiting for you. We can clean up." He ignored the rearing of Harper's head. Connie disappeared and came back with a bowl of bisque. "We were just talking about your shopping expedition. Is that shirt new, Bella?"

"Do you think it's pretty?" She traced the neckline with one hand. His daughter was preening. The simple feminine gesture made his throat swell and he swallowed hard.

"Very pretty." He raised his brows at Harper, who seemed to be waiting. What? Did she think he didn't know how to give his own daughter a compliment? Nodding her head, she dipped her spoon into the bisque.

For a second the only sound came from their spoons and the muted traffic on Victory Drive.

"Harper, why don't you tell us how your first week is going?" As long as she was here, she could damn well carry her share of the conversation.

"Well, I..." Her flush rivaled the tomato soup. "I think it's just fine. I know my way to Bella's school now."

"She only got lost once, Daddy." Bella sounded so proud. He almost hooted out loud as Harper's blush deepened.

"Really? Well, I suppose some things are bound to be new."

Eyes dropped, Harper shoved her hair back. A rogue memory of her swinging those tresses back as she stood on his bar swamped him. He sucked in a breath.

"They are, sir. Ah, Cameron."

The image in his head faded fast. She had a way of making him feel older than the hills.

"Why don't you tell us a little bit about dinner at your own home?" His question came out sounding smug but he didn't mean it that way. After all, she'd almost made it through one week. At this house, that was saying something.

Harper's spoon circled her soup bowl. "Well, I, ah, have five brothers and one sister so dinners were kind of noisy."

"Wow." The yearning in Bella's face took a hold of his heart.

"Sounds like fun. All those people." Sure, he remembered a crowded dinner table. But it hadn't been fun and they'd called it supper, not dinner.

"Yeah, it was fun. My dad's kind of a character and well, the boys could be rowdy."

"Rowdy?" Bella frowned.

"Wild. Disruptive," Cameron supplied, waiting to be corrected.

But Harper grinned. "Yeah, we were wild. But our mother would smack us with a spoon if we got out of hand. More a warning than anything."

"Did you get s-smacked, Harper?" Bella could hardly get the word out. There would be no smacking in this house so she had no idea what it was. Sitting back, he tried to visualize the Kirkpatrick dinner table. If any smacking had gone on, it certainly hadn't toned her down a bit.

"Of course I did. And I earned it." Harper laughed as if being disciplined had been more fun than a barrel of monkeys. Connie appeared with the main course. Stifling her giggles, Harper took the platter of brisket while Cameron helped himself to the bowl of butter beans. The food smelled wonderful and he realized he hadn't eaten lunch. That wasn't unusual unless he had a lunch meeting.

The brisket broke with his fork. He savored it slowly while across from him Harper wolfed dinner down with the enthusiasm of a trucker. But she blotted her lips like a lady.

"You have outdone yourself again, Connie. I do believe these mashed potatoes could levitate right off the plate." Harper laughed politely and Connie blushed. The conversation moved on. Connie left and Harper cleared the table when they were finished eating and then brought the tapioca pudding to the table.

"Want some?" She lifted a goblet to Bella, who shook her head.

Clearly disappointed, Harper slipped into her chair. She actually cared about his daughter's eating problem and that touched him. Some of the girls just didn't get it. One had tried to force feed Bella. At least that's what it looked like to him when Bella's shriek brought him to the kitchen. He'd dismissed Meredith, or was that Madeleine, on the spot.

Later he tried to help Harper clean up. "Usually I put the plates in the dishwasher and then leave the pans in the sink for Connie."

"Oh, no pans left out. My mother would have a fit." Harper attacked the roaster with gusto. "This was my job at home. Not a very good cook but cleanup duty? I'm on it."

She was as good as her word. Feeling a little lost, Cameron opened the dishwasher. Didn't take long before she hipped him aside. "No, no. Big plates in back."

He stepped aside. Another flashback sent him to the nearest chair. She'd really known how to use those hips as Catwoman and he didn't need another reminder.

As she organized the dishwasher, Harper swiped her eyes toward the TV room. Bella had curled up on the sofa and looked almost asleep. "So it's always like this? Not even puddings?"

Back to that again. When it came to Bella's eating issues, he felt so helpless. "I'm afraid so. I take her to a therapist every other Saturday. She thinks we're making progress but there's no easy solution. You might as well know that now, Harper. This isn't a case where one cup of tapioca and she'll be cured."

She closed the dishwasher and flipped the knob. "I didn't say it would be easy. I'll take her up to bed."

"No, I'll do it." Truth was, Bella wasn't much of a cuddler. Carrying her to bed was a treat.

After the two of them got Bella into her PJs and she'd curled up on her side, Harper disappeared. He locked up and made a quick call to Kimmy.

"Are we still on for this weekend?" she asked with an audible yawn. She had to get up so early for her TV show.

"Of course." He struggled to recall the plans.

"Good. Don't forget it's black tie."

The gallery opening. He thought the black tie thing was a little over the top, but this was some sort of relative of Kimmy's. Very high brow. "Of course." He'd need another sticky note.

But as he tried to read in bed that night, Cameron wasn't thinking about the gallery opening or even the meeting with Darcy, which had gone well.

Harper was on his mind.

But she wasn't sitting at the dinner table or wrestling with a roasting pan.

And she most certainly wasn't wearing that green shirt.

Chapter 6

Friday and a great day for the park. Harper was so glad Bella's grandparents had called. In the back seat of the BMW, she looked so cute in a blue and green flowered top and blue knit pants. Ever since Cameron's compliment about Bella's clothes, she'd insisted on wearing a new outfit every day. February sunlight shone through the live oaks arched overhead. Harper had always loved this boulevard and never dreamed she'd ever be living here. The engine of the BMW purred as they sat at a stoplight. She was feeling pretty good.

Harper had made it to the end of the week. For the first time since her arrival, she felt like she knew what she was doing. Singing along to Adele's "Burn," she stepped on the gas when the light turned green.

One of Bella's new Hello Kitty tennis shoes beat against the front seat.

"Hey, Bella, no kicking, okay? You'll leave a mark. Your dad won't like it."

Harper was discovering that the word "Dad" worked magic. Bella stopped kicking but tucked her fingers in her mouth and began to suck. Made Harper crazy, but one thing at a time.

The call from Bella's grandparents had been such a nice surprise that morning. Connie was busy with the laundry, so Harper had answered the phone. The ring of the landline startled her, and she'd rushed to answer it. "Bennett residence. This is Harper."

There'd been a pause on the other end. "Hello, this is Bella's grandmother. And, well, we were just wondering if we could see little Bella?" The voice quavered, like the woman was either very old or sick.

"Why, of course. We don't have anything scheduled for today." Was she owning this nanny role or what? Cameron had mentioned that his own family lived out of town, so this must be his wife's family. She didn't know much about Cameron's wife, only that she'd died tragically. Since she'd planned on taking Bella to Daffin Park anyway, she quickly agreed to meet the couple near the fountain. Linda Sue Goodwin told her they would be on the bench at the edge of the pond around ten o'clock.

When Harper pulled into the park, the Spanish moss swayed from the trees in a soft breeze that promised spring. "We're going to see your grandma and grandpa this morning, Bella. Won't that be nice?" She looked in her rearview mirror. The little girl was eyeing the swings across from the pond.

Stepping out and hooking her canvas tote bag over one shoulder, Harper opened the back door and helped Bella from the seat. Taking the little girl's hand, she surveyed the area. "Now, where are they?"

Bella's attention was still captured by the play area.

"Look, is that them over there?" An older couple huddled together on a park bench under one of the trees. When they spotted Harper and Bella walking toward them, they stood, although the man had trouble getting to his feet.

Bella pulled back on Harper's hand. "I want to swing," she complained in a whiny voice.

"And we will. But first we'll talk to your grandparents, okay?" What was this? Gently she tugged Bella forward.

How well Harper remembered Sunday dinners at her grandmother's house, before the Kirkpatrick clan became so large that Grandma Nora had to come to their place. Roast chicken and dumplings had been Grandma's standard Sunday meal. To this day, that smell made Harper's mouth water. Her grandmother had died five years ago and Harper really missed her. Grandpa had been gone a long time. Bella was lucky.

Leaning heavily on a cane, Mr. Goodwin tried to keep up with his wife as she sprang toward them. Her wire-rimmed glasses didn't hide her pretty features.

But Bella balked. "I want to swing now!" She kept tugging at Harper's hand.

How embarrassing. Stopping and squatting to eye level, Harper said, "We'll go to the swings later, Bella. Don't be rude."

The only response was "the lip." Bella had a habit of thrusting out her lower lip whenever she didn't agree. That happened a lot.

With Bella tight in hand, Harper walked toward the attractive couple. At one time, their pewter hair might have been as dark as Bella's. That would make sense since in the pictures, their daughter had raven hair. In spite of a slight limp, Mr. Goodwin looked like he'd just stepped off a golf course in his navy slacks and jacket over a yellow polo shirt. His wife also trended toward L.L.Bean in tailored beige pants and a pale blue sweater set with pearls. The smell of Heaven Sent was unmistakable as Harper drew closer, extending one hand. She liked them already. "Hi, I'm Harper Kirkpatrick. Bella's new nanny."

She could have been invisible as Linda Sue shook her hand. Her eyes were riveted to Bella.

"Oh, Harvey. Isn't she just the picture of Tammy?" Mrs. Goodwin's pale eyes watered.

"She certainly is. The very picture."

Good grief, were they both going to burst into tears? The whole scene began to feel strange. Bella had ducked behind one of Harper's legs, hands knotted on her purple jeans until Harper could feel the pinch. "Come on, Bella. Say hello."

The little girl remained rigidly attached to Harper's thigh. Those tiny fingers might even leave a bruise.

"Why don't we just sit down," she suggested. Anxiety cinched Harper's chest. Bella's grandmother was checking Harper out with a puzzled frown, taking in the purple and orange striped scarf in her hair. The husband hung back.

"She doesn't know us. That's all, Harvey. Let's sit down, dear." Bella's grandmother coaxed her husband back to the bench where he maneuvered onto the worn slats with some effort.

"Arthritis," Linda Sue told Harper in an undertone.

The unease in Harper's body broke into a nervous chatter, like the squirrels dashing through the trees overhead. Something felt so off. Pulling Bella onto her lap, she faced the couple. "When was the last time you saw Bella?"

"Oh, well." Linda Sue looked to her husband, who gave a dismissive snort. "You see, we haven't seen her. Not since she was a baby."

Please, would the ground just open and swallow me?

"Never?" Harper's arms tightened their hold and Bella squirmed.

"Did you say that you were a *new* nanny?" Linda Sue looked as confused as Harper felt.

"Yes. I started this week."

"I see." What looked like sympathy softened Linda Sue's features. "Well now, Harper, we're sure glad you brought Bella to see us today. She looks just like our darling little girl."

The lump in Harper's throat felt like a golf ball until anger dislodged it. Why in heaven's name would Cameron keep this poor couple from seeing their granddaughter? They seemed harmless as they chatted with her about the weather. When they asked about her background, this felt strangely like another interview. The older couple barely listened, eyes on their granddaughter. Bella was bored. Her swinging legs made that obvious. After two kicks to Harper's shins, it was time to head for the play area.

"We should go. I promised Bella she could swing. Maybe we could meet again sometime." *After I know what I'm doing.* Harper slid Bella from her lap and stood.

"Oh, we'd like that." Something in Linda Sue's pinched expression told Harper she realized a mistake had been made. "Thank you for bringing her today."

"Not a problem." Only it probably was.

Opening her arms, Linda Sue beckoned to Bella. "Do you think I could have a hug? Just one hug for your grandmother?"

Bella lowered her head and the lip went out.

Mr. Goodwin put a hand on his wife's shoulder. "Don't, Linda Sue. She doesn't know who we are, darlin'." Sadness echoed in his voice.

Regaining her feet, Linda Sue managed a small smile. "Thank you so very much. Harper? Is that right?"

"Yes, my name is Harper."

After they said goodbye, Harper took Bella's hand. With a wild shriek, the child broke free and raced toward the play area, arms outstretched. Lord, she was a wild spirit. After settling Bella onto one of the swings, Harper began to push. From the corner of her eye, she could see the couple sitting in the black Lincoln, watching them. It creeped her out.

Her mind reeled as she pushed Bella higher. What kind of guy was Cameron Bennett? Forget his gentlemanly grooming and the soft southern burr to his voice. Was he so busy with his business and his girlfriend that he couldn't share Bella with his wife's parents? Seemed so cruel.

"Too high!" Bella's screech snapped Harper back to reality.

"Sorry. Sorry, honey." Harper grabbed the rubber swing and slowed its course. She didn't want to terrify the girl.

But she may have already done that with grandparents she didn't even know.

"I took Bella to meet her grandparents today," Harper told Connie about an hour later when they were having lunch. No use beating around the bush. She'd been raised Catholic and was always ready to repent. Connie was making soup for dinner, and the smell of chicken and onions filled the kitchen.

"Grandparents." Connie fixed her with an empty stare and stopped stirring.

Grabbing her glass of lemonade, Harper took a sip. "Yes, Tammy Goodwin's parents. I guess." Cripes, she felt like such a fool.

Connie's eyes widened. "You'll have to tell him. I'm not."

Harper straightened in her chair. "Of course I will. No big deal."

"I'm sorry, Harper. I should have told you." Connie pushed a wisp of grey hair back and returned to stirring. "I always take a message when anyone calls, just so you know. What Mr. Bennett does with those messages, well, that's not for us to know or say."

But she could tell from the housekeeper's expression that it bothered her more than a little. She had to tell "Mr. Bennett" herself? Harper might need some of those southern smelling salts to get the job done.

Bella paid no attention to their conversation, shoveling in the cereal. Her appetite gone, Harper tucked the leftover half of her turkey and cheese sandwich into a baggie and stowed it in the refrigerator.

She'd been feeling so good about her position and now she'd blown it. When would Cameron get home? Did he go out with the guys after work on Fridays? She sure hoped so. Or maybe he'd meet Kimmy—wasn't that her name—after work for a drink? Part of her would be relieved if he didn't come home, but she wanted this to be over. Would he fire her?

After putting Bella to bed, Harper took up her post in the library. A stack of magazines had arrived that day. She paged through *Kiplinger* and then went on to *Money Magazine*. You could tell this was a man's house. Absolutely no articles about clothes or makeup. She set the magazines aside and looked over the library shelves.

A book about historical Savannah in her lap, Harper was nodding off when she heard someone in the kitchen. She jerked awake and the book fell to the floor. The last thing she wanted was another confrontation in the library. Scooping up her reading material she slid it back onto the shelf and hot-footed it down the hallway. She found Cameron in the kitchen standing in front of the open refrigerator.

"Mr. Bennett?"

Carton of milk in hand, he slammed the refrigerator door shut and turned. "Harper, Mr. Bennett makes me feel like...like I'm your father or something. Call me Cameron, please."

But this was a Mr. Bennett conversation and she knew it. Nothing cozy about what she had to say.

He took a swig of milk from the carton, absolutely forbidden in the Kirkpatrick household. A drop of milk rolled from one corner of his lips, and she almost swiped it away. His tongue darted out, and warmth cascaded through her body. She was having totally inappropriate thoughts. And enjoying them.

Harper curled her hands into fists, reminding herself that she was furious.

"My, oh, my, have I missed one of our dinner dates?" He wore a puzzled frown.

Dates? She stiffened. "No, but I did want talk to you, Mr. Ben— ah, Cameron."

Tugging off his tie, he returned the milk to the refrigerator. When he pulled out one of the chairs from the round table, it squeaked against the tiles in protest. "Why don't you have a seat?" He threw her a guarded look, like he wanted to be sitting down if he had to take a hit.

"Don't worry. I'm not leaving." She perched on the edge of the chair. "Although you might ask me to after this."

"Really? This should be good. Let's hear it." Tipping his chair back, he laced his hands behind his head. He'd unbuttoned his shirt, revealing some promising chest hair—one of Harper's personal weaknesses.

Delete. Delete. She didn't want to think of her employer that way. Now she could think of nothing else. Arms. She'd study his forearms. The sleeves were rolled up, and a dusting of hair glinted gold in the light that glowed above the sink.

Best to get right to the point. "Bella and I met with the Goodwins today. In the park."

His chair hit the floor with a thud. In a heartbeat his expression shifted from tired to tyrannical. "Are you friggin' kidding me? The Goodwins?" A vein throbbed in his forehead.

"Bella's grandparents." She could hardly get the words out. Was she too young to have heart palpitations?

He was furious, a flush blazing up his cheeks, but the memory of the tears in Linda Sue Goodwin's eyes gave Harper courage.

"Why in hell's name would you do that?" He bit off his words like he was yanking apart cold taffy.

"They called. I didn't think anything of it."

"Saints be praised. I do believe you didn't think at all." Vaulting to his feet so fast the chair tipped over, Cameron began to pace. Coins jingled in his pockets as he fingered them.

Yes, she was certain these were heart palpitations.

"I thought I was helping out, that this happened a lot. I didn't know." Her face must have told the rest of the story. But she would not cry.

She just. Would. Not.

Cameron ran one palm over his eyes. "They saw her as a baby, but not since then. And trust me, there's a reason."

Well, it better be a good reason. Lips trembling, she waited.

Cameron sucked in a tight breath. Just what he needed. The past chasing him down like a yapping hound.

Righteousness sparked from Harper's eyes. As usual, his nanny was a walking parade of color. The wide purple and orange scarf wrapped around her head made her look like a pirate. The huge orange flower tucked in her head scarf looked Carribean.

Carribean and hot.

She'd gone crazy with his credit cards, lugging home boxes and bags. Bella's smile made the bills a worthwhile investment. But if he let this go on, he probably wouldn't even recognize his daughter. Still, Bella had smiled at him at the dinner table last night and asked him if she looked pretty.

That's the only reason preventing him from firing Harper on the spot for breaking a cardinal rule. If she headed for the hills like the others, he was burnt barbecue. He struggled to rein in his rage.

"I have never been on good terms with my former in-laws. They never approved of me."

Approved? That was putting it mildly. They'd burned so many bridges it would make Sherman's March to the Sea look like a marshmallow roast.

"But they're her grandparents." Harper's hand shook as she adjusted the flower in her scarf. Artificial, he supposed, or she'd be gasping for breath.

She may have a fake flower stuck in her hair, but there was nothing artificial about Harper Kirkpatrick. She was authentic as hell and Bella needed her around. Time to go easy.

"Let's just say they weren't particularly kind to us. Bella only became important to them *after* her birth. And after my wife's death." Memories sliced through him like the damn carving knife hanging from Connie's magnetic strip next to the stove.

Eyes softening, Harper sat perfectly still. He could see her mind working. She wanted more details. He hated giving them. What could she possibly know about fathering a motherless child? How could he help her understand without having her run out the door?

He yanked the chair out and sat back down. "And what are you doing with your days, Harper?"

Her lips opened and closed. Was she at a loss for words? That was unusual for Harper. "We read books. We go to the park." Then she froze because of course the park hadn't turned out so well.

He could see her swallow in that long delicate throat. The heat that pulsed through his body shocked him. Every time that damn Catwoman suit came to mind, it made him crazy.

"And I take her to school, of course." She folded her hands in the lap of her purple jeans. A frown formed between her eyes that could turn from green cat's eyes to brown suede when she got really serious. "Could you tell me more about Bella's eating problem? What does the therapist say? I suppose I ought to know that."

She'd changed the subject, thank God.

"We don't know." And here came the kicker. But Harper might as well know what she was dealing with. "There's a chance it might be psychological. At least, that's what the therapist says. The eating thing might be her way of controlling what she can."

Harper's eyes swirled with sympathy and he wanted no part of it. "That's so sad. Could I ask, how old was she when…"

"When her mother died? Bella was only two, so we don't really know what she remembers."

Harper's hands knitted together as if she were in prayer.

Sometimes this house seemed almost like a mausoleum, so closed up. Jumping up, he pulled the back door open and inhaled. The cool air set his thoughts to rights. Calm and a sense of control returned. The sound of the fountain in the garden always soothed him. Harper seemed genuinely invested in Bella, and he liked that. He didn't need another girl's sudden departure. The nanny position had become a damn revolving door.

"Harper, I wonder if you could do something for me."

The fake flower bobbed. "Sure."

"I'd like you to give me a report on Fridays. Tell me about how you spent your time during the week and what you feel you accomplished with Bella."

Harper jerked like he'd hit her with a cattle prod, but he wasn't backing down. There would be no more meetings with the Goodwins.

"And just what would you like in this report?"

"The facts. Your activities and accomplishments." He'd tossed his jacket on one of the other chairs, and now he searched an inner pocket for one of his business cards. "You can just send it to my e-mail."

Cheeks flaming, she nodded. "Fine. Is there anything else, sir?" Her eyes glinted like sparklers on the Fourth of July as she took the card.

"No, that will be all." Good Lord. He sounded like an officious prick. Was he becoming the type of man he avoided when he moved to Savannah?

Harper leapt to her feet with agile grace that reminded him of a bachelor party he was trying desperately to forget. "Fine. Well. Glad we had this little talk." Her sarcasm had a Midwest directness, not the southern swirl of molasses he usually heard. He wasn't going to take this sitting down so he stood. But before he could say a thing, she turned and was gone.

Watching her leave, he wondered just how mad she was.

Chapter 7

Saturday was Harper's first day off. After the cozy chat with Cameron the night before, she needed it. Raging hungry when she woke up, she dashed downstairs to grab some breakfast. Connie caught her in the kitchen. The housekeeper's face was flushed. "I don't suppose you cook?" she asked as Harper dug around in the walk-in pantry.

"Heck, no." Her idea of cooking was nuking a pizza in the microwave. Billy had complained about it all the time.

With a resigned set to her shoulders, Connie pulled a crockpot from the lower cabinet. "Oh, dear. I thought not."

Now, was that an insult or what? Finding some cinnamon chex, Harper grabbed a handful and began to munch. "What do you need? My mother always says if you can read, you can cook. I can read." But Maureen Kirkpatrick didn't give up her stove easily, which was why Harper and McKenna never got in any practice time on that court.

Relief flooded the housekeeper's face. "Oh, thank you so much. I will write everything out. Make it very simple. Mr. Bennett usually has sandwiches on Sunday but he's invited, well, *her* for dinner."

"Who?" Harper's chewing slowed.

"Miss Carrington."

Oh. Well. Harper had to munch on that a minute. She'd finally get to meet the woman who dressed little girls in linen. Should be interesting. "No problem. I can totally rock this dinner. Martha Stewart, here I come." She could add the meal to her "list of accomplishments" next Friday.

Relief eased the tension from Connie's face. It was way too early in the day for this nice woman to have her panties in a knot. "Today, I'll cook this pork roast for Sunday dinner. It'll be in the refrigerator overnight in the crockpot. Just heat it up tomorrow. I'll leave detailed instructions." She grabbed a pad of paper from a drawer and began to write. "You can roast some brussel sprouts in the oven. Do you know how to bake potatoes?"

That was definitely an insult. "Of course. Ten minutes in the microwave."

Yanking open one of the enormous refrigerator doors, the housekeeper pointed. "Vegetables in the left hand bin. Use the brown-skinned potatoes."

Harper's chest swelled. This had redemption written all over it. Except for the disastrous meeting with the Goodwins, she was totally owning this job. "No problem, Connie. Don't worry about a thing."

While Connie finished preparing the meat, Harper stowed the cereal away and poured a cup of coffee. Time to get dressed.

The sound of canned laughter floated into the kitchen from the TV room where Bella was watching cartoons. The little girl's giggles made Harper smile. Bella didn't laugh enough, in her book. Coffee in hand, she trotted up the stairs.

Showering in the clawfoot tub was a trip. She had to step indecently high to even get into the thing. Thank goodness for the wide shower head that must have been added later. After shampooing her hair, she climbed out and dried off with one of the plush pink towels. She ran jelled fingers through the damp strands and let her hair fall to her shoulders in loose curls. No styling today. Then she pulled on a lime green knit shirt with pink stripes and pink jeans. You never know who you might see driving around town.

Like it mattered. Harper had a numb spot in her chest where her heart used to be. When would she be over Billy? Sometimes she'd hear a song, like "Unchained Melody" and oh, yeah, she was back longing for the boy. Billy was a key thread in the fabric of her college years. They'd had so much fun together. The fact that he preferred the fast life in California left her feeling confused, like she'd never really known him.

After she brought up the color in her cheeks with some blush, she emptied the contents of her leather sack into her bright pink peony purse. A little lip gloss and she was ready to go. Before she left, she poked her head in the TV room. "See you later, Bella."

The little girl's eyes grew round.

Too late, Harper remembered the history in this house. How many nannies had said the same, never to return? "I'll be back this afternoon."

Lips set like she was thinking *sure, I've heard that before*, Bella blinked and went back to the screen.

Harper grabbed the car keys from the hook. "If I don't run into

you later today, Connie, have a nice day off. I'll see you Monday."
The housekeeper threw her a good-natured wave. They were getting along great. Harper's green flip-flops threw up a fine spray as she made her way through the dewy garden. The climate-controlled garage felt cool, a faint nip of gas and oil lingering in the air. Beyond the SUV were Cameron's Jaguar, a Bentley and his prized Porsche. The man liked his boy toys.

But he was a man, not a boy.

She dropped the car keys. Picking them up, she turned them over in her hands. Was this an ah-hah moment? She slid into the front seat. Her curiosity about Cameron almost embarrassed her. Just on principle, she'd resisted Googling him. After all, what was happening here? Maybe Cameron had the "Not Available" appeal.

That must be it. He was safe.

And much older. At least, she was pretty sure about that.

He must be at least in his mid-thirties.

She could dream about Cameron Bennett because he was totally out of reach. Settling back in the soft leather, she started the vehicle. McKenna thought she should start dating again.

"Look for Dad or one of our brothers when you check out guys," McKenna had advised her. "Billy may have been missing a sensitivity chip."

"Now you tell me?"

"You were happy with him. Billy could be a lot of fun. And he had that bad-boy ponytail. But maybe he didn't have husband qualities." McKenna's eyes had grown sad. "Next time, be choosy and careful."

"Next time won't be anytime soon."

"I know what you mean, but we can always hope." McKenna had her own problems finding Mr. Right.

Out on the street, Harper gave the SUV a good rev and punched on the sound system. How great was it to drive a vehicle that started on the first try? During the week, she'd downloaded some of her music and as she turned out onto Victory Drive, she blasted it. Is it ever too early in the morning to listen to Adele? But the sad, angry songs always made her think of Billy, so she changed to the radio and tuned in country music.

Stopping at a Starbucks for a chai latte picked up her spirits. The day was heating up fast, and Harper almost wished she'd worn shorts. Still, it was only February. She was just nutso because she'd made it through the first week of her new job. But would she make any progress at all with this position? Bella Bennett was one angry kid.

With nothing to do, she buzzed her old neighborhood. Left hand draped over the steering wheel, she laughed, picturing Cameron's face when he opened the e-mail with her "list of accomplishments" for the past week. She'd worked on it until about two a.m.

Coming to her old street, she slowed down. One week in another neighborhood and she looked at the ramshackle houses with new eyes. Most of these houses needed some serious work. Structures leaned and paint peeled. Harvey, one of her former neighbors, was hoofing it toward the coffee shop on the corner.

"Hey, Harvey!" She waved to him from the window.

How she enjoyed his look of amazement as she glided past.
After a quizzical smile, Harvey continued on to Cuppa Joe, shirt
tails flapping.

When she reached the two-flat she'd lived in with Billy, she
slowed to a crawl. The windows of the second-floor apartment
yawned empty. Still too soon for Charlie to have it rented out. The
blue and yellow batik window curtains she'd created by hand were
stowed in Cameron's attic. The green philodendrons and maiden
hair ferns that had once crowded the apartment windows had all
died after Billy left. She'd been so darned sad that she hardly got
out of bed for about three weeks. Those dead plants had been
nothing but a hurtful reminder and she'd cried carting them out to
the trash.

She stepped on the gas and took a right at the corner. Feeling a
magnetic pull to the place where she'd been so happy—and so
sad—she circled the block. On her third pass, she pulled up short.
Dressed in a black T-shirt and cutoffs, Adam stood barefoot in the
center of the street, one flat hand held up like a police cop.

Smiling, she pulled over.

"Nice set of wheels." Adam eyed the SUV with approval as she
jumped out.

"Not mine." She gave him a good hug.

"No kidding?" Taking her elbow, he maneuvered her toward
the green frame house where he rented the first floor. He snagged
the morning paper from the lawn before following her up the
steps. "Had coffee yet?"

"I have had my breakfast and my coffee." The apartment

smelled familiar and friendly. She followed him back into the kitchen.

"So how'd it go this week?" Opening *The Savannah Gazette* on the table, he motioned for her to sit down.

"Pretty darn good." Dropping her purse on the floor, she slid onto one of the stools. Even Connie would approve of the neatness of Adam's kitchen. His serious collection of spices hung in a rack next to a stove. If she opened a drawer, she'd find the coffee containers in alpha order.

"So what are you doing over here?" Adam gave her a skeptical look. "Guess you didn't get fired yet if you're driving the guy's car."

"Maybe I missed the old neighborhood."

"Maybe you missed the old boyfriend." He poured the cup of coffee she hadn't asked for. "Harper, Billy is not the prize in the crackerjack box, got it? Let him go. He was an idiot."

She bristled. "That's why he got such a top job in Hollywood, right? While I have only been able to nail down waitressing jobs…and, oh yes, my latest babysitting gig."

"Quit slamming yourself." Adam's carefully groomed eyebrows drew together as he took the stool across from her. "I would hardly call a nanny position in a historic mansion a 'babysitting gig.' Especially for Cameron Bennett."

Her ears perked up. "What do you know about him?"

"The Internet is a wonderful thing."

"Spill."

Adam could have the most annoying Cheshire grin. "Boy wonder. Restoration genius. The city worships at his feet. Even volunteers for Habitat for Humanity. Widower. One daughter." He dropped information on the table like warm toast. "What's the little girl like?"

"Mad at the world."

"If you lost your mother, maybe you'd be mad too."

"Probably." Outside, the finches were in a feeding frenzy, nudging each other off the posts of Adam's birdfeeder. "Her father doesn't seem to have much time for her."

"Not a surprise since he's now half of a power couple." When Adam wiggled his eyebrows like that, he had a tasty tidbit. "According to the news, he's dating Kimmy Carrington."

"I've heard the name. Why is it familiar?"

Leaning over the table, Adams said a dramatic whisper, "Kimmy in the Morning."

Surprise nearly toppled Harper from her perch. "No way. *That* Kimmy?" Hard to picture Cameron with the TV pop psychologist. When Harper lived in the dorm, the girls would all mock Kimmy while they got ready for class. Kimmy dished out mind pills that were laughable.

"You've got it. Master of the obvious. Solving the world's problems, one trivial suggestion at a time."

"But beautiful." Harper fingered her damp curls. As she recalled, Kimmy's hair fell to her shoulders in a sleek blonde wave. She didn't like picturing Cameron with Kimmy.

"So, how's he turning out as your boss?"

What could she say about Cameron? Even though Adam was a close friend, she didn't want to admit that she'd made a major mistake with Cameron's former in-laws that week. Instead, she told him about the family dinners she'd scheduled.

"How's that going over?"

"I'm not sure. It turned into more of a question and answer period. I felt like I had to explain myself."

Adam's lips curved. "Maybe he wants to learn more about you."

"I doubt it." She wrinkled her nose. "Besides, he's old."

"What? Late twenties according to Wikipedia."

"Wow. Really?" The world shifted. "I just don't think of him that way."

"Kimmy does." Adam laughed. "Have you met her yet?"

"Sunday. She's coming for dinner."

"Hmm. I'll have to catch up with you next week. Get all the delicious details."

Acid churned in Harper's stomach.

Delicious? She sure hoped so.

Chapter 8

At four o'clock Sunday, Harper stood in the kitchen, staring at the crockpot in the refrigerator. What had Connie told her? And where was the note? Maybe it got thrown out with the newspaper. Mousse stood in crystal cups, so dessert was taken care of. The rest of the meal—total puzzle. She pulled out the drawer of the crisper. Right. Brussel sprouts.

Although she thought Bella was upstairs with Cameron, suddenly the toddler appeared, pulling at her aqua shirt. "I want to play outside." They had spent Sunday afternoon out in the porch, but Bella had been a total brat. Coloring was "boring," and she didn't want to learn how to play checkers. Cameron had spent most of the afternoon working in his home office.

"Maybe later, okay?" Harper sucked in a deep breath. After all, it wasn't Bella's fault that her nanny was a Martha Stewart wannabe.

"Anything wrong?" Cameron's voice made her jump.

She slammed the refrigerator closed and turned. "Nope. Not at all."

"Great." With his oxford cloth shirt sleeves rolled up neatly and khaki pants, he was very much the Sunday southern gentleman. "Anything I can do to help?"

She gripped the kitchen counter with both hands. "Got it covered."

And if he believed that, she had a Florida swamp she'd like to unload.

"Terrific." His gaze dropped to Bella, who looked so cute in her pink play pants and flowered shirt. The new tennis shoes they'd bought at the Oglethorpe Mall lit up with every step. "Hey, Bella, I have something in the car for you."

When Cameron swung his daughter into his arms, a lump formed in Harper's throat. Black hair wild, she looked at her dad with cautious adoration.

As Cameron opened the back door, he turned back. "Harper, I meant to tell you that a friend will be joining us tonight."

"Oh, Connie mentioned that. Looking forward to meeting her."

Cameron nodded. "Kimmy was fascinated when I mentioned these family dinners." He said "family dinners" with wonder, like he was referring to Disney World. "I asked her to join us."

"No problem." Anxiety blazed across Harper's chest. She watched the two of them take the back stairs to the side yard, where Cameron put Bella down. The little girl was so excited she was practically skipping down the stone walk toward the garage.

Harper turned back to the crockpot. First step, plug it in. Where should she put the dial? Medium sounded safe. Opening the refrigerator door, she grabbed the sturdy porcelain pot and plunked it in the metal liner, clapping on the Pyrex top.

Now for the vegetables. From what Harper had seen, there was no big trick to this. Just spread the vegetables out on the pan and cover them with oil. Rummaging through the cupboards, she pulled out one of the larger baking pans and set it on the counter. How hard could this be? Next, she cut the brussel sprouts in half before arranging them on the baking sheet. With a liberal hand, she brushed them with the olive oil.

As Harper worked, she heard Bella giggling in the side yard. Peeking out, Harper saw that Cameron had put up a badminton set. Bella looked a little young to be whacking a racquet around, but she dodged toward every white birdie Cameron sent her way.

Hard for Harper to drag her eyes away.

But there was dinner. With Kimmy.

In Harper's home, meals had been a ritual. Her mother cooked huge amounts of food. Spaghetti with juicy meatballs that had to be cut with a knife and swiss steak tenderized by pounding with a heavy plate. Grandma Nora had taught them all how to "lay the table." Heaven forbid if the blade of a knife faced the wrong direction.

Speaking of which, it was time to get organized. Rooting around in the ornate credenza, she found some green placemats and set them out. This would be a special meal.

About an hour later, she felt ready. Still not able to smell anything cooking, she turned up the crockpot. The vegetables were in the oven. Dashing upstairs, she pulled on a khaki mini skirt and a black V-neck. Wasn't black a dinner color? Pretty subdued so she pulled her hair back with a black and orange scarf and stuck an artificial orange poppy under the scarf. Better. Then back to the kitchen. Cameron and Bella were in the TV room.

When Kimmy arrived, her sultry voice rolled toward the back of the house like a thick wave of warm grits. If Harper closed her eyes, she could almost imagine the pop psychologist was conducting one of her interviews. Couldn't help one quick peek.

Talking quietly in the foyer, Cameron and Kimmy made a striking couple. Her blonde hair shimmered, a striking contrast to the blue dress hugging her figure in all the right places. And those platform shoes? To die for.

But Bella was hiding behind her father.

"Come here, darlin'," Kimmy coaxed. "I have a gift for you, sweetheart."

Bella's head stayed plastered between the backs of Cameron's legs.

"Don't you want to see what I have for my special girl?"

Kimmy looked up at Cameron, who clearly didn't know what to do. Nudging open an expensive looking box, the TV personality shook out a yellow voile dress with a ruffled collar and puffy sleeves. She held it out as if a camera were zooming in on it. "Isn't this the prettiest thing you have ever seen?"

Peeking around her father, Bella frowned. "Yuk. Harper says I don't have to wear dresses. Not if I don't want to."

Oh, lordy. Harper crept closer.

Cameron looked way in over his head. "Well, now, darlin', Kimmy went to a great deal of trouble for you. Aren't you going to say thank you?"

Folding her arms over her chest, Bella stood silent. Tears glimmered in the corners of her eyes.

"Good girls are always grateful," Kimmy said primly.

Bella's bow lips trembled.

That did it. Harper stepped up to the plate. "It's, well, really something."

Kimmy looked over, her gaze settling on Harper's hair. Maybe it was the flower.

"Kimmy, I'd like you to meet Harper, our nanny."

"The new one? Charmed, I'm sure." She threw Harper a tight smile, hands still gripping the horrible dress.

"Bella's just not used to seeing...well, so many ruffles." Gently taking the dress, Harper folded it back into the tissue. She turned to Cameron. "Maybe I'll just put this where it belongs?" *Like the trash?*

"Thank you, Harper. So thoughtful of you, Kimmy, to think of Bella." Taking Kimmy's elbow, Cameron steered her into the library. "Would you like a key lime martini?"

Kimmy cooed approval, and Bella trotted behind Harper into the kitchen where she put the box on the counter. "Want to watch me cook?"

Lower lip protruding, Bella nodded and climbed into a chair.

Tying on her Wonder Woman apron—a Christmas gift from Adam that she'd never worn until today—Harper figured it was time to channel Martha.

Cameron came into the kitchen to fix some drinks. He sniffed and grinned. "Smells great in here. Nice apron."

"Gift from a friend." After lifting the cover of the crockpot, she poked the roast with a fork. Connie did that a lot and so did her mother. "How's it going out there?"

"This is really nice, having dinner together. I appreciate it, Harper." His smile flowed over her like warm chocolate.

"Family meals are always... good." Kimmy wasn't family, although that may be the plan. Harper gave the meat another stab.

"Dinner at six?" Martini glasses in hand, Cameron turned.

"Right." She spun the crockpot dial briskly. Almost felt like she knew what she was doing. Grabbing the bowl of olive oil, she opened the oven and brushed one more coating of oil on the vegetables. Cameron's footsteps moved down the hall.

In the dining room, Harper took her time laying out what looked like the good china. The Kirkpatrick clan had always used their everyday dishes. Her grandmother's china was only used on holidays after the boys broke a plate or two washing them. Cameron's china was beautiful with a thick black band that looked blind embossed. The pattern suited the green placemats. She was fussing with the table when Cameron appeared at the door, Kimmy right behind his shoulder.

"Everything all right?"

"Sure." She sniffed. "I'll be back." Harper scurried for the kitchen and was met by billowing smoke. *Oh, mercy.* She yanked the crockpot cord from the outlet. Too late. The smoke alarm went off. When she pulled the oven door open, searing smoke blinded her. The luscious green brussel sprouts had become charcoal briquettes. Grabbing two hot pads, she pulled out the baking sheet and set it on the unlit burners. Her nerves jangled and the alarm continued to wail. Grabbing a dish towel, she found the device and waved the towel under it. Tears stung her eyes, but she'd be damned if she'd let Cameron or Kimmy see them. The three of them clustered in the doorway, Bella in her father's arms. This dinner had turned into fifty shades of hell.

"Is Harper going to burn the house down, Daddy?" Bella looked at her father for confirmation.

"I think she just might, sugga." Kimmy flashed a satisfied smile.

Picking up the meat fork, Harper turned.

Chapter 9

Cameron's eyes were glued to the fork. "Harper? Everything okay?"

She could hardly breathe. Avoiding Kimmy's eyes, Harper eased in a tight breath. Her death grip on the bone handle of the fork relaxed. No sense losing this job on a mere technicality, like stabbing a guest. Lifting the cover of the crockpot, she gave the darn roast a hearty poke. Cameron stepped over to the smoke alarm and the screeching stopped. Harper's ears still rang with rage and heat surged up her cheeks.

Probably her redhead genes. One glance into the pot and she slammed the cover back on tonight's dinner before Kimmy got a good look at the charred mess.

"Goodness sakes alive, what in heaven's name happened here?" Kimmy surveyed the kitchen with barely concealed satisfaction.

"I'm hungry, Harper," Bella whined.

"Oh, sweetie." If only she could produce a miracle.

Cameron studied the burned vegetables. "Why don't you feed Bella and I'll order takeout."

By that time, Kimmy had grabbed a hot pad. Almost looked like she knew what to do with it. The expression on her face when she checked on their dinner didn't hold any hope. "Why, I never knew meat could turn black like this, sugga."

You'd think a psychologist would be more kind.

"Harper." Bella pulled on her leg. "I wanna eat."

"Okay, we're going to fix that." Harper had to put the kitchen drama behind and step back into her nanny role. Quickly, she got Bella into her chair with a sippy cup and mixed up the cereal. Cameron and Kimmy disappeared. Even after Harper opened the back door, the burnt smell lingered. She sure as heck didn't want Connie to come in Monday morning and smell this.

While Bella spooned in the slop, Harper studied the freezer. No frozen meals. Besides, those would never make the grade with Kimmy in the Morning. What a relief to hear Cameron in the hallway, ordering takeout. Kimmy's voice was also audible. "How can you keep her when she's incompetent?"

"Harper is a nanny, not a cook," Cameron countered. Harper's tight shoulders eased. "And please keep your voice down, Kimmy. She'll hear you."

Right. As if Kimmy cared.

Watching Bella eat her warm bowl of pablum, she decided Cameron was right. She was a nanny and she better act like one. She had to find a way to help Bella gain an appetite for regular food. She may have failed big time tonight by pretending to be a gourmet cook, but with Bella? She was going to succeed.

The words rang hollow in her mind. Fleeting confidence sifted through her like sand. What did she know about a child's eating habits? Tears prickled behind her eyes, and her nose began to run. Grabbing a paper towel, she blotted her face. Maybe she should pack it in. Billy's parting words penetrated her despair. *You never finish anything.* He'd thrown those words at her like a Molotov cocktail as he grabbed his duffel bag and headed for the airport and California.

That was before the break-up call.

Harper pulled herself up so sharp in the chair that her back muscles protested. No way. Billy was wrong and she had to prove it. Come hell or high water, Bella would eat toddler food. And Harper would learn how to cook. Never in this lifetime would she be humiliated like this again.

After Bella finished eating, Harper slipped the bowl into the dishwasher. She could hear Cameron and Kimmy in the library. When the ribs, coleslaw, and sweet potato fries arrived, Harper threw everything into serving bowls and had the meal on the table in seconds. Tummy full, Bella was content to sit with them, jabbing her napkin with a fork.

Seated at the table, Harper found herself facing Kimmy. Although the ribs were mouthwatering, Kimmy was on a diet, of course. She cut meat from the bone with ladylike precision. "You know, Cameron, ribs are not good for your heart, darlin'."

"That's one rule I'll never follow." Cameron ripped into those ribs like he hadn't eaten in days.

"My goodness, are we celebrating Christmas?" Kimmy pointed to her placemat.

Harper glanced down.

Holly hellfire, swallow me please.

Sure enough, holly sprigs patterned the corners of the green placemats. How could Harper have missed them? Her face flared, her throat closed and she put her fork down.

The sticky corners of Cameron's lips lifted. "I do believe green is good at any time."

Harper's stifled laugh turned into a coughing fit, and Kimmy's frown deepened.

"Well, really." Kimmy turned to her coleslaw.

Like Kimmy, Harper had been carefully cutting the pork from the bone, as if this were biology lab. When she noticed Cameron taking the direct route, she grabbed a slippery length in her fingers and dug in, Chicago style. Heck with being a southern lady. She'd missed that train a long time ago.

She had given Bella a small bowl of applesauce. From a jar, it was probably the same consistency as the cereal and looked just as appetizing. Head propped on one hand, Bella swirled a spoon through the applesauce but never lifted the spoon to her mouth.

"Darlin', could you stop that please?" Cameron finally asked.

"Shouldn't play with your food, Bella," Kimmy said while she toyed with her slaw.

Bella's sigh weighed on Harper. Every bite became more difficult. When she put her fork down, no one seemed to notice.

Kimmy didn't have any trouble filling the silence. As Harper listened to Cameron and his girlfriend talk about events and people she didn't know, it struck her that Kimmy was older than Cameron. The TV personality had to be in her mid-thirties.

Cameron went for older women. Interesting.

Harper was almost disappointed when no one wanted coffee.

Hard to mess up with the individual portion coffee machine and the mudslide creamer she'd picked up. A stop at "Back in the Day" bakery had yielded lavender and Mexican hot chocolate cookies, along with drunken brownies. She arranged her peace offerings on a plate.

"Way too many calories for me." Kimmy sniffed, passing on dessert.

But not Cameron. "Bakery? One temptation I cannot pass up." He sank his teeth into a brownie with a wicked smile that earned him only a tolerant glance from Kimmy– the kind a mother would give a misbehaving child. Under her disapproving eye, Harper had her pick of the plate. No use holding back now.

"My, oh my." Kimmy shook her head.

"Never did believe in diets." Harper could hardly get the words out around a mouthful of brownie.

Kimmy folded her napkin into a neat square and then announced she had to "skedaddle." Had to prepare for her show the next day. After setting Bella up in the TV room, Harper cleared the table. Felt like she was cleaning a crime scene. What would Connie think when she discovered what had happened to her beautiful roast?

As Harper worked in the kitchen, being super careful with the china, Kimmy said good night to Cameron in the foyer. "Thank you for, well, dinner—or what there was of it." Her words carried clearly.

Wow, now that stung. Harper almost dropped a plate.

"I'm just walking Kimmy out to her car, I'll be right back,"

Cameron called out.

Putting some serious elbow grease into cleaning the crockpot, Harper worked out her anger. What was she doing here? Her earlier resolve dissipated, along with the smoke in the kitchen. She wanted to go home to Oak Park. Enough of the dysfunction in this crazy household.

After loading the dishwasher, she left the crockpot in the sink and shepherded her charge upstairs where she drew a bath in the clawfoot tub. Bella had buckets full of bath toys, and Harper had fun playing with the plastic fish that squirted water.

Didn't take long for them to get into an all-out water fight. At the end, their hair was stringy and they were both giggling uncontrollably. Bella's laugh eased Harper's heart. Quickly, she got the little girl into her Tinkerbell nightgown and towel-dried her hair.

"Can I do it?"

"Sure." Harper handed her the towel. Didn't matter if Bella's efforts only put more knots in her hair. In the end, Harper worked some conditioner through the little girl's dark tresses. "You have beautiful hair, you know that?"

Bella looked pleased. "I do?"

"Gorgeous, sweetie. You are a gorgeous girl." Probably like her mother. Spreading the towels on the edge of the tub to dry, Harper felt an unaccountable wave of sadness. She shook it off. A February wind blew outside as she chased Bella down the hallway and into her huge bedroom.

"What book should we read?" Harper scrutinized the shelf.

"Peter Pan," Bella pleaded, pulling up the pink comforter.

"Right, you're the girl with the Tinkerbell pajamas," Harper teased, grabbing the book.

Before Harper started reading, Bella snuggled up next to her. "I'm sorry, Harper."

"For what?"

"I took Connie's note." Bella's lips trembled. "I made you make a mess."

Surprise gutted Harper. "Oh, honey. Why?"

One tiny shoulder lifted. "I don't know but I'm sorry. I'll never do it again. Okay?" Bella's eyes begged for forgiveness.

Somehow Harper swallowed her disappointment. "That's okay, Bella. Guess I should know how to cook a roast without the note. You don't have to be a wizard to use a crockpot."

Darkness was falling. Outside on the long porch, the hanging ferns were outlined against the night sky. After snapping on the bedside lamp, Harper began to read. She practically knew the story of Peter Pan by heart. When she got to the part about the motherless boys, the pictures in the library came back to haunt her. Did Bella remember her dark-haired mother? What would it take for Cameron to allow the Goodwins to spend time with Bella? She needed people around who cared about her. Kimmy sure didn't make the cut.

By the time she reached the end of the story, she felt another presence in the room. Arms crossed, Cameron leaned against the doorframe. He looked beat. "Almost asleep?"

Harper nodded. Bella's hands were tucked under her cheek on

the pillow. Snapping off the bedside lamp, Harper tiptoed through the door. Cameron bent to turn on a night light along the baseboard.

As Harper glanced back from the hallway, Bella looked so peaceful. But this had not been a calm week. "Look, I am so sorry about dinner. I am such a klutz—"

Cameron regarded her with steady eyes. "I hired you to care for Bella, not to cook."

"It's not like I couldn't if I tried." She didn't want to be a one trick pony.

"And you're doing great."

He was stretching it, and they both knew it. Cameron just didn't want another nanny to leave. She got that.

"But I know you want things to be nice for K...your friend." Man, she had trouble just getting Kimmy's name out.

"Life isn't something you read on a teleprompter, Harper, that's for sure." A bleakness swept his eyes but was gone so fast she wondered if she'd really seen that sadness.

"Maybe I should pick stories more carefully," Harper mused.

"Why?" In the dim light, his blue eyes turned gray.

"Some children's fairy tales are so sad."

He pondered that for a moment. "But life's sad. Right?"

"Sometimes." But her kind of sadness—having Billy Colton dump her—couldn't compare to Cameron's and Bella's loss. In fact, she felt silly mooning over her boyfriend when this poor guy lost a wife he dearly loved.

"Don't worry about the story. Bella likes to have you read to her." Reaching out, Cameron softly swiped one thumb under her left eye and glanced at his blackened finger.

She probably had major raccoon eyes and cupped her heated cheeks. "The water fight."

Rubbing his fingers together, Cameron smiled. "Looks like Bella won." Digging into his back pocket, he offered her a handkerchief.

"Thank you." The handkerchief smelled like his aftershave. She pressed it gently to her face.

"Don't beat yourself up. You're good for Bella...and you're good for this house."

Wow. His comment distracted her from the mixed signals her body was giving her. She tucked the handkerchief in her pocket.

Hand on the banister, Cameron started downstairs. "I better lock up."

Was he embarrassed by his own compliment? Wanting to clear the mess in the kitchen before Connie got here in the morning, she followed him. Her breathing had almost returned to normal.

When he stopped in the kitchen five minutes later to lock the back door, he paused. The light over the sink cast a golden glow on his hair. "Whatever are you doing?"

"Cleaning up."

"Connie will take care of that."

"Oh, I don't want her to start the day with this mess."

His slow grin sent warmth curling through her stomach. "Well, now, that's very considerate of you, Harper. Your mama trained you well."

"My mama would tell me to clean up this mess or else. It's not easy to burn food onto a Teflon surface."

Cameron's gutsy chuckle tickled Harper's funny bone. Soon they both were laughing until she was snorting like one of her brothers. Nice. Very feminine. She pulled out his hanky and wiped her eyes.

"I declare." Cameron pushed back from the counter. "Harper Kirkpatrick, this house needs more laughter."

"I think you're right." Gosh, he was so close. She could almost taste the spicy barbecue sauce on his warm breath. How had she missed his thick eyelashes? Cameron's sculpted lips stopped laughing. A muscle twitched in his cheek. For one crazy moment, she thought he might kiss her.

Even crazier, she wanted him to.

This was so wrong.

Giving his head a jerk, he bent and snapped the dishwasher closed, broad shoulders pulling on the oxford cloth shirt. Harper wielded Connie's pot scrubber while wicked, random thoughts sent heat crackling through her body.

He was easing away. "Night now."

When she looked up, Cameron looked dazed. "Good night. Sleep…" Harper clamped her lips shut. Good grief, she almost told him to sleep tight—the phrase that made Bella smile each night. A curious tilt of his head and he turned, footsteps slowly crossing the hall until she heard the third and the seventh stairs creak.

Hadn't taken long to learn the noises some stairs made.

Or the tread of his feet on them.

Picturing Kimmy in the Morning in Cameron's arms made Harper's chest ache. She attacked the pot with a vengeance.

Chapter 10

Following the disastrous dinner with Kimmy, Harper settled into a schedule. She took Bella to school and then dashed home to do research on eating disorders. The information wasn't encouraging. One day, when she was trying to persuade Bella to try a chopped-up banana, the little girl threw her cereal bowl, splattering everything. The mess even hit the stove and refrigerator. Bella burst into tears. "My shirt! My new shirt!" Her little arms shot out like she'd been hit by a paint ball.

Harper's heart pinched. "I didn't mean to upset you."

"You're mean." Bella's attempts to wipe off the mess only made it worse.

Grabbing a dish towel, Harper wet the corner and began to dab. "Not on purpose, sweetheart. I'm just trying to help. Want to play badminton?"

The lip was making its appearance but Bella retracted it with a smile. "Sure."

In her research Harper had learned that diversion was the best way of handling these incidents, not that it was easy.

"Sometimes I am in totally over my head," she told McKenna during one of their Sunday night chats.

"This might not be about chewing or eating, although I'm no expert."

"You went to nursing school."

"Any experience I have is with infants, but I've seen enough to know that a lot of these disorders that crop up with kids can have a psychosocial component."

"You're losing me." Mind numb after another stressful Sunday dinner with Kimmy, Harper stretched out on her bed. At least this time Connie had been there for the preparation.

"I'm talking about emotions. This eating aversion might come from Bella's heart and head, not her body." Her usually talkative sister fell silent for a couple beats. "Are you thinking of throwing in the towel, Harper? You can always come back to Chicago. You might find more design work in a larger city. You don't have to stick it out in Savannah just because you went to school there."

Her bed creaked when Harper swung up to a sitting position. "I'm not leaving, McKenna. No way."

"That's my girl." Harper could hear the smile in McKenna's voice. Had her sister been goading her on?

"Helping with Bella's eating issues and learning how to cook are two of my goals. I even have them penciled in on my calendar."

"Whoa! Cooking? Mom will be so proud." McKenna hooted way too loud for Harper's comfort.

"If she'd ever let us near her stove, I wouldn't be behind in all this."

"If you can read…"

"…you can cook," Harper supplied. But she'd never believed it.

What the heck was a pinch of anything?

But she dug in her heels after that talk with McKenna. Going home would mean failure. That wasn't going to be her. She'd started hanging around the kitchen and it wasn't Connie's crusty personality attracting her.

"Are you hungry or just curious?" Connie finally asked one night.

"Both," Harper admitted. "Sure would like to learn the basics. You know, how to cook a roast or chicken...that type of thing." She didn't want to explain that her mother had remained queen of her kitchen. The Kirkpatrick kids were strictly the set-the-table-and-cleanup crew.

"Be glad to teach you a thing or two," Connie said with a pleased smile. "Every woman should know how to cook. The way to a man's heart—"

"I'm not going there," Harper broke in. Like Billy could have cared. He'd been a health food nut, so they'd always had plenty of tabbouleh and hummus around.

"We'll see. Whatever you think, men do enjoy home cooking. Just ask Jack."

Yeah, well, Jack was a little overweight in Harper's book. That's what Connie's skills had brought her husband, not that Harper would mention that now. The housekeeper had pulled a hunk of meat from the refrigerator. Connie was oh, so casual when she said, "Fixing any meat is just a matter of having the right temperature. If you turn the crockpot dial to high, you might have a mess."

"Well, of course." An incriminating heat burned Harper's

cheeks. Did Connie know about the debacle that Sunday?

Hard to tell when Connie was bent over one of the crisper drawers. "Then you peel the carrots. Slice them up, along with the potatoes."

Harper grabbed a peeler, trying to look as if carrots and potatoes were the most interesting thing she'd heard about all week. Had Connie noticed the plastic sack of potatoes unopened in the vegetable drawer after the disastrous dinner? If the housekeeper had noticed, she was totally cool about it. Harper secretly felt that Connie liked her. She'd overheard the housekeeper tell her husband Jack that Harper had "staying power."

The potatoes were rough and cold in her hands while Harper hacked away with the peeler. Connie kept the lesson going and settled the roast into the crockpot like a baby. Amazing how she flitted from one task to another, talking in a low, melodious voice, like this was some initiation rite. "There now. Then you pour a can of onion soup over the roast and cook at medium."

After that day came a lesson with cinnamon chicken and then apricot-glazed salmon. Harper kept notes on bits of paper in a little box that used to hold her hair clips. Once she stopped hurting herself with cooking implements, she used the lesson time to mine Connie for information. Just curious, that's all.

"How did Bella's mother die?" she asked Connie one day when Bella was at school and they were making celery seed coleslaw together.

"Car accident." Connie looked away. "Terrible. Just terrible."

Harper stopped shredding. The choked words conjured up a

paralyzing image. Questions ricocheted through her mind. Questions she could never ask. A heavy sadness had seeped into the room.

As time passed, Harper got to know Connie and her husband Jack. They lived in a small cottage out back that used to be servant quarters in the 1800s. Quite a pair. On their days off, they took in the countryside on their Harleys, of all things. The first time she was treated to this sight, Harper had to suppress a smile. Roaring off in helmets and black leather, they looked like a couple of bobble-head dolls. The next day Connie would fill Harper's ears with stories about small towns Harper had never heard of before. They'd poke around antique stores and eat in roadside restaurants. Connie made even the smallest outing with her husband sound like an adventure. "Jack and I ..."

Connie and Jack were good friends. Someday Harper wanted that. Love *and* friendship.

Her time with Billy started as friendship. They'd been in the same classes. A few beers one night and it progressed to more. They moved in together. Sure, eventually they used the L word. Looking back, she wondered if her feelings for him had been love – the kind her parents had for each other. The kind Connie and Jack shared.

Harper hadn't heard zip from Billy. Pictures of the two of them together remained in a box under her bed. But she sure didn't pore over the photos at night, the way she had in the beginning. She was spending more time at her drawing board, not that she'd ever use the sketches—at least, not here in Savannah.

Three times a week, Cameron dutifully joined them for dinner. Sundays with Kimmy shouldn't have counted as one of the family meals, in Harper's mind, but they did. Couldn't Cameron see that those dinners only gave Kimmy a chance to bore them with an unending monologue? And the girl sure didn't need any cue cards. Rail thin and picking at her food like a bird, she filled the silence with her incessant chatter.

Harper began to look forward to their Tuesday and Thursday dinners. Bella seemed a lot more relaxed with just Cameron and Harper there. Usually Cameron quizzed Bella about school. But the little girl could be evasive. "Nothing." She'd run her spoon through the oatmeal. Her father never pressed her.

Maybe Cameron just wanted to fill the silence when he turned to Harper one night and asked, "What did you do today?" Her weekly reports had fallen by the wayside at his request.

"I, ah, took Bella to the park."

As his startled look, Harper added, "We didn't meet anyone. Don't worry."

Whether or not the Goodwins had called again, Harper had no clue. Connie usually took any calls and she'd already told Harper what the protocol was. Did Bella's grandparents realize the meeting had been a mistake, one that Cameron would probably correct?

Although she'd like to just treat her position like a temporary job, her curiosity grew with each passing week. Cameron never said anything about his own parents. Passing through the kitchen one Saturday afternoon, Harper found a woman sitting at the table with Cameron. He introduced her as "Lily, my sister." The woman had a narrow face, like Cameron's, and kind eyes when she smiled. "How long have you been here?"

Harper had to count. "Five weeks maybe?" She looked to Cameron.

Lily looked surprised and Cameron laughed. "Right, Harper might be a keeper."

"I should say."

"Uh, nice meeting you, Lily." Flustered, Harper escaped into the hallway.

"A keeper"? For sure she'd never stay if Cameron married Kimmy. The thought weighted Harper's steps as she made her way up the stairs.

The weather warmed enough for Harper to drive with the sunroof open. Bella shrieked with laughter while they bombed around town one afternoon, hair flying in the breeze. Then Bella started to wheeze.

"Sorry, sweetie." Heart pounding, Harper pulled over, grabbed Bella's inhaler and climbed into the back seat. She held the device to Bella's lips, her own breathing increasingly restricted by the scare.

"I'm okay," Bella pushed the inhaler away.

"You sure?"

"I hate that thing. It's stupid." Looking out the window she settled her chin on one hand. Harper couldn't miss the tears trembling in the little girl's eyes. She ran one hand softly over Bella's dark hair and kissed her forehead.

"Let's hit the road, okay?"

Bella nodded. As Harper climbed back into the driver's seat, she heard Bella heave a sigh. Life seemed so difficult for her and Harper didn't know what would cure that. Cameron said very little about the sessions with the child therapist on Saturday mornings. Harper didn't want to ask.

Driving home after the attack, Harper realized she'd never expected to care so much about Bella. But she did.

Later, Harper wondered if the wheezing came from the pollen or the excitement. For Harper stress was more a trigger than dust or pollen. But Bella's situation might be completely different. So frustrating. All around them azalea buds plumped. Soon the boulevards of Savannah would be a riot of pink and orange. But from then on they drove with the windows closed.

Bella's school began to have outings, and Harper dutifully volunteered for a picnic in the park. Everything went fine until it came time to eat.

"Hey, you're eating baby food!" one of the other little girls pointed out in a loud voice. They were all seated at picnic tables under the live oaks. Harper had brought Bella's lunch in a small padded lunch pack.

Ms. Lucy, their teacher, quickly stepped in, but the damage had been done. Bella pushed her plate aside and buried her face in her arms. Harper's heart broke. When the other children ran screaming toward the slide, Bella stayed put, despite Ms. Lucy's attempts to make up for the mean comment.

Harper just had to do something about Bella's eating. If she brought it up with Cameron, would he be insulted? He took things so personally sometimes. Someone had to take this on so Bella didn't become the odd kid out because of her eating habits.

After putting Bella to bed that night, Harper zipped upstairs and tore open her art supplies. Her design work had always been an outlet but it had been a while. The park had filled her with ideas that day, before it all went downhill. Now she sat at the drafting table and sketched leaf patterns until they just clicked. When she glanced outside, a faint light hit the garden from the long porch outside Cameron's room.

Some nights she smelled the distinct aroma of a cigar. Did he sit on that long porch in the darkness? His smoking struck her as elegant and illicit. A cold shiver moved through her when she pictured Cameron lounging in a rattan chair like the ones outside Bella's room. He'd probably have one ankle balanced rakishly on the other knee as he puffed on the fragrant cigar...a true southern gentleman. She'd never heard Kimmy's voice out on the porch. Any time they spent together was at her house, or so Harper assumed.

Her eyes were drawn to the light. What was Cameron thinking as he sat there alone? Her imagination made her shift on the stool in her third floor garret, as she laughingly called her room. That night, his light stayed on almost as long as hers and she did not go to bed until way past midnight.

But she could not sleep.

Since the first dinner with Kimmy, Harper hadn't been alone with Cameron. Fine with her, or so she told herself. So it was a surprise one Friday evening when she was dashing out the door to have a drink with Adam and Cameron waylaid her, stepping out of the library. "Could you spare a minute?"

"Sure." She felt foolishly glad that she was wearing new skinny jeans and her hot knee-high boots.

Usually Cameron had that southern way of circling the subject, so very different from the direct Midwest approach. But not that night. "Do you have plans for the weekend?" He was nipping his full bottom lip, so distracting.

"Um, could I ask why?"

"Well, here's the thing…" Had she ever seen him this uncomfortable? "There's an event tomorrow night. Command performance and Kimmy's sick."

Harper's stomach took a dive. The kind of gala Cameron would attend with Kimmy was definitely way out of her league.

"And I'll pay extra for the night—"

She jerked back. Did the man think he could buy anything?

Cameron was unbelievably cute when he blushed. "Sorry, Harper. This isn't coming out right. I need an escort for this event. Well, not really an escort…"

Harper almost was enjoying his discomfort.

"I mean, I need an attractive woman to go with me to the Telfair Ball, make polite conversation, that kind of thing." By this time, his cheeks were the color of the brocade drapes. "Connie turned me down."

They chuckled together. So he thought she was attractive?

"What's the dress code?"

"Formal. My credit cards are at your disposal."

She worked her heel against the marble floor, wishing she'd escaped earlier. But he looked so darned desperate. "Don't want your credit cards, but thank you. You're on."

"Bless the lord." He slumped against the doorframe. "Thank you, Harper."

"Don't mention it."

His eyes had slid to her boots.

"What, you don't like them?"

"Oh, no. I've always liked them."

Ah, huh. His cheeks were bright red when she bounded out the door and down the steps. She felt his eyes hot on her back. Heart pounding, she climbed into Adam's pickup. Grabbing her inhaler, she sucked in some deep breaths.

"So I make you that nervous?" Pulling away from the curb, Adam shot her a sly grin.

"Smart aleck." The hot and cold chills whipping through her body made Harper wonder if the dreaded early menopause her mother complained about could hit a girl in her twenties. She gave Adam the news about the gala.

"The Telfair Ball? You are coming up in the world."

Harper hardly heard Adam's teasing. Where could she get a dress?

"And you're going to wear?" Her friend was a mind reader.

For the rest of the night, they strategized. Having Adam's input helped calm the plague of locusts circling in Harper's stomach. When she was in college, she'd done some modeling during fashion week. Sarah Lynn Gilbert had charge of the gowns, although

Harper hadn't seen her since graduation. She planned to be at the college early in the morning to wheedle a dress from the collection. Of course, Adam would do her hair.

"This whole gala thing scares the crap out of me, okay?" By that time, they were both on their second Cosmo.

"Not to worry. Come to my salon at four tomorrow. I'll juggle my schedule. Easy, peasy."

"I really appreciate this, Adam."

"Anything for you and Mr. Wonderful."

"Oh, he isn't—"

"Look, I saw him staring after you tonight. Trust me, he was not looking fatherly. He may be fooling himself but I didn't just fall off the stupid truck. That boy is into you."

"He's dating someone. And he's old."

Adam hooted. "Kimmy Carrington is a mannequin, not a woman. And twenty-nine's too old for you?"

"Twenty-nine?" Strangely unsettling.

"Told you. I do my homework."

While Adam continued with his foolishness, Harper's mind galloped on to the gazillion other things on her list before tomorrow night. In Savannah, the Telfair Ball was one of the social events of the year. She'd seen the pictures plastered in the paper and online but never imagined she would ever actually attend.

How surreal, almost like Cinderella.

But wait. Did that make Cameron her prince?

That early menopause stuff or whatever else caused these hot flashes kicked in again. She opened her window but that didn't help her breathing. Once home, she headed straight for the refrigerator and opened the door. The frigid air blasted her body until she shivered. Her thoughts still could have melted the ice cubes.

Chapter 11

The look in Cameron's eyes as Harper came down the stairs Saturday night made her clutch the banister. Wouldn't be cool to do a face plant with him. Again. Legs trembling, she carefully picked her way down the Oriental runner in her strappy sandals. Over her arm was a black shawl, and her free hand clutched the tiny black file bag she'd had since her first prom. The borrowed citrus green gown fell softly from one shoulder. She loved the way the fabric moved on her body. Adam pointed out that the amber undertones caught the highlights of her curls when she brought the dress to his salon for approval. That one hour searching in the costume vault with Sarah Lynn had been totally worth it.

"Well, I declare." Cameron's dropped jaw unnerved her.

"So I look that bad, huh?"

His lids lowered. "No, darlin'. You look that good."

Oh, mercy.

The hand he offered kept her from stumbling from that last riser. Thank goodness she'd remembered to tuck her inhaler in her handbag. She would definitely need it tonight if he kept looking at her like that. Ruggedly handsome but elegant, Cameron took her breath away in that tux. The mauve bowtie? Perfect and so him.

Bella drifted from the kitchen, followed by Connie.

"You look beautiful, Harper," Bella whispered.

"Thank you, sweetheart."

"One handsome couple, I would say." Connie wiped her hands on a towel.

What the heck?

Cameron still stared.

"Which car are we taking?" Harper struggled to keep her tone business-like.

"Jack is our chauffeur this evening." Whisking the black shawl from her hands, Cameron draped it over her shoulders. One touch sent fire coursing over her skin.

Long evening ahead and this had to stop. She moved briskly through the open front door.

Outside, the Bentley sat waiting and Jack pulled open the rear door. A cool February breeze skimmed through the treetops as she sank into the soft leather in the backseat.

"Evening, Jack," she said.

He threw her a wink in the rearview mirror. "Evening, Miss Kirkpatrick."

"Oh, please, Jack. Just Harper." She fussed with her shawl.

Closing the door behind him, Cameron overheard. "What's this? You would never be *just* Harper. Don't you agree, Jack?"

"Absolutely, sir."

The car pulled away from the curb, and Harper wouldn't have been surprised to hear the clatter of horses' hooves or see a glint of pixie dust. Jack turned onto Victory Drive, and they glided through the gathering darkness. Certainly this was a dream. Soon, she'd wake up and drag herself downstairs for coffee. She wasn't really going to the Telfair Ball, for cripe's sake, with a man who rocked that black tuxedo.

Jack maneuvered smoothly through the traffic and they were soon on Bull Street. Coffee shops, salons, and historic churches spun past. How many times had she met friends at the Foxy Loxy Cafe for a brownie sundae when she was a student? Four years ago, she never could have imagined this happening to her. Squired to a ball by one of Savannah's most eligible bachelors? At least, that's what Adam had told her.

Back then, she'd been a sophomore in college and all things were possible. Billy Colton came into her life that year and she thought he was her forever man. What a sobering thought. Did she wish she were with Billy tonight? The mental picture wouldn't come into focus.

Cameron and Jack were talking sports. She tuned them out. The only thing she heard was the thudding of her heart while she arm-wrestled with her memories. She could hear Adam's voice as surely as if he were sitting here. "Billy belongs to your past." The Bentley passed Forsyth Park and soon they were deep in the heart of the historic district.

Her anxiety spiked while Jack maneuvered the Bentley around the succession of squares that dotted Bull Street. In the darkness the squares took on fairy-tale magic. Surely this couldn't really be happening. When they finally reached Telfair Square, Jack pulled up in front of the historic Telfair Academy. The Jepson Center, kitty-corner and part of the Telfair holdings, had been hosting a collection from the Uffizi in Florence, striking the Renaissance theme for this evening. Dear Adam had filled her ear with details while he worked on her hair that afternoon.

Thank goodness she'd also had a quick conversation with McKenna, who'd advised her to "Just have fun tonight."

Sure. Like that was an option.

"Harper, pretend you're one of the women in those Renaissance paintings— elusive and mysterious." McKenna's voice had held a note of mischief.

"All right. I'll try."

"Be a babe." Her sister had laughed. "A ladylike treasure but a babe underneath."

Harper took a deep breath as Jack pulled over to the curb and jumped out.

But Cameron was ahead of him. Quickly circling the car, he opened her door and extended one hand. "M'lady."

"Thank you, C-Cameron." Just saying his name made her woozy, but the cool air slapped some sense into her. Stepping out, Harper dropped his hand as soon as she got her bearings. The uneven sidewalks in the historic district could prove dangerous but she'd risk it. Safer than these feelings rioting through her body.

"Y'all have a good time now, you hear?" Jack's voice followed them up the stairs.

Hand on her elbow, Cameron turned. "Thank you, Jack. I'll let you know when your services are needed further."

"I've always loved this old building," she murmured as Cameron led her past the statuary and through the stately pillars.

"Neoclassical Regency architecture."

He laughed in surprise. "Spoken like a true student."

She flushed. "You don't get through design school without knowing the local architecture."

"Fascinating, isn't it?"

For the first time she wondered about his work. "You love the history of Savannah, don't you? After all you grew up with it."

Cameron shrugged. "Not really."

They'd entered the building and a crush of people swallowed them, ending their conversation. Cameron returned greetings as they edged down the main hallway toward the stairs leading up to the Rotunda. She'd never been this close to him, well, except for the night she fell into his arms in the Catwoman suit. His cologne might be subtly understated, but it hit her like a brick.

"Thanks for coming tonight," he murmured, voice warm on her neck.

"Part of the job, right?"

"Not really."

You got that right, Baby Blues.

Excited voices echoed off the paintings of the permanent collection. She pushed back her hair with a shaking hand. Adam had spritzed almost half a can of hair spray to subdue the coppery brown waves that fell past her shoulders. Still, her hair resisted. In the Rotunda, waiters circulated with trays of appetizers and flutes of champagne. Cameron deftly scooped up two glasses and handed her one.

While they sipped, Cameron introduced her around until her

head spun with names. Amazing how he managed to intersperse business with his quick greetings. After quickly emptying her first champagne split, she decided to slow down. Falling flat on her face tonight was not an option.

Her job depended on it. So did her self-esteem.

"My, oh, my, and who would this lady be?" With his dark hair and arresting eyes, the handsome guy who'd approached them could be on the cover of *GQ* magazine.

"Kimmy is indisposed, Mallory. May I introduce you to Harper Kirkpatrick? Harper is Bella's nanny."

"Charmed, I'm sure," Mallory murmured, bending over her hand. "Bella is a lucky girl."

Dazed, Harper mumbled something in response. Adam would never believe this. She was bookended by male southern glory. The man was hot but not as attractive as Cameron—at least, not to her. Remembering her sister McKenna's advice, she wondered if she was looking mysterious enough.

"Mallory is CEO of Thornton Enterprises. One of their holdings is a string of high end jewelry salons." Cameron exchanged a smile with his pal. "In fact, my guess is you've offered more than one contribution for our bidding pleasure this evening."

The auction items were showcased in one of the side galleries. And although they'd rushed through that room, Harper had been awed by the fabulous display, everything from paintings to Oriental rugs and trips to faraway places.

Mallory laughed. "If you like emeralds, I expect to see your paddle in the air. A get-well gift for Kimmy?"

"Maybe."

Emeralds for Kimmy...as in an engagement ring? Harper fought to squelch the feelings twisting her stomach so tight she gasped. Both men turned. She patted her chest. "Excuse me. The champagne."

"So sorry to hear of your separation, Mallory," Cameron continued. "I didn't know Rhonda well."

"Let's call it what it is, Cameron. A divorce." Mallory's voice dropped and so did his eyes.

"Then, indeed, you have my condolences."

"I'm sure you understand my awkward position. Being thrown back into the Savannah social scene is like being fed to the lions."

"I know the feeling."

Mallory's head jerked up. "Cameron, I am so sorry. Didn't mean to bring up sad memories."

Cameron was brushing aside the apology when across the room, a stately brunette beckoned to Mallory. Harper knew an irritated woman when she saw one.

"Seems I'm being called to duty." Mallory upended his drink. "A pleasure to meet you, Harper."

Cameron followed his friend with sad eyes. "Poor guy. Single men in this town? Open season takes on a whole new meaning. He'd better team up with someone fast or the single women will tear into him."

Was that what he'd done with Kimmy? Had he "teamed up" as a safety measure?

Somehow the thought pleased her.

"I didn't see him at your party." Oh, good grief. She'd never mentioned she was Catwoman.

A sly smile played along Cameron's lips. Had he known all along? "No, he wasn't at the bachelor party. Travels a lot on business and was out of town. Entirely his loss. So...you might be interested?"

"Of course not." As if she could ever date a man like Mallory Thornton.

"Let me know if that changes. The way you looked in those boots last night, I'm sure you don't lack for dates."

But she hadn't gone out with anyone since she'd come to live with him. She snorted. Not at all pretty and definitely not mysterious. "Right. Like that's going to happen."

"Let's circulate." He took her arm. Electric prickles traveled across her skin. Maybe this dress was too revealing, the back dipping too low. Her body became a lightning rod for his touch.

As she spun through the room on Cameron's arm, he smiled and nodded. The noise level was high and no one really expected conversation—at least, not from her. Some of the guests looked familiar, like she'd seen them in a news article. She was hobnobbing, as her mother would say.

But McKenna had been right. The less she said, the more people seemed to accept her.

When the auction began, she was almost relieved. The lights dimmed and all attention turned to the auctioneer spotlighted in front of a huge screen at the podium. The painting of a pheasant sold for an outrageous sum, as did the street scene of downtown

Savannah.

Paddles flashed discreetly. The room was full with what Chicagoans would call high rollers.

"See anything you like?" Cameron's breath tickled her bare neck.

"Not really. I'm a sightseer tonight."

His chuckle circled her stomach and squeezed. "My dear lady, you are one of the sights."

She cut him a side glance. "No need for flattery, Mr. Bennett."

"None given, Ms. Kirkpatrick."

The auction picked up speed. So did her heartbeat. An easy camaraderie knit this group together, and she felt woefully out of place. They encouraged each other with private jokes born of familiarity. Cameron held back in the bidding. "Last thing I need is another painting or a Limoges porcelain box for Bella to throw."

"She would not!" Bella had never shown that kind of physical anger.

His glance held what sure looked like appreciation. "Your loyalty to Bella touches me."

"Isn't that my job?"

"Not for the others."

"I'm so sorry." But the backwash of guilt was followed by remorse. Hadn't she considered leaving too?

"No more than I was when we parted ways." Sad acceptance laced his words.

A child's birthday party had come up for auction.

Cameron met her eye. "Now?"

"Go for it." She had no idea when Bella's birthday was, but having a party already packaged sure would save her a lot of work.

If she still had the job. Could Harper stand to live with Bella if she couldn't help her?

Could she bear to leave?

The auctioneer went into overtime, warbling the climbing numbers. Everyone there probably had a child or grandchild. Paddles beat the air. But in the end, Cameron prevailed, buying the birthday package for an outlandish amount. Many in the audience raised their glasses to him. Obviously Cameron was well liked. Probably went to prep school with these men. Standing in the nest of his cronies, she felt entitled wealth ooze around her like liquid gold.

"A prize for Bella!" one man's voice rang out.

"Such a good father," an elegant woman commented.

The auction rolled on, the people-watching the best ever. Her mother had always taught Harper it was impolite to stare, but darn, so much to see. Women posing in expensive gowns. Men exuding power and old money.

In her opinion Cameron outshone them all, with Mallory Thornton coming in a close second. Both were southern gentlemen to the core, no doubt with the pedigrees to prove it. And she was a girl from the west side of Chicago.

What was she doing here? Harper shifted in her strappy sandals that had cost a week's pay. The night felt endless. The women in their subdued black or white gowns made Harper feel garish and out of place, her citrus green way too conspicuous. The reddish brown hair? Too much of it and Adam's curls, way too girly compared to their sleek knots and short bobs.

Remembering McKenna's advice, she pasted a Mona Lisa smile on her face.

Relax. Breathe deeply.

"Are you feeling all right?" She turned to find Cameron considering her with concern.

"Of course. Why?" Her smile slipped.

He shrugged but definitely looked worried. "You have the strangest look on your face, like indigestion, but we haven't even eaten dinner yet. Hang in there, girl."

So much for Mona Lisa. Harper's stomach flopped over at the thought of food. But she wasn't going to let him down, even though escaping to her cloistered bedroom was looking really good right now.

Following the auction, the group filed out of the historical Academy to trail down the street past Trinity Methodist Church to the more modern Jepson Center for dinner. Woman donned shawls in the light evening breeze, and Cameron helped drape the black pashmina around her shoulders. The gleaming white marble of the newer building beckoned, but Harper concentrated on her feet as they negotiated the uneven sidewalk. Cameron steadied her with one hand.

"My, oh, my. If it isn't my old buddy Cameron...and friend."

The snarky voice whipped her head up. Cripes, she'd almost run right into him.

Blocking the path stood the idiot from the bachelor party,

mustache twitching and a drink spilling from his hand. "What have we got here tonight? And how much did you pay her?"

Harper gasped.

Anger rolled off Cameron in hot waves. "Randy, I do believe you have had a bit too much to drink."

The sneer didn't budge, not even in the face of Cameron's warning. "So where is Ms. Kimmy tonight?"

"Home sick, Randy. You've had too much to drink, and I do not care to repeat myself."

Wow, every syllable slit the air like a dagger.

The other partygoers gave them a wide berth. A scene? Really? Harper shivered in the darkness while the limbs of a live oak swayed overhead. Moving in front of Harper, Cameron muscled his friend out of the traffic pattern and into the side street. Not wanting to be left behind, Harper followed. Cameron widened his stance and fisted his hands.

Cameron, a street fighter? No way. But the pose looked shockingly natural.

Thank goodness Randy got the picture and backed off into the darkness. When he was gone from sight, Cameron relaxed and ambled back to her. "You okay, Harper?" The same hands that had been ready to duke it out gently took her shoulders. She shivered.

"Yes. Fine." She had no breath. The constriction began in her throat until it throbbed in her head. Ripping open her handbag, Harper grabbed her inhaler and sucked.

Cameron's hold tightened. "You don't look fine to me. Sure you're okay?"

Finally her lungs released like an escape hatch. The blessed oxygen rushed in.

"Yeah. Yeah, I think so."

"Positive?"

"Cameron, I'm not Bella. I can handle myself." Twisting away, she tucked the inhaler away.

Cameron raked one hand through his blond hair. He was a guy who looked good mussed up. "This breathing thing worries me."

She squared her shoulders. "You don't have to worry about me. Bella? Something else entirely."

His surprised laugh bubbled into the night air. "Spoken like a girl from Chicago."

"Ready to push on?" She wanted to get this over with.

He held out his arm, and she took it. "Madam, I am at your service."

Her annoyance eased. Really, he could be so darn sweet.

They moved toward the light pouring from the Jepson Center. By the time they were shown to their places at a long narrow table, she'd managed to stop shaking. The room glistened with colorful swirls of ribbon and silk flowers, reflected in the huge glass windows that fronted York Street.

She was easily the youngest person at this event, and Cameron might come in a quick second. More than half the guests had grey hair. And the rest? Dye jobs that Adam would highly approve.

"Hungry?" Cameron whispered.

"Not really."

The woman on the other side of the table looked up. "Oh,

don't you look lovely, dear." Unlike most of the other women, her silver hair was set in marcelled waves that brought to mind black and white movies.

"Thank you."

"The dewy beauty that comes with youth," she continued in a voice accustomed to being respected. "No fussy jewelry can take the place of that." Her sizeable broach, earrings and bracelets glimmered. She was the real thing.

"Amelia Grafton, I would like you to make the acquaintance of Harper Kirkpatrick." Cameron promptly introduced them. The man knew everyone.

"So nice to meet you, Mrs. Grafton," Harper murmured.

"Please call me Amelia, dear." The older woman nodded her head at Cameron. "Aren't you the lucky man."

"Oh, I'm not..." Harper began.

"You are quite right and I thank you." Cameron jumped right in with his elegant southern manners.

Then her companion spoke to her and the matron turned away.

Cameron snapped his napkin open. "Well, at least we have Bella's birthday taken care of thanks to the auction."

"When is her birthday?"

"May second."

"Oh, I'm a May baby too. We're both Taurus." Harper's bond with Bella grew stronger.

Cameron's eyes sparkled. "Well, I declare. A joint celebration might be in order."

Not the time to tell him she didn't know if she'd be here.

Chapter 12

Harper felt relieved when the waiters served the salads. The
thought of not being with Bella for their birthdays struck a sad
note. She may have assured McKenna that she was in this for the
long haul, but tonight that comment rang hollow in her heart.
Surrounded by people who didn't know or care about her, she felt
out of place and isolated.

The noise level in the room settled as guests sampled their
hearts of palm salad. Harper liked her palms green and rustling
overhead. Picking at the lettuce bed, she wondered if she were
using the right fork. An amazing amount of silver gleamed at each
place. With a sigh, she set the fork aside. Not hungry. Cameron
kept up polite conversation with those seated around them. When
the beef Florentine entrée was served, she barely touched it.

How great it would be to be tucked in bed with a book or
sketching at her drawing board.

Dessert was served with a flourish by white-jacketed waiters.
Harper stared at the two perky pale mounds on the plate in front
of her. "What are these?"

Cameron checked the menu. "Nipples of Venus."

"W-what?" An embarrassed heat zipped up her chest.

"Must be an Italian delicacy." Giving her an outrageous grin, he teased one mound lightly with his dessert fork. "So this isn't popular in Chicago?"

Her face burned while her breasts peaked. "Not that I'm aware. They never serve nipples or any other part of Venus in Chicago."

Cameron broke into hearty guffaws that prompted Amelia to glance over. "Whatever are you laughing at?"

"Sorry. I can't stop telling jokes," Harper explained. She'd die before she'd share her comment with this lovely bastion of Savannah society. "Ignore him."

Cameron unleashed another round of chuckles. Harper had never seen him this way. She wished he'd let loose with his daughter like this. Bella would probably love this side of her daddy.

Waiters circulated with steaming carafes and the rich scent of coffee soothed her. The night was almost over. Harper took her first sip. "What's in this? It's so sweet."

"Anise. Tasty, isn't it?"

"Wonderful." She took a deeper gulp. Soon she'd be home, snug in her bed.

"And now for the dancing."

"Dancing?" Setting her coffee cup down, she almost missed the saucer.

"What, you're not up for a few spins around a dance floor?"

She sighed. "Sure. Whatever it takes."

"Your enthusiasm warms my heart."

"Really? Sarcasm is needed here?"

His lips were twitching again. She hadn't danced in a long time. Maybe it was time. Cameron had been fun and flirty tonight.

Or was that her imagination?

Soon the festively dressed group filtered outside again, like butterflies searching for a place to perch. At the curb valets opened the doors of luxury cars. Not everyone was going to dance the night away. Silver-haired matrons were helped into the vehicles by husbands ready to go home. She wanted to ask for a ride.

But not tonight. Together with the younger group, she trouped across Telfair Square with Cameron, who had laced her hand over his arm. This time, Randy was nowhere to be seen and she exhaled. Her earlier fatigue had disappeared.

Maybe it was the coffee. Or maybe it was her employer and those darn baby blue eyes. By the time they reached the Telfair Academy, she was itching to dance. And only with Cameron.

Cameron's mind moved a lot faster than their feet as they strolled back to the Academy. Amazing that he was enjoying the evening. He'd bought the tickets at Kimmy's insistence. She was big on these fundraisers. The last time they attended a gala, she begged him to dance, but he wanted no part of it. For Kimmy, hitting the dance floor meant posing—not his thing. Dating a TV personality had its drawbacks. Truth be told, he had to take a close look at this relationship.

But tonight he just felt like dancing.

Of course, he had noticed Harper often treated him as if he were two days older than water. The horror on her face when Amelia Grafton assumed they were together had amused and then annoyed him. In fact, Harper's long-suffering attitude tonight—like he'd invited her to a wet T-shirt contest—was an insult. Cameron's competitive nature roared to life. She was going to have a good time if it killed him.

Music flowed through the open doors. Guests made their way to the rotunda where the evening had started. High tables were arranged around the perimeter, a respectful distance from the paintings. The musical group was playing a slow number with lots of saxophone that suited him just fine. He led the way to a table.

Harper settled onto one of the tall stools, crossing her long legs that seemed to go on forever. All long gowns should have slits to the thigh. And all women should have legs like Harper's.

No way was he sitting down. "Ready to dance? You can leave your purse here."

She clutched her bag to her chest. "Think I'll keep it with me, thank you."

The inhaler. "Sorry. Of course." He held out one hand.

Eyes wide, Harper looked like Bella the first time he took her for swimming lessons.

"I won't bite, Harper."

With a blush he found very becoming, she moved into his arms.

But a truck could have driven between them. She held him off like the flu. "Really, I won't bite," he repeated. The thought of his lips on her long pale neck came out of nowhere. A rush of heat nearly buckled his knees. His grip must have tightened because Harper became ramrod stiff. Cameron recovered but her left arm kept pushing him away. Time for a distraction.

"You look stunning this evening. What are you wearing?" He

drank in her scent, so delicate and enticing. Kimmy had a rather heavy hand with perfume.

"Spellbound. Thank you. So do you."

"Look stunning? I look stunning?" He wanted to see that pink deepen in her cheeks again.

"Handsome. But you don't have to flatter me, Cameron. I know you'd rather be here with Kimmy. This is just part of my job."

That didn't sit well so he ignored it. "You certainly didn't eat much. Are you on a diet? Not that it's any of my business."

She pinned him with doleful eyes. "You're right. It is none of your business."

He choked back a chuckle. "Sometimes you can be sassy."

"Sometimes I think you like it."

Damn. She was right.

"And you're a pretty good dancer," Harper continued, relenting a little until he had her close enough to glimpse golden sparks in her hazel green eyes. "Lessons, I suppose?"

"I never attended Mrs. Pritchard's dance school, if that's what you mean." Perish the thought.

"Probably off playing polo with your friends instead?"

The thought of wielding a mallet while riding a horse cracked him up. "No indeed. That would be dangerous for the poor horse."

The dance ended, drawing polite applause. More people had filtered into the rotunda where a small bar was set up in the corner.

"Would you care for anything?"

"Some kind of un-caffeinated soda would be great."

"Be right back. If your honor should need defending, just tell them you're with me." His eyes searched the room. He hoped Randy had gone home. His blood pleasure rose just thinking of their earlier clash. Alcohol was the road to ruin.

Cecile Mason greeted him when he joined a long line in front of the bar. "And where is Kimmy this evening?" Her eyes sliced to Harper with the subtlety of a searchlight. Cecile didn't miss a trick. He'd always steered clear of Kimmy's friend.

"She wasn't able to come, Cecile, as Kimmy no doubt told you when you spoke today." Kimmy seemed to be Cecile's on-call therapist.

Her lips pouted. "Well, I see you've found a substitute."

"Bella's nanny graciously agreed to forfeit her free evening." Couldn't this bartender pick up the pace?

Continuing to regard Harper with some interest, Cecile raised her brows. "How very convenient. Since you're single, a nanny makes sense."

"Bella needs supervision and company." Sometimes he thought his daughter needed more than that, but he couldn't wrap his mind around it. "And now, if you'll excuse me. So nice to see you, Cecile."

As he gave his order to the bartender, Cameron couldn't help but feel a little peeved by the comment about being a single man. He certainly wasn't in any hurry to tie the knot again, not with his history. Lately, Kimmy had been dropping broad hints about their future. How long had they been dating? Not long enough. He wasn't about to be rushed into another marriage. Leaving a generous tip, he grabbed the two drinks.

Making his way through the crowd was no easy task. The music had brought everyone to their feet. Cameron was surprised to see Harper dancing with Bubba. She probably remembered him from the bachelor party. In any case, she'd make the man's night. Harper's buoyant laugh floated toward him. How refreshing that she didn't bother with the restrained simper of some women. Bubba moved pretty well for a man his size. A blue blood, he probably *had* attended Mrs. Pritchard's School of Dance. Cameron wasn't used to envying his buddy, but as he slid onto the stool, he felt a little jealous of the warm smile Bubba had somehow elicited from Cameron's date.

Date? He took a deep sip of bourbon. Damn, this sure did feel like a date. "Are you behaving yourself?" he asked his old friend when Bubba returned Harper to the table.

"As always." The guy was beaming.

"Bubba saved me. He was one familiar face in the crowd and had pity on me." Harper's playful little punch to his shoulder made Bubba blush even more.

"Harper told me she's having fun with Bella," Bubba said with a smile. "She's one lucky little girl."

"Why, thank you, Bubba." Harper looked pleased. "That's so sweet."

"Two girls playing together." The words were out before Cameron had a chance to think.

Harper's mouth fell open.

"In case you haven't noticed, Harper's not a little girl." Quite a statement from Bubba.

"Trust me, I *have* noticed. No harm intended." Notice? Tonight would strobe in his memory for quite a while.

Now it was Harper's turn to blush.

"See you two later." With a nod, Bubba left, but not until after Harper had given him a heartfelt hug.

"My word, you've charmed him." He watched Bubba stop to greet Winchester and Flo Fields. Savannah born and bred, Bubba fit so easily into this world. Cameron shifted his shoulders in the tight-fitting tux. Not an easy accomplishment for some.

"What a sweetheart." Harper's gaze followed Bubba with affection.

Kimmy never had time for his friends. She seemed to merely tolerate them unless they were a CEO of some company. And it would be a cold day in hell before she'd grant Bubba a dance, even if he asked her.

The music shifted up a notch. The fundraiser usually drew an older group that loved to let down their hair with people they knew. Savannah could be like that. Humming under her breath with shoulders moving to the beat, Harper shook one little shoe. Her toenails were painted bright orange.

"Care to dance?"

"To this? Really?"

"What? You think I'm too old?" He slid out of his jacket and loosened his tie. That sealed it. Damn straight they were dancing. "I'll just leave my walker here."

Without another word, Harper slid off the stool. He took her hand. The handbag was left on the table. Maybe she was finally relaxing. Harper moved right into the center in the group, her shoulders grabbing the beat. Cameron was right behind her. Seemed like so long ago but he'd had a good time at parties at the University of Georgia in Athens. Now the drums resonated deep in his gut. They both got into it.

"You're pretty good." He'd never seen Harper move like this.

"I had a job where I got to practice."

"Really?"

Eyes sparkling, she burst out laughing.

What a minx. "You mean on top of my bar?"

"Could be." Arms raised and hips moving, Harper rotated again. As Catwoman, she'd been sexy. Tonight she was mind blowing. Not just a girl but a woman.

Stop staring at her hips.

But who could blame him? Harper was teasing him and she wasn't getting away with it. His hands found her waist. With a tiny jerk only he could feel, she stiffened, then sighed and released. Coming closer, she rested her hands on his shoulders. His hands tightened and so did hers. Never mind that Cecile caught his eye across the floor and raised her eyebrows. Was she digging her phone from her blasted gold handbag?

Harper snapped those hips again and she had his full attention.

He didn't give a rip. Not tonight.

The past few years hadn't been easy. Long time since he'd let his hair down. Wasn't this why he'd hired Harper? She was fun. Fun for Bella, he reminded himself. And tonight? Fun for him. Downright witchy and working her voodoo. Snapping her fingers, she pulled away with a little smile, almost out of his reach. He didn't miss the looks cast by other men. Harper cut quite a figure in the slinky green dress. Not only did she sing along, she made all kinds of faces...like she felt the music clear through to her soul.

Something shifted inside. His life had veered off course and hurtled down a track he never saw coming. Sometimes he felt more like forty than twenty-nine. Tonight felt like college again. He was out to have a good time, dancing with a very hot girl.

Hot? Blow torch torrid. Harper's heat could incinerate him.

But she was totally unaware of her charm.

She moved back into him and he flipped her around, tucking her slim hips against him. That was his first mistake. Good God, he had to think about a cold shower or this could become embarrassing. But a shower was the last thing on his mind. The feel of her hips against him. The scent of her outrageously soft hair brushing his cheeks. The shimmy of her shoulders that sent other parts of her body swaying. Total overload.

Whipping Harper around, he jerked her closer. Her eyes widened. But she didn't push away. Legs apart for balance, they swayed together, tight and in sync. She kept her hands on his shoulders while he hung tight to her waist. They'd be the talk of the town tomorrow.

And he did....

Not. Give. A. Damn.

The drummer nailed it and the music ended. They stood there panting like race horses, eyes lost in each other. Sweat rolled down his back. Her moist heat had rumpled his shirt and his tuxedo pants. Loosening his tie, he stripped it off and undid two top buttons. Harper's eyes flicked to his open shirt and she backed away, driving orange fingernails through her hair. When she dropped her eyes, tawny lashes feathered over her high cheekbones. How long would it take his breathing to return to normal?

"Hey, that was fun." She sounded surprised.

"*Fun?*" He felt like he'd just run a mile.

But running wasn't what he had in mind.

She gave him a curious look before turning back toward the table. For a second he stood there, trying to sort this out. He had to get a grip. Mallory caught his eye across the floor and threw him an amused grin.

Cameron didn't give a rip. He'd had enough of order and duties. That wasn't where his mind was right now. No, he was looking at the sweep of Harper's porcelain back, wondering where it led and how those curves would feel in his hands. Uncertainty broke his stride. He stumbled and then caught himself. After all, she was his employee. If he offended her, she could take off tomorrow. Bella would be lost again. He had to get it together. When they reached the table, she slid onto one of the high chairs and crossed her legs. Grabbing his glass he tossed back a mouthful of bourbon.

Her chest heaved in the most distracting way. "What?"

He had to choose his words carefully. "Nothing. You're, ah, a great dancer. Always knew you had a lot of spirit. Getting up on that bar at the bachelor party in front of the guys…"

"…wasn't easy." She shifted in the chair.

"I could see that. But you did it. Bella needs that." Time to circle back to Bella.

When her lips curved into a smile, relief banished the nausea swishing through his stomach. She chuckled, naughty and provocative. Or maybe that was him? "Didn't know you had that in you, Mr. Bennett."

"Right back at you, Ms. Kirkpatrick." They grinned at each other like fools and the air cleared. She could make him feel crazy and comfortable at the same time. "Why are you giving me such a hard time tonight?"

"What if I am?" Harper flashed that cheeky grin again.

"I'll, ah, give you ten minutes to cut that out."

Her peal of laughter turned heads. He laughed right along with her.

Then the smile slipped from her face. "Bella needs some fun, Cameron. She also needs attention."

What? "Do you mean I work too much? We have those family dinners." His head spun. What was he missing here?

Her long silent look pinned him. Good God, was she going to quit? He knifed one hand through his damp hair and looked away. Maybe he'd totally overstepped his bounds tonight. Maybe he was no better than Randy. Harper's departure would be so hard on Bella.

And it would be hard on him.

The realization hit him broadside.

But Harper didn't say another word, thank God.

They sipped their drinks in silence and left fifteen minutes later.

The car was quiet all the way home.

"So, you two are really wiped out, huh?" Jack finally asked.

When Harper cuddled in the corner and yawned, she looked downright kittenish.

"Yep. Sure are." Cameron's pulse sped along with the hum of the tires.

Tired? Maybe. But he sure as hell knew sleep wouldn't come easy.

Chapter 13

When she woke up Sunday morning, Harper luxuriated in the smooth cool feel of the sheets. Connie made a point of mentioning the six-hundred-thread count when she handed Harper her "bed linens" on Mondays. Somewhere in the garden below mourning doves cooed. The scent of coffee teased her awake.

Memories from last night jerked her upright.

What the heck happened? Harper pulled her knees to her chest. She wasn't thinking about the gorgeous dress, the food, the dancing. Nope. Just Cameron. He'd literally rolled up his sleeves and gotten down on that dance floor. The flashing eyes. The grinding hips. And when he'd torn open his shirt? She squeezed her eyes shut. Couldn't even go there. Her heartbeat started doing scales. She'd had a great time with Cameron.

Her eyes flew open. When had Baby Blues become Cameron to her?

A chill sent her burrowing deeper under the blankets. When he'd put his hands on her hips, she'd totally melted. She sniffed her own skin. Sure enough. She could still detect a faint whiff of his cologne on her body. They'd been that close. Thank goodness Jack had picked them up. Being alone with Cameron in a dark car? Her thoughts embarrassed her.

So ridiculous. He was involved with Kimmy and he was her employer. Leaping out of bed, Harper streaked to the bathroom to brush her teeth and take a shower. She needed coffee. Bad. Champagne always gave her a headache, but that hadn't stopped her last night. Now her head throbbed under the showerhead. Taking the hot needles of water felt like a much needed punishment.

Today was her Sunday off, and she was meeting Adam at the Omelet House. When she got downstairs, the laugh soundtrack from a children's cartoon show zapped her headache like an electric bolt. She leaned into the TV room. With his daughter cuddled at his side on the green sofa, Cameron looked so cozy in gray track pants and a T-shirt. Harper's heart stuttered at the thought of the soft gray cotton, warm from his body.

"Hey." He raised his mug in greeting.

Baby Blues had become Sleepy Blues.

"Hey, back."

He zapped her with a megawatt grin. She twisted her wet hair tighter, ignoring the drip onto her jean jacket and pumpkin turtleneck. On the screen, Ninja warriors screeched. Cameron went back to the show. Harper shuffled into the kitchen to fill her travel mug with coffee. She had to get out of here. Once she'd twisted the top of the mug tight, she ducked her head back into the TV room. "Okay if I take the SUV?"

Cameron hadn't shaved yet. The brown stubble defined his chin, so very cuppable. "Of course. Have fun."

"Thanks. See you later." Almost felt like she was reporting in to her dad.

But Cameron totally was not her father.

She left them snuggled together. The cozy sight warmed her heart. Bella adored her daddy. When Cameron was around, she was on him like a magnet. After last night, Harper totally understood. Grabbing the keys to the SUV, she dashed from the house.

Adam was already waiting for her at a table near the windows in the barebones restaurant on Ferguson. The scent of fried bacon flipped Harper's hunger switch. She'd hardly eaten anything last night. As soon as she plopped into a chair, Adam began firing questions

"So how'd the evening go? Did they like your hair?"

"Everyone loved my hair, and the evening went fine."

Adam gave her The Look. The one that said he knew she was holding out on him.

She grabbed a menu, even though she knew it by heart. "Adam, I was a stand-in for Kimmy. Okay?"

He lounged back. "You're more than a stand-in, darlin'. You've got main event written all over you...when you want to be."

Harper rolled her eyes. "I'm the nanny, for Pete's sake."

His eyebrows raised in slanted exclamation points. "If you say so. Only, sugga, it's nice to have aspirations."

"My aspirations are to go into design. Somewhere." Knowing how he'd take it, Harper had never mentioned that she sometimes considered moving back to the Windy City.

With a thoughtful frown, Adam stirred more sugar into his coffee. A waitress arrived and took their order. The double waffle sounded good. Harper ordered two eggs on the side for protein.

"You aren't thinking of doing anything stupid, Harper, are you?" Adam asked when they were alone again.

"*Moi?* God forbid." She pressed one hand flat on her chest.

"Don't play cute with me. I mean it. You'd never go back to New York, would you?"

"Absolutely not. I've never been a fan of indentured servitude." That summer internship had been a nightmare.

New York, no. Chicago, maybe.

Easing out a sigh. Adam sat back. They'd gotten along so well from the first moment they sat next to each other in class freshman year.

"So tell me about the clothes. What were the darlings of Savannah wearing?"

Harper smiled remembering all the gowns that had probably come from high-end stores in Hilton Head or Atlanta. The waitress brought the food.

"What's that smile about?" Adam buttered his waffle before dousing it with syrup.

"You've never seen so much sophisticated black." For the next hour, she dished on dresses and hairstyles while she wolfed down waffles and forkfuls of egg. A few comments about the silent auction were also in order. But when she described the Nipples of Venus, Adam roared and she joined right in. How good it felt to hash things over with her old friend. Adam was one part of her past she never wanted to lose. He always had her back.

Still, she couldn't tell him everything.

When they finished their last cup of coffee, it was almost noon. What to do with the rest of the day? Harper didn't want to go directly back to the mansion. Last night still bothered her and thank goodness Adam had not pried details out of her. This was her free day, and she never got tired of exploring Savannah. After saying good-bye to Adam, she drove back toward the historical district and parked near Forsyth Park. Kids were playing near the fountain, laughing as they raced each other back to the slide. She had to bring Bella here.

Harper made frequent trips to Daffin Park with Bella. After all, the park was practically across the street. But Daffin didn't have the same historic feel of Forsyth. The pathways of the downtown icon radiated from a central fountain that dated back to 1858. Taking a seat on one of the benches rimming the fountain, she tipped her face toward the sun. She could listen to the water splashing from the cupids all day. The laughter of the children bubbled above the sound of the water.

But the park would never cure all Bella's problems. Harper's spirits sank. Maybe Bella needed more help than she could give. If Harper left, what then? She couldn't just toss the vulnerable little girl to the wolves...the next desperate nanny who may or may not love Bella.

A man with a camera was blocking off space in front of the fountain. Must be a wedding today and Harper settled back to watch. Didn't take long for the wedding party to arrive. The bride wore a red plaid taffeta gown and the groom, a kilt. Ceremonies here were usually short and individualized. Only the minister and a few friends witnessed this one, including a guy with bagpipes. Over in five minutes, the wedding still brought a lump to her throat. The couple gazed at each other with visible adoration. Other park visitors stopped to gape. When the girl tossed her bouquet, Harper felt like running to catch it.

She had to get out of here. Bagpipes split the air as she left the park. Strolling up Bull Street past the Mercer Mansion, she checked out the shop windows, where the trinkets and furniture were way beyond her budget. Since her position covered her room and board, she was finally getting a grip on her credit card bills. A buying spree was not in her immediate future.

As she walked along the cobblestone street, her thoughts turned back to the ball. Last night almost seemed like it had happened to another girl. She could still feel the touch of Cameron's reassuring hand on her elbow. Southern gentlemen sure had exquisite manners.

But the times when he hadn't exactly been a gentleman were the moments she replayed mentally in delicious detail. The day felt cool, but she unbuttoned her jacket.

When Harper reached the college gift shop, she stopped in. But the place just reminded her of Billy. How many times had they wandered through here? They'd been so young, so unaware of what life was really like. Harper pushed through the doors and headed back to the SUV.

The mansion was quiet when she got back. For a while, she worked at her drafting table. Felt good to feel the pencils in her hands, and the sketching came easily. Letting her pencils do the talking, she ended up with designs for Bella's room. A castle would stand in one corner, and that dusty canopy over the bed was stripped away. The colors were green with the metallic blue of the Ninja warriors.

After her enthusiasm burned off, she felt sleepy. No noise from the back yard, just the low hum from Victory. Cameron must have taken Bella somewhere, maybe over to Kimmy's. Kicking off her flats, she flopped onto the bed. Some time later, her phone woke her up.

"Hey, what's happening?" her sister asked when Harper picked up.

"Just another sleepy Sunday afternoon, McKenna."

Her sister snorted. "Doesn't sound like you, Harper."

McKenna always fussed over her, not that Harper minded. She described the Telfair Ball but skipped over the dancing part. No need to mention the lusting part either.

"Wow, sounds like you're hobnobbing with Savannah's finest," McKenna remarked when Harper wrapped up.

"I am so not a part of that group."

Her sister fell quiet for a second. "Hey, are you letting this job get you down?"

"That would be putting it mildly," Harper admitted. "I'm taking care of a little girl who still eats mush at all her meals. I don't like failure, McKenna. Her father seems to feel as helpless as I do."

"Sounds like they really need you."

"Sometimes I think you should have been a psychologist."

"Told you before, I may deliver babies but I am not an expert with toddlers."

"Enough about the job." Going to the window, Harper pulled aside the gauzy curtain. In the bright Sunday afternoon sunlight, Bella sat on the stone bench, kicking her feet. "Are you dating anybody?"

"Not really. Are you?"

"No. Touché." She turned away from the window. Where was Cameron? She didn't want Bella down there alone. "McKenna, I don't know what I'm doing here."

"You're helping out a little girl who really needs some support."

"But am I equipped for this?"

"You have one of the biggest hearts in Oak Park and don't you forget that." McKenna slipped so easily into her coaching mode. "You're the girl who used to bring home hungry mutts and mewling kittens. What you're doing isn't in line with your degree, but these are different times now, Harper. The fashion industry was hit hard. People might not have the income they did before the recession to spend on clothes."

Harper felt the doors to her future closing. Her chest seized.

"Hey, Harper? You still there?"

"Hang on." Fumbling for her purse on the bed, she grabbed her inhaler.

"Harper? Honey, you're scaring me," her sister's voice hollered through the phone.

After a couple quick inhalations, Harper felt her throat ease. She knew on the other end, McKenna was counting to ten. She grabbed the phone. "Sorry. I'm fine. Funny, the pollen stuff doesn't seem to affect my asthma as much as stress does."

"Talking to me is stressful?"

"Oh, no. Not at all." But her own thoughts were. Silence stretched between them and McKenna felt so far away. What Harper needed right now was a good hug from a sister.

"Maybe you need me to come down there and shake some sense into you."

"You don't have to do that, McKenna." But hope flickered in her heart.

"Sure, try to discourage me. I love Savannah. Remember what fun we had when I visited you for that awesome St. Patrick's Day parade?"

"Second only to New York's." The thought of seeing her sister lifted Harper's weird mood.

"Great. I'm due for a couple days off. Selena will cover for me. Maybe you could suggest a hotel?"

"Let me talk to Cameron. He probably won't mind if you stay with me. The mansion has a gazillion rooms."

"Mansion. I like the sound of that."

By the time they hung up, Harper was feeling so much better. Maybe she was just homesick. Maybe she missed the tree-shadowed streets of Oak Park. It would be great to see her sister and the parade would be a perfect time for McKenna to visit.

The Kirkpatricks were no strangers to St. Patty's Day parades. Although Chicago had stopped dyeing their river green for environmental reasons, they still put on a gangbuster of a parade. Every year, a committee chose the queen. When Harper was a senior in high school, her father had nominated her for the honor. To her amazement, she'd won and ended up waving to the crowds from the float, her green gown rippling in the stiff March breeze. Smiling with the memory, she headed downstairs to make sure Bella wasn't still sitting outside alone.

A visit from McKenna could provide a much needed distraction.

Chapter 14

Connie was cooking in the kitchen when Cameron came down from his home office. He hated taking business calls on Sunday but sometimes it couldn't be helped. At least that's what he'd always told himself. Now Harper's words came back to him. Maybe being a good dad took more than putting food on the table. He should know that.

The smell of cooking helped soothe the sting of losing a prime property in the historical district. The trust had decided not to sell at this time. He'd made it clear that he would be ready when they were. In the past, his patience had paid off. Plenty of other projects needed his attention.

Including his daughter.

"What are you cooking up?" He peered over Connie's shoulder.

"Ham and double-baked potatoes. One of your favorites," she reminded him while he sniffed the air with appreciation. Cameron loved double stuffed potatoes heaped with melted cheese. "Harper asked if she could help."

"Thought this was her day off." He'd heard her on the stairs. His ears had become attuned to her light step.

"It is. She's got it in her head that she wants to learn how to cook."

"And you don't think she can?"

Connie wielded that mixer like a weapon. "Not that hard. Harper's a bright girl."

"She sure is." Pushing the kitchen curtain aside, he watched her kicking a soccer ball around with Bella. Harper was as graceful at soccer as she'd been on the dance floor. Letting the curtain drop, he popped a coffee container into the Keurig, not that he needed more caffeine. Since last night, he felt jumpy as a cat.

Bella's shrieks rose from the garden as she chased after the ball. Now why hadn't he thought of doing that with her? "Do you think it's going to work out?"

Turning off her contraption, Connie said, "Your guess is as good as mine. I guess anyone can score a ham and punch in cloves. She'll learn."

"I'm not talking about the food. I'm talking about Bella and Harper."

Connie gave him one of those glances that made him feel about five years old. "You just don't want to interview again. I don't blame you." Going back to the stove, she tossed something in the pan that sizzled.

He wandered over to one of the huge Bosch stoves he'd had installed when he first renovated this house, not that Tammy ever used one. "What's for dinner?"

With a shake of her head. Connie chuckled. "I already told you. Where is your mind today?"

He stared at her back. What could he say? She was right.

"Georgia ham and double baked potatoes. Collard greens on

the side." The smell of onions rose from her pan. "Is Miss Carrington coming for dinner?"

"Don't know. She's been sick."

"Did you ask her?"

"Not yet." He wasn't up for the Grand Inquisition.

The wooden chopping board rang as Connie attacked some celery like she was using a nail gun. "Have a good time last night?"

"Why, yes, I did. Had to beat the men away, including Bubba."

Connie laughed. "I'll just bet."

"Didn't Harper look d-d-delightful?" He'd almost said, "damn hot."

"More than delightful. More Chicago than Savannah, I might add. None of that sedate black or simpering lilac for that girl."

"Well, Connie, why don't you tell me what you really think?" Leaning one hip against the counter, he took a sip of coffee. "I do believe you're right."

Connie pushed the celery from the cutting board into the pan. "Bella might be a case where Chicago is called for."

"Right again."

Time to take his troubled thoughts into the library and he grabbed his mug. Settling into his favorite leather chair, he called Kimmy. She assured him she'd be delighted to come to dinner. Her response was so quick he suspected Cecile had already talked to her.

"Are you sure you're up to it?" he asked. Kimmy's voice still sounded hoarse.

"Well, now, you are so sweet to ask but, sugga, I am feeling so much better. Really I am. Five o'clock or so?"

"I will await with breathless anticipation."

Strong words that felt foolish. He'd been breathless last night. As he hoofed it upstairs, he wondered if he'd feel that way tonight.

When Kimmy rang the bell early that evening, he was there to answer. "You don't have to ring the bell. You can come in and give a shout."

Stepping inside, she offered a beautiful but pale cheek. "So sweet of you, Cameron. Did you manage without me last night?"

Yep, Cecile had definitely made that call.

He closed the door, and her strong perfume held him hostage. "Everyone was devastated by your absence. Why don't we sit on the back porch?"

The day was cool but not too chilly. He needed some fresh air.

"Mint juleps, Connie?" he asked as they swept past the kitchen on their way outside. "Would that be all right with you, Kimmy?"

"Perfect. Hello, Connie."

Did Connie even answer?

By that time, Harper and Bella had moved from the garden onto the porch. Pushing back a long curl, Harper looked up from a game of checkers. "Hello, Kimmy. Like your green outfit."

"It is pretty, isn't it?"

In fact, it was about the same shade of green Harper had worn the night before. He supposed Kimmy's blonde hair made the difference in how it looked. And of course she'd been sick. "Teaching Bella to play checkers?" he asked. Connie must have shown Harper where the games were stored in the study.

"Yep. She's darn good too."

"Harper, I understand you filled in for me last night." Kimmy settled into one of the rattan chairs.

So charming the way Harper blushed. "I tried. Pretty big shoes."

"Not really." Kimmy glanced at her feet. Her shoes looked like they were honed from pewter. No doubt she'd bought them in a Savannah boutique for an outrageous price.

Bella pretty much ignored them, intent on the game.

"You don't want me to be able to hop over you, Bella," Harper explained. "You want your man to reach the other side and get a crown. Then he can move every which way."

To his surprise, Bella followed her nanny's suggestion and blocked her.

"Way to go, girl." Harper gave her a high five.

The smile on his little girl's face tugged at Cameron's heart. He leapt to his feet. "Think I'll just go check on those drinks."

Thirty minutes later, they were seated in the dining room. The group Sunday dinner had turned out to be a splendid idea, one of many from Harper. Bella, of course, had her bowl of mush in front of her, and he tried not to look at it. He had no idea what he could do about her eating problem. When he was growing up, he ate everything on his plate, glad to have it. He figured when she felt hungry enough, she'd eat.

Still, the child was thin as a rail. Clearly that approach hadn't been working.

The ladies discussed the upcoming St. Patrick's Day parade

while he feasted on Connie's ham, the taste of cloves on his tongue. No one could fix a ham like Connie.

At some point in the meal, Kimmy excused herself and returned with a bowl of banana, sliced very thin. "Bella, why don't you try this? It's so easy to eat."

His daughter just stared at the bowl. Harper's face drained.

"You might enjoy it, sweetheart. I'll take a bite. See." Kimmy lifted the spoon to her lips.

Bella was not impressed. In fact, she drew back.

"Oh, now, darlin', you must open your mouth. Yes, you must." Kimmy's voice thinned as she scooted the spoon closer.

Bella batted Kimmy's hand away and his favorite potatoes turned to a rock on his tongue. "Kimmy, maybe this isn't such a good idea." He put down his fork.

"She doesn't want it." Harper looked ready to vault right over the table.

Chin up, Kimmy filled the spoon again.

"Kimmy, I do believe Harper is right. Please put the spoon down." Slowly he got to his feet.

Setting her lips as only Kimmy could, she inched the spoon closer. "Nonsense. The girl has to eat."

The fact that Kimmy was a psychologist stopped him from saying more. Bella pulled at the collar of her little top, something she did when she was nervous. "Kimmy, stop."

Face set, Kimmy tried again. With a wail that could be heard out on Truman Parkway, Bella shoved the spoon away.

The slop hit Kimmy's top and everything else in the near

vicinity. She gasped. "Oh, for heaven's sakes."

Harper was on her feet.

His ears rang as Bella let out another screech. Connie came to the doorway. The place was up for grabs. He didn't miss the look Connie exchanged with Harper while Kimmy dashed off to repair her outfit. Clucking to her gently, he lifted Bella into his arms.

Disbelief numbed him. Sure, he'd wanted to Kimmy to display some interest in Bella, but not like this. Connie cleaned up the dining room with stern disapproval, and Harper excused herself without even trying the peach cobbler. Bella disappeared into the TV room. Connie must be having a bad day because the cobbler had never been so tasteless. Despair churned in his stomach. Obviously still not feeling well, Kimmy kept dabbing her eyes with the napkin. She got up to leave before she'd even finished her coffee. He trailed her to the front door, his temples throbbing.

"I'm so sorry, Cameron." Kimmy's nose was red, whether from her cold or the episode, he didn't know. "Maybe I shouldn't have come."

"You meant well, Kimmy."

"I did. I really did." More dabbing. "Really, Cameron You have to know that."

She was blinking those eyelashes up at him. He patted her on the shoulder, which only seemed to make her mad.

After they air kissed, she left, her heels clicking on the pavement. Staring after her, he wondered why he didn't feel more. Struck him that her cold wasn't the only reason he hadn't felt like kissing her good-bye. Cameron stood in the doorway and waved as she drove away. That red convertible made it clear she was Kimmy in the Morning. Everybody in Savannah knew that car.

Maybe that had been her charm when he was a new widower. Closing the door, Cameron remembered how numb he'd been after the crash. And there was Kimmy at that Chamber event, all condolences and sweet words. His business depended on connections. Together they could work a room like no other couple.

"Want me to take Bella up to bed?" Connie asked when he wandered into the kitchen. "I'll take care of the dishes later."

"No I'll do it. But thank you." Bella had been so upset.

"Come here, Pipsqueak," he said sitting down next to her on the sofa in the TV room. He'd taken to Harper's nickname for Bella.

Wordlessly, his little girl crawled onto his lap. Kissing the top of her head, he rocked her, felt her ease out a sigh. His hold tightened. "Maybe I'll just carry you up to bed." She snuggled closer.

Bella weighed no more than a sack of potatoes but she felt so frail in his arms. After he had her in bed, she asked for a story. He'd do anything to make up for the scene at the table. He never should have allowed it. Remorse left a bitter taste in his mouth while he read. When he finished one Dr. Seuss book, she handed him another and he gladly opened *Old Hat, New Hat,* reading in a ridiculously high voice that got her giggling.

"Sorry about tonight, baby girl," he whispered before he turned out the light. "Sometimes I don't think I'm a very good dad."

Good God. How it hurt to admit that.

"Oh, no, Daddy." Bless her heart, Bella threw herself against his chest. Those skinny little arms gripped his neck. "You're the best, the very best. Really."

He smoothed her hair. Couldn't blink fast enough. Last thing he wanted was for Bella to see her daddy in tears. "So are you, sweetheart. So are you."

She snuggled back down. He turned off the bedside lamp. The night lights were on. "Night, sweetheart."

"Night, Daddy."

Taking the back stairway, he circled back downstairs and wandered onto the side porch. From his favorite rattan chair he could see the moon through the live oaks. Usually he felt like lord of the manor sitting here. Not tonight. Every nerve in his body jittered. When he heard the clatter in the kitchen, he went in to talk to Connie. But Harper stood at the sink, arranging the plates in the dishwasher.

"Connie will do that."

Glancing up, Harper drilled him with fiery green eyes. "I need something to do."

He eased out a sigh. "Quite a ruckus, tonight wasn't it?"

She slammed another dish into the rack. "Kimmy never should have tried that with Bella. For heaven's sake, she's a psychologist…" Her voice broke and she pressed her lips together.

"She was only trying to help."

Tossing her head, Harper gave a harrumph he could feel deep in his gut. After jamming a pan into the bottom rack, she turned. "Do you mind if my sister comes to visit in March? Guess I don't have vacation days, but I'll make up the time somehow. McKenna loves the St. Patrick's Day parade."

So she'd called in the family troops. Was it that bad? The flashback of how Harper had felt in his arms the night before rocked him. Suddenly he was on sensation overload. He shook it off.

"Of course not."

Harper swiped at a piece of hair, the hair that had mesmerized him while she gyrated last night. "She'll stay in a hotel."

Stubborn, the hair fell over one eye, and he tucked it behind her ear. "That's nonsense, Harper. We have plenty of room. I'll just let Connie know." She could have all the damn days off she wanted. He couldn't stand the thought of her leaving.

Bella wouldn't be the only one left hurting.

Turning, Harper stripped off the rubber gloves and tossed them under the sink. The move was so homey. Suddenly he was back with his sister in the small kitchen that always smelled of burnt cooking lard.

But Harper wasn't his sister. The clenching in his gut told him that much.

Chapter 15

Harper's heart just about leapt right out of her chest when McKenna swung up the ramp at the Savannah Airport. With a wild whoop, she fell into her big sister's arms.

"Glad to see you too." Pulling away, McKenna gave Harper a searching glance. Nowhere to hide with this woman. "What's up with you?"

"Just glad you're here." Harper linked one arm through McKenna's.

The days following the Telfair Ball had been a jumble. So hard to undo the damage Kimmy had done. Now eating even less, Bella had withdrawn. Not even promises of a visit to the park brought a smile.

"We had such a row at dinner last Sunday." On the way to the parking garage, Harper described the horrible incident with Kimmy.

"And this woman is a psychologist?"

"Pretty darn incredible."

Stopping at the BMW, Harper clicked open the back. McKenna stowed her bag. "Nice wheels."

"Just one of the job perks. Nothing can beat your jeep, McKenna." They climbed into the front seat.

Her sister's gaze swept the console. "I'd say this is a close second."

Harper exited the garage and before long they were on the highway. She could feel McKenna relax as palm trees and tall cedars flew past.

"Will you just look at this?" McKenna craned her neck. "And it's at least thirty degrees warmer here than Chicago. I'm almost thrilled you had a crisis so I could come down again."

"Not a crisis. Nothing I can't handle myself." But she wasn't so sure.

"Ah, huh. So, tell me about your boss."

Too many words came to mind. "Ah, successful. Probably a Savannah mover and a shaker. Devoted dad but clueless sometimes."

"After all he is a man."

"Frustrating! And a good dancer." The last came out on a chuckle.

"Whoa. So you've danced together?"

Heat flooded her cheeks. "Think I told you about the Telfair Ball. Yep, we sure did dance. Cameron has some, ah, pretty good moves." Her stomach shimmied.

"The way you talk about him, I didn't know Cameron was that young." McKenna's tone had turned thoughtful.

"He might act older than his age. But not that night." She smiled, remembering.

"Maybe losing your wife does that to a guy," McKenna said thoughtfully. "Matures you fast."

"Especially if he has a little girl."

Thank goodness they'd reached Victory Drive. She wasn't comfortable dissecting Cameron. Way too personal, even with McKenna. "He's been a good employer."

"And Bella? Can't wait to meet that little tyke."

"She's really special, but I'm not sure Cameron's girlfriend feels that way."

They'd reached the mansion and Harper pulled into the garage.

"Wow." McKenna eyed the stately brick home while she grabbed her bag from the back.

"Pretty awesome, right?" Harper led the way through the garden.

"And a fountain? Some people have it really tough." McKenna gave Harper's shoulders a quick hug. "I'm happy for you. Thanks for inviting me."

"Yeah, well, looks can be deceiving. Most days this job really is work. Wait till you meet everyone."

As they mounted the back steps, muted laughter floated from the kitchen.

Connie, Cameron, and Bella were sitting around the kitchen table when Harper pushed open the back door. "We're home."

Home. The word had slipped out. Blushing, Harper introduced McKenna.

Scraping back his chair, Cameron stood and extended one hand. "Glad you could visit. Harper gets tired of us, I'm sure."

She didn't miss the widening of McKenna's eyes. "Thanks for putting me up. I would've been glad to stay in a hotel."

Hands on his slender hips, Cameron shook his head. "Wouldn't think of it. Bella and I rattle around in the place, don't we, sweetheart?"

But Bella wasn't paying any attention to her father. She was too busy admiring McKenna. "You're pretty. I like your red hair."

Squatting until she was eye level, McKenna said, "Well, Harper told me all about your pretty black hair. We gotta take what we're born with, I guess."

Bella giggled. McKenna could talk to a tree, and it would answer. Harper was used to comments about McKenna's hair. Sure, she had some reddish streaks in her own caramel curls when the sun hit it just right, but McKenna was flaming all-out red.

McKenna turned to Cameron. "Harper tells me you gave her some time off. Thank you."

"Trust me. She deserves it."

McKenna was leaving on Tuesday, and Harper had been relieved by Cameron's immediate generosity.

"Guess I'll get McKenna settled in." Harper led the way through the foyer.

"Geez. I had no idea." McKenna's head swiveled as she took in the chandeliers, carved sideboards and gilded mirrors.

"Tough job, but someone had to do it." She'd never told her sister about her first trip to Cameron's house. This weekend might be a time for revelations. They began their trek up the stairs.

Connie had put McKenna in one of the rooms across the hall from Harper on the third floor. "You know, so you can do your girl talk thing."

"Not bad digs," McKenna murmured, taking in the room that was a mirror image of Harper's except McKenna's was blue compared to Harper's green. Both rooms felt like postcards from a past era. Somehow that suited Savannah with its southern comfort.

After McKenna had unpacked, they drifted back down to the kitchen. Cameron was in the TV room with Bella. As usual, she was mesmerized by some galactic battle. Cameron was reading the paper. Sometimes Harper wanted to swat him over the head with that darn sports section.

"You girls going out?" He lifted his blue eyes.

"Gonna show McKenna around. We're going to Back in the Day Bakery for lunch."

"Can I come?" Bella's plaintive question stopped Harper in her tracks.

"I don't see why not." McKenna looked at Harper. "Think I saw a car seat in the SUV?"

Anything to get her away from the TV. "Why don't you get your jacket, Bella?"

Cameron put the paper aside. He hadn't shaved and the stubble dusting his cheeks gave him a disturbingly rakish look. "Now, you don't have to take Bella, Harper. Today is your day off, especially since your sister's visiting."

"Of course she can come." Harper tousled Bella's hair. "McKenna and I are going out tonight. Don't worry about it. I'll just grab some lunch for her." The delicious salads and sandwiches at the bakery wouldn't tempt Bella, that much Harper knew. Working quickly, she mixed up some cereal in a plastic container.

Lunch with Bella would make Harper's challenges here clear.

Cameron had taken Bella upstairs and she was back in a flash, dragging her jean jacket. Bella often insisted on dressing herself, and she was wearing a pink T-shirt with a pair of red pants. Her hair needed brushing, but Harper knew if she started to make changes there might be a scene.

"Let's ride," she said, helping Bella on with her jean jacket.

Cameron watched them from the kitchen doorway as they made their way to the garage. "You'all have fun now!" His voice carried on the early afternoon air.

Looking back, McKenna muttered, "Kind of a lonely guy. Definitely hot, but lonely."

Lonely? Harper never thought of him in that way. She buckled Bella into the carseat and they were off.

When they reached the bakery, she parked on the street and helped Bella out. The three of them trooped into the glass-fronted structure. Inside, the mismatched furniture added to the casual charm.

"How kitschy and cute. I love this, don't you, Bella?" McKenna asked. But Bella was too busy taking it all in.

A section of an old-fashioned booth faced out, and Harper placed Bella between them on the padded seat for a bird's eye view. After scanning the menu, they both ordered the rosemary chicken sandwich with the ciabatta bread. By the time one of the girls delivered their order to the circular table, Harper had opened Bella's cereal and had her sippy cup ready. But Bella had slipped out and wandered to the bakery case with McKenna right behind her. The two stood with hands on the glass, eyes fixated on the chocolate cupcakes smothered with jimmies. "Want one?" McKenna asked.

Eyes solemn, Bella nodded. The clerk approached them.

"Six blonde brownies, three Mexican hot chocolate cookies. Same for the lavender ones too. " The list rattled on. "Oh, we'll take that chocolate cupcake too," McKenna told the girl. "Want one, Harper?"

She shook her head. "Trying to lose weight before summer."

"Right. Me too. We'll take three," McKenna told the girl.

They settled back into the booth with a huge box of pastries, and the food came right away. Twisting open one of the bottles of root beer from the self serve refrigerator case, Harper wished she could meet her sister for lunch every day. "I'm so glad you've come."

"Me too."

When Harper handed Bella a plastic spoon, the little girl dug into her cereal. She often seemed hungry but ate without any enjoyment. McKenna's eyebrows rose, but she didn't make a comment. Harper loved that about her sister. She took life as it came. While Bella ate, the two sisters chatted about home. McKenna filled her in about Vanessa, a close friend who'd just scored a spot on the TV show *Eye of the Tiger*, where entrepreneurs begged for backing from a group of successful businessmen.

"Randall Bakery is kind of the tipping point that could make or break them," McKenna explained. "Vanessa thinks they have to go national with their whipped cream cakes."

"How's Bo?" Harper asked. Vanessa's little boy was such a cutie and McKenna was his godmother.

"Terrific. Took him to the zoo last weekend."

"The zoo?" Bella piped up, eyes wide.

"Maybe we'll do that some day." Hadn't Cameron ever taken his daughter to see the animals?

The conversation moved on. Harper had so many questions about her five brothers back in Oak Park and McKenna loved telling stories. Before they knew it, the salads were gone and they were munching on the fragrant bread. After Bella finished her cereal, she sat staring at the cupcake, tiny chin propped on her hands.

Harper held her breath. "You gonna eat that?"

Bella gave her head a solemn shake.

"Would you like to taste one of those jimmies?"

Bella shook her head again, but her eyes never left the mounded top. Harper and McKenna went back to talking about the sites McKenna wanted to see during her visit. From the corner of her eye, Harper saw the little minx dust the top of the cupcake with one finger. Lips parted, Bella studied the jimmies clinging to her hand as if they were stars dropped from the sky. Then she rubbed her fingers together with a frown and the bits of chocolate plopped to the table. Harper exhaled.

"Can we take this home, Harper?"

"Absolutely." Harper exchanged a look with her sister as they cleaned up the table. Minutes later, they were in the car headed for Forsyth Park. After Harper found a parking spot, the three wandered over to the swings where children played.

While McKenna lazed in the sun on one of the benches, Harper pushed Bella on a swing. The spring sun fell softly on the park, but it was breezy. The huge rhododendron bushes were beginning to open. So beautiful but pollen was thick in the air. When Bella began to wheeze, Harper stopped the swing and grabbed the inhalers from her bag.

"Got a problem?" McKenna had wandered back to the play area.

"Nothing we can't handle." Harper ruffled Bella's curls as they both pulled on their inhalers. Maybe she was foolish to bring Bella here but sometimes Bella seemed so insulated from life.

Five minutes later, they were back in the car and driving north. McKenna pointed to the Mercer House, the red brick mansion that had been featured in the movie *Midnight in the Garden of Good and Evil.* "Wouldn't mind touring that mansion again."

"You're on. Let's go tomorrow."

"Can I come?" Bella's voice came from the back.

Looking in the rearview mirror, Harper hated to disappoint her little charge but the mansion held treasures and Bella always wanted to touch things. "I don't think it's something for children, okay? We're going to the parade on Monday, and you'll love that."

The momentary disappointment on Bella's face lifted. "A parade?"

"Did you go to the St. Patrick's Day parade last year with your dad?" McKenna asked.

Bella's forehead wrinkled. "Maybe."

McKenna caught Harper's eye. No child could forget a parade. When they got to Broughton Street they stopped at Leopold's ice cream parlor.

"This place reminds me so much of Peterson's in Oak Park," McKenna remarked after they'd placed orders for hot fudge sundaes.

"Maybe that's why I love it so much." Harper looked around the antique wooden counter, soda fixtures, and the bentwood chairs in the eating area. "Sometimes I really miss Oak Park."

"You can come home any time."

Harper grabbed some napkins from the dispenser. She couldn't admit her silent longing for home, not in front of Bella. Her need to hang in and try to help the little girl motivated her every day. But she wasn't helping her. Lunch at the bakery had really brought that home.

And since the ball, being around Cameron had become strained and difficult. But maybe that was just her.

When they got home, Cameron was working in his office but he sprang down the steps, picking Bella up and whirling her around in his arms. "How's my girl? Did you have a good time?"

"Yep." And she proceeded to tell her dad about the swings. "But I didn't eat the ice cream."

"Maybe next time." His gaze found Harper's, as if commiserating.

Resting her head on his shoulder, Bella nodded. "Maybe, Daddy."

That night, Harper and McKenna hit the town. They ended up

at the brewery on Broughton, talking more than drinking. For a while, Adam joined them with some of his friends. McKenna had met Adam before and they picked up right where they'd left off. Soon, Adam and the guys drifted off and Harper took McKenna to Lulu's Chocolate Bar for coffee and thick slices of key lime cheesecake on a coconut macaroon crust. No diets tonight.

"Good thing they only weigh the luggage at the airport and not me," McKenna quipped. "But I'm sure having fun."

"Me too." Harper settled back with a sigh. Lulu's usually had entertainment, and a guitarist was playing love songs in the corner. She wished he'd stop. This place reminded her way too much of Billy.

"What are you thinking about all the time?" McKenna gave her a searching glance over the rim of her coffee mug.

"Billy, sometimes," she admitted on a sigh. *And sometimes Cameron*, she added to herself.

McKenna set the mug down. "Don't."

"I can't help it."

"Harper, four years together and the guy dumps you long distance?"

Harper snorted. "Pathetic, right?"

"An adult conversation about why you're breaking up would be nice."

"Guess he just got busy in California."

Didn't look like McKenna was buying it.

The vocalist's rendition of "Unchained Melody" brought back so many memories. How many times had she sat here, Billy's arm around her?

Usually she felt worse, thinking about the past.

Not tonight. The realization shook her.

McKenna squeezed her hand. "Come on, Harper. Sometimes a guy's just a habit. Don't you think you've outgrown Billy?"

"Outgrown him? McKenna, a guy's not like a training bra."

Her sister narrowed her x-ray vision eyes. "You've changed, Harper, and you don't even see it."

"What do you mean?"

"You're older. Wiser. Maybe this job has done it."

Flabbergasted, Harper almost reached for her inhaler.

Her sister fanned out both hands. "Hey, I'm telling you straight. You are different."

She hated the tears swelling in her throat. "Maybe. Still, sometimes I want to come home."

"Fine, but are you running from something or to something?" McKenna asked with her maddening practicality.

"Good question." Did she want to leave Savannah just because Billy wasn't here anymore?

Or was she running away from someone else?

The skin at the back of her neck prickled.

When they reached the house that night, Cameron's Porsche sat in the garage. Saturday night and he hadn't gone out. The light glowed over the sink. Using her key, she pushed open the back door. Past midnight and the house felt quiet. They called it a night when they got to the third floor.

The following day, they walked along River Row and visited the tourist shops. McKenna picked up a box of chocolates for her staff, along with some for Vanessa and Amy, her other close friend who had just gotten engaged. McKenna was going to be a bridesmaid in Amy's wedding. Per McKenna's request, they toured the Mercer house before trekking over to Zunzi's for a takeout lunch.

"You're ordering a meatloaf sandwich?" McKenna asked after Harper placed her order.

"What's wrong with that?" The smell was so tempting.

McKenna's eyes softened. "You really must be homesick."

Wolfing lunch down in the park across the street didn't make Harper feel better. City workers were setting things up for the St. Patrick's Day parade the next day. Cameron was taking them. Last year, she'd gone to the parade with Billy.

Tonight that didn't bother her at all. She could hardy wait for tomorrow.

Chapter 16

Cameron was probably as excited as Bella about the parade.
Although he'd offered to take out a room at the DeSoto Hilton
along the parade route, the girls had howled.

"Are you kidding me? That's the whole idea of a parade,
Cameron. To be there." Harper had looked at him like he'd lost his
mind.

"What would you hear…or smell inside a hotel room?"
McKenna asked, shaking her head. "The crowd's an important part
of the experience."

"All right, all right." He'd thrown up his hands. "Some of the
family men I know make a reservation at a hotel. Just trying to do
the right thing."

"Have you ever seen a parade from a hotel room?" Harper
crossed her arms.

He was starting to get that are-you-an-old geezer look from her.
The answer was no.

"Not many parades where I come from, so no to that. But I did
visit Savannah for this parade in college. Drunken brawls and I
don't want Bella near that."

McKenna's eyebrows rose. "We intend to stay away from
drunks and brawls."

Fair enough. So here he sat waiting in the kitchen, checking his watch. Bella was the first to barrel into the room, looking so cute in her green jeans and sweater. "I'm ready, Daddy!" McKenna followed close behind.

His little girl smelled like baby shampoo when he swept her into his arms. The glittery shamrocks wired to her headband nearly took his eye out. "Where did you get that?" As if he couldn't guess.

"Harper. Do I look pretty?" She shook her head and the shamrocks on her headband quivered. Greasepaint shamrocks decorated her cheeks.

"You look beautiful." Cameron nuzzled her ear until she giggled, swatting him away.

Harper arrived dressed in her usual bright colors. Took his breath away. "Like the cheeks."

"Do you?" She blew out a breath that made each green shamrock larger. McKenna rolled her eyes.

They were off. Took a while to get downtown.

"Is it always this crowded down here?" McKenna asked.

"The parade has a huge draw," he told her. Savannah knew how to do things right. Harper's question about the parade touched a sore point. He'd never even heard about a parade as a kid. And he definitely wanted Bella to have that experience.

Downtown, he parked behind a business owned by a friend not too far from the parade route. They walked three blocks to Drayton. Bella seemed to be a calling card. Some kind people let them weasel their way closer to the front.

"Where's Kimmy?" Harper asked.

"In the parade. She hates crowds, but her station has a float."
Kimmy did like people clamoring for autographs, however. That
much he knew.

Wasn't too long before Harper cried out, "Look. Here they
come!" In her slim jeans and bright green hoodie, she caught more
than a few eyes.

The parade moved slowly, music swelling. When the first band
marched past, the horns blared. Bella looked beside herself.

"Have you ever been in a parade?" She looked at her nanny
with adoration.

"Has she been in a parade?" howled McKenna. "Honey, she
was the queen of the Chicago St. Patrick's Day Parade."

"Did you wear a pretty dress?" Bella blinked up at her idol.

Harper nodded, brushing Bella's hair back from her forehead.
"Sure did. The dress was long and green. Yes, it was very pretty.
McKenna made sure of that."

Harper had gone up another notch in Bella's eyes.

After doing battle with a purse large enough to hold one of the
Savannah squares, McKenna pulled out a wallet and flipped it
open. "Here ya go."

"You look beautiful," Bella whispered, taking in the shot of
Harper that was, in his opinion, pretty spectacular. "Like a princess.
Doesn't she look pretty, Daddy?"

"*Very* pretty." Did his tone say more?

Harper turned raging red. "That was a long time ago. I was in
high school." She handed the wallet back to her sister.

With the sun on his face and excitement in the air, the day

seemed like a cause for celebration. "Drinks?"

The girls nodded and he dashed into a nearby restaurant. Harper and McKenna wanted a beer but he was sticking with water for the moment. Nothing worse than a drunken bash on St. Patrick's Day. Took him a bit to buy the wristbands that allowed drinking in public.

When he was in college, he'd been part of a group of guys who always drove back to Savannah for this parade. When had it become too much trouble? Maybe he'd been missing out on the fun and so had Bella. No question that on the street there was a lot more activity. The air was filled with the smell of bratwursts grilling and caramel corn. Everyone was decked out in green, and he was glad he'd worn his pale green polo. At least he hadn't messed up there.

"You need a necklace." Harper laughed, taking one from her neck.

"I don't want to take yours." A guy in a necklace? He didn't think so.

"I've got plenty. Come on." Standing on tiptoe, she looped the beads over his head. The crowd moved. Her breasts brushed his chest.

He heard her sudden intake of breath and gave her an inch, much as it killed him. "Thank you."

"You're welcome."

Her eyes glittered, so close he could see the gold around each iris.

"Daddy?" Bella tugged on his jeans. "I can't see."

Dazed, he looked around. More people had arrived, cutting off their view. "Okay, Pipsqueak. Want to get up on my shoulders?"

Bella nodded. Bending, he scooped her up. She was light as the cotton candy a clown was selling. Her tiny hands hugged his neck, feet beating against his chest to the music.

A float came by from one of the local stores, and they all cheered. Professional clowns and bicyclists trekked across the street, tossing candy at all the spectators, but Bella didn't seem interested. Before long, he had to do something about her eating habits. The therapist helped by making him feel better about his situation. But the sessions hadn't changed anything for Bella.

With McKenna and Harper cheering and applauding next to him, they watched the parade. Before too long, the float from WFAV came past.

"Look, there's Kimmy!" Bella pointed.

Kimmy looked almost regal in a green sweater set as she waved to the crowd. She could be stunning, which was what had attracted him in the beginning.

"Kimmy, Kimmy!" Bella screamed again.

Finally she turned. Her hand moved in that queenly wave she had. She seemed very distant. Although she threw some kisses to the crowd, she didn't aim for Bella.

Sinking back on his shoulders, Bella said. "She's not as pretty as Harper. She doesn't have a pretty dress."

"Oh, Bella. Kimmy looks, well, beautiful," Harper said.

A guarded reply if ever he'd heard one. What did the nanny really think of his girlfriend? And why would her opinion matter?

Harper's scarf rippled in the breeze. Her beads glittered in the sunlight and those shamrocks on her cheeks? Didn't look childish, that's for sure. Harper didn't try to look pretty, not really. She was having fun, the way she had at the Telfair Ball. Cameron couldn't help but smile.

"What's so funny?" she asked, nose wrinkling.

"You and you don't even know it."

When Harper pouted, she looked so much like Bella. McKenna glanced over before turning back to the parade. Felt good to be here with the group. Almost like family. He turned his face up to the sun.

The clown had circled back, sheaf of cotton candy cones now half empty.

Harper darted forward. "We'll take two. Want one?"

"Nope. Go ahead and have your fun."

Handing a huge pink puff of candy to her sister, Harper broke off a chunk and trailed it into her mouth. Her lips closed over it, eyelids fluttering closed.

He had to look away. So sexy and she wasn't even trying. But his attention snapped back when he heard Bella ask, "Can I have some?"

Harper stopped chewing. Bella never asked for food. *Never.* While he gripped Bella's ankles, Harper held out the cone, a tremulous smile on her lips. Bella's tiny fingers swooped toward the cone. He couldn't see Bella's expression but he sure as heck could watch Harper's face register surprise and, yes, hope. "Just let it dissolve on your tongue, Bella. Like this."

Tipping back her chin, Harper did something with her tongue that tightened every muscle in his body. McKenna had turned to stare. Her expression told the story. Apparently Bella was following Harper's lead.

"Isn't it yummy?" Harper grinned up at his daughter.

"Uh, huh."

"Want more?"

"Uh, huh."

Were those tears brimming in Harper's eyes? Cameron's throat swelled. Might be just cotton candy but this was huge in his book.

The clop of horses' hooves turned his attention to a carriage pulled by four prancing horses but Bella wasn't interested. She was still all about the cotton candy. Amazing. Finally, Bella's attention must have turned back to the parade because Harper said, "Maybe more later?"

"Maybe." He welcomed Bella's sticky fingers on his neck.

A good day had just gotten better.

When one of the militia units came marching by, girls dashed into the street to give the best-looking guy a kiss, another Savannah tradition. Of course the soldiers didn't mind a bit.

"How come those girls are having all the fun and we're here?" McKenna tossed her empty cotton candy cone into a trash barrel.

"I don't see anyone stopping you," Harper challenged.

McKenna fisted her hands on her hips. "Maybe we should have a contest."

"Sounds good to me." Harper handed him the rest of her cotton candy.

"I think that's a great idea." The words were out before he could stop them.

"Can I play?" Bella asked.

"Heck no. Not yet, sweetheart." His daughter kissing a stranger? Not on his watch.

Harper tugged Bella's foot. "But you can keep score. How about that?"

"Okay. Great." Bella settled more firmly on his shoulders, like she was getting down to business. Every once in a while, he thought he felt a pull on the cotton candy he continued to hold up, ignoring the ache in his arm.

An Army unit marched past, smiles gleaming on the faces of the troops. Harper dashed into the crowd to kiss a tall blond, and Cameron's stomach twisted. The covert grin indicated the guy wasn't about to complain. Her sister was right behind her landing a kiss on a curly-haired guy who could have been all of eighteen.

"Harper and McKenna are being silly," Bella said with a giggle.

"They certainly are." They weren't the only women making spectacles of themselves. Just the only ones he wanted to watch.

Not that he was enjoying it.

"Don't you think that's about enough?" Irritation rasped in his throat. He'd taken over the counting when Bella passed ten.

"Just getting started," Harper hollered over a brass band.

"Who's winning?" Bella called out.

"We both are." McKenna leapt toward the next military group.

The air was filled with voices, music and laughter that didn't lift his testy mood. One guy took Harper's shoulders in his hands while he enjoyed a quick kiss. Heat peppered Cameron's annoyance. He could almost feel those lips on his.

"Oh, look!" shrieked Bella. "Harper is popular, Daddy."

Another good-looking guy in uniform had just landed a sound kiss on his nanny. Game changer. A peck on the cheek was one thing but this? Too long and the guy looked way too pleased. Handing Bella to McKenna, he pushed through the group in front of them. But by the time he reached the curb, Harper had trotted back to the sidelines. "What are you doing?"

The shamrock on one of her cheeks was smeared. He didn't even want to think about how that had happened. "Ah, defending your honor?"

"Figured as much. That's so sweet." Reaching up, she ticked his chin with one finger and he grabbed her hand. His irritation cooled but the heat riddling his body didn't. She cocked her head to one side, saucy and smiling. "I can take care of myself."

"You sure about that?"

"No question about it." She tugged her hand away, looking pleased. Damn. She was enjoying this. And so was he.

"Good reflexes," McKenna told him when he reached for Bella again.

"You have to be fast where your sister's concerned." He settled Bella back on his shoulders

Now, why did McKenna find that so funny?

Chapter 17

Harper felt so bummed out taking McKenna to the Savannah airport Monday. She didn't realize how much she missed her sister until she spent time with her again. The parade had been such fun. She'd felt something shift. Was it Bella's bites of cotton candy or something else? The following morning Bella marched down to the kitchen and announced to Connie, "Guess what? I ate cotton candy."

"I know it's sugar and I shouldn't have been so thrilled but I was," Connie told Harper later, wiping damp eyes with her apron.

"I know. I felt the same way."

The picture of Bella's face as she sampled the confection would stay with Harper a long time. Small victories like that kept her in Savannah.

And then there was Bella's father. Had Cameron been flirting with her? And had she teased him right back? Made her stomach queasy.

Harper and McKenna plodded into the airport in silence. Sunlight beamed through the skylights onto the brick courtyard, but Harper wasn't feeling cheerful. When they hugged, Harper hung on tight.

"Hey, you okay?" Brushing back a strand of Harper's hair,

McKenna gave her sisterly scrutiny.

Harper managed a shaky sigh. "I'm going to miss you. Sometimes going home to Chicago seems like a good idea."

"But maybe not the right thing, okay? We find our mission in different ways, Harper. I go to Guatemala and work with pregnant women with little access to care. You have a great opportunity to make a difference with Bella. Her dad's too busy and he's a guy, okay?"

Passengers pushed past them, boarding passes in hand. Flights were being called overhead.

"That little girl idolizes you. Live up to it, missy. She needs you." McKenna grabbed the handle of her carry-on. "Now, the father? Can't wait to hear how that turns out."

"What are you talking about?"

With a mysterious smile, McKenna disappeared down the ramp. Harper wanted to squeeze her until she coughed up whatever was on that scheming mind of hers, but McKenna's bright head of red hair receded. No time to confide that Bella's father posed another reason why Harper should leave. After yesterday, the feelings she was having for Cameron Bennett troubled her. Billy didn't fill her dreams anymore. Nope, just a tall blond with a rock hard body and a killer smile.

Harper stopped at the airport Starbucks for coffee and carried the cup out to her car. On the way home, all the reasons why she should stay ran through her mind. No evictions on her horizon. She'd been making payments on her bills. Lived in a beautiful home and had most evenings off, along with two days. Sure, she wasn't making any advances toward finding a job in her field, but she was learning how to cook. At least now when she showed up in the kitchen, Connie didn't look at her like an intrusion.

Then there was Bella. Harper's heart squeezed thinking about the tyke with rebellious eyes and hair to match. When she started this job, Bella had presented a daunting challenge. She still did. In May she'd be five years old, heading for kindergarten and still eating baby food. What could she do to change that? Harper turned her radio to cool jazz.

When she pulled into the garage, Cameron's Porsche was still there. Usually he was at his office by now or out on a job.

Connie was in the kitchen when Harper pushed open the door and hung the car keys on the hook.

"The boss wants to see you." Connie nodded toward the back stairway that led upstairs. "He's in his office."

Whoa. Her mouth dried. She'd never been summoned like this and tripped on her way upstairs. Had something gone wrong during McKenna's visit?

Palms damp, she knocked on the door of his bedroom. Cameron's office lay just beyond his personal space. She'd never ventured inside this room and rarely even came down this end of the hall. That's how uncomfortable she felt about seeing where Cameron slept.

When Cameron opened the door, the wave of spicy aftershave tightened Harper's stomach. In suit pants and a white dress shirt with sleeves rolled up, Cameron looked unbearably handsome. "Hey, Harper, can you take a look at something?"

"Sure." Mystified, she followed him back to the office, the tension in her stomach ratcheting tight. This wasn't the time to stare at the black comforter, leather chair, and contemporary furnishings that sure didn't come from a resale shop. Her nervousness eased when they entered the bright office beyond the bedroom. Sunlight streamed through the windows.

Tucked under the angled drafting table, Bella sat coloring at a small table. "Hi, Harper. McKenna was fun. I like her."

"McKenna liked you too, Bella." The little girl beamed.

"We both enjoyed her visit. I hope she'll come again." Sliding onto a high stool, Cameron motioned her over. Sketches of a room interior were spread out on his drafting board.

Okay, so she wasn't in trouble. Harper drew closer. The drawings were streaked with eraser marks. She sure recognized the signs of frustration. Why didn't he use his computer to generate his work? On a desk off to the side, a laptop stood open.

Cameron followed her eyes. "Sometimes I like to use my hands to figure out a project."

"Me too. I get a better feel for the work when I put my hands to it."

He squinched his lips to one side. The pucker unleashed a warm roll of heat through her body. "You have design training. I could use another set of eyes." The bright sunlight streaming through the leaded glass panes lightened his blue eyes to the color of the sky, a shade not available on the Pantone Matching System charts.

Not that she'd tried to pinpoint the exact shade of Cameron's eyes. Yet.

"Daddy said a bad word this morning," Bella said, her voice somber.

"He did?" Harper glanced at Cameron in mock surprise.

"Just frustrated. I apologized." The guy was so cute when he flushed. "Having trouble moving this job along."

Suppressing a grin, she turned back to his drawings. Cameron sure had changed from the uptight man she'd met at the bachelor party.

"This is the main room for a renovation I'm involved in. The couple wants an open concept for their older home—a common request right now but not always easy." Frowning, he bent over the table. She followed his fingers moving over the page. A hot flash made her shift positions. She could almost feel the touch of those hands on her hips when they were dancing.

Time to concentrate. And not on dancing.

"By taking down this wall to the dining area, I can open up the room, but the wall with the fireplace bothers me. There's a woods in back of this place, and I want to somehow incorporate a view."

Harper studied the drawing. The room held tremendous potential. "Can you take out part of the wall on either side of the fireplace? Add some shelves below for driftwood and vases, with a window above. Let the light in that way." Her mind creaked into action like a rusty clock. Long time since she worked on something like this. Even then, in school the work had consisted of assignments.

Cameron nodded. "Great idea. I'll check with the contractor today."

Harper's mind spun. "Maybe get some weathered doors to block off the second floor overlooking this area. Use colors that mimic the Savannah marsh. You know, that warm grayish brown. Add some golden highlights with glass work, woven b-baskets..." Looking up, she stuttered at the intensity in Cameron's eyes as he listened. Like it mattered.

When had Billy ever given her attention like this?

"Yes?" His appreciative smile skittered across her skin, raising goose bumps. Good God, as Cameron would say, what was going on here? She pushed her hair back from heated cheeks. Way too much sun in this room.

"Harper, you're brilliant." He'd already picked up a stick of graphite. Cameron had the hands of an artist, and she swallowed hard as he blocked and sketched. While they worked together, Bella colored quietly at her little table. She was drawing a house.

For the next twenty minutes, they tossed ideas back and forth, each new point feeding another. All the training she'd had in school, all the fabulous field trips her classes had taken came roaring back, only this time the project was real.

And this time she was working with Cameron.

Time passed quickly until finally Bella said, "Harper, I'm hungry."

Pulling her phone from her pocket, Harper checked the time. "Gosh, it's past noon."

"Damn. I have a lunch meeting." Cameron began to carefully roll up his drawings and tucked them into a cardboard tube. "Thank you, Pipsqueak, for reminding me."

Bella smiled up at him with adoring eyes.

"Come on, Bella. Lunch time." Harper opened one hand. Maybe lack of food was responsible for her own spinning head.

"Thank you, Harper. These are all great ideas," Cameron said, walking her to the door. When their shoulders touched, electricity zinged through her. "I, ah, I..."

Did he feel it too?

One of his shoulders rolled back, oh, so casually.

Yep, he felt it.

"I hope you're willing to work with me on this? I can, well, compensate you."

Not again. She felt offended. "Look, I'm already well compensated. Working on this project is fun, not work." Turning to face him, she felt buoyed by recklessness. Their brainstorming had felt better than the best sex she'd ever had. Were her cheeks red?

He pursed his lips, like he didn't agree. Too bad. Her terms. Cameron followed them downstairs, briefcase in hand. On the way, she noticed the paper still clutched in Bella's hand. "Can I see your picture?"

They'd reached the foyer and Bella held it out. "It's my house."

"Bet you have your daddy's talent." Harper took the paper. Three stick figures stood outside the house, a plump bluebird overhead. Cameron must be the figure in the tie and Bella, the smaller stick figure with the dark hair. Harper pointed to the figure in the short skirt. "Who's this?"

"The mom. Every house needs a dad and a mom."

Cameron looked like he'd seen a ghost.

"Very pretty. Can I take it up to my room?" Rolling up the sheet, Harper felt like she was hiding the evidence. Who was this mother figure in Bella's mind? Kimmy? The woman who wouldn't even look Bella's way when her parade float passed by?

"Nope. I'm going to hang it on the refrigerator." Grabbing the paper, Bella marched into the kitchen. The picture went up, anchored by Bella's ABC magnets.

Harper couldn't even look at Cameron.

Sessions in Cameron's home office became more common and the house in the historical district began to take shape. One drawing led to another until they spilled over onto Harper's drafting table upstairs. Her work focused on window treatments, furniture, fabrics and accessories. For the first time since graduation she was doing work her education had prepared her for…and it felt wonderful. Some nights she almost felt giddy. Hard to get to sleep.

Was the project keeping her awake or was working so closely with Cameron the problem? The excitement in his voice, the light sparking his blue eyes while they tossed ideas back and forth played on an endless loop in her head while she lay in bed. She found herself analyzing each comment, the slightest gesture. Crazy making. Harper had to remind herself that the interest was about the project, not her.

April arrived with a burst of warmer weather. When Cameron suggested a day at the beach for the coming Sunday, Harper was all for it. "Kimmy's coming with us," he added.

"Sounds like fun." *Not.* "Do you think the water will be warm at Tybee?"

He squinched his eyes like a little boy. "Probably not warm enough to swim, but you can splash along the shore. This isn't Chicago and Lake Michigan."

"You mocking my city?" She socked him playfully in the arm.

Surprise brought a smile and he rubbed his arm. "You're hurting me!"

"Want me to kiss it and make it better?"

His eyes slid to her lips.

Would both her feet fit in her big mouth?

Two beats of silence felt like ten. Flustered, Harper dove back into conversation and motor-mouthed, like she was swimming for her life. "Don't, ah, you give me a hard time about the Great Lakes. Your beach at Tybee isn't that much better."

Bella appeared in the doorway. "Did you say beach?"

Cameron expelled a deep breath. "Would you like that, Pipsqueak?"

"You bet." Bella came tripping toward them, clutching the hem of her Tinkerbell nightgown. "Could we go, Daddy? Really?"

He looked to Harper. "Pack a picnic lunch?"

"Absolutely."

"Hooray!" Bella's bare feet slapped the tile floor while she jumped up and down. Cameron smiled at her antics. A day at the beach. Harper didn't care if it was only seventy degrees. A day with Kimmy? Maybe Harper needed a reality check right now. A stern reminder. Anything to cool the heat raging through her body like a bad sunburn.

Connie had come in from the living room, dust rag in hand.

"Did I hear something about a picnic lunch?"

"On second thought, you don't have to bother, Connie."

Cameron scooped Bella onto his lap. "Plenty of places in Tybee to grab some food. Maybe just some snacks."

"And cereal for me," Bella interjected.

"Right. Cereal for you." Cameron ruffled his daughter's hair, and she rested her forehead in the hollow of his neck. "Kimmy would probably like a day at the beach."

Bella jerked back, wrinkling her nose. "Does she have to come?"

Cameron's smile dissolved. "I think it would be nice to invite her, don't you?"

"I guess." Bella's resignation made Harper swallow a chuckle.

She really had to work on her attitude. Kimmy was Cameron's girlfriend and Harper should respect that. But as she lay in bed that night, her thoughts ran wild, overstepping that boundary by a mile.

For the rest of that week, Bella was in high gear. Harper would find her singing as she danced around the house.

"That child is wild." Connie was cutting carrots and celery for them to take along.

"High spirited," Harper offered.

"You've brought a change in that little girl."

"Me? No."

Turning on the disposal, Connie shook her head. "Never was

this happy around here before you came."

"Thank you, Connie." Bella sure wasn't the sad little girl who'd been coaxed into the library for Harper's interview only months ago. Maybe she was succeeding in this position. Quiet satisfaction buoyed her steps all day.

On the coast just east of Savannah, Tybee Island was only twenty minutes away. Kimmy decided to drive herself. Apparently she had work to do at the station that Sunday. Harper figured the TV figure wanted an escape hatch. Kimmy seemed so restless, flitting around the area hoping the media would spot her. At least that was Harper's take on it and the thought turned her stomach. How would Kimmy ever have time for Bella? As Cameron and Harper rode down Highway 80 with Bella in the backseat, she was glad she didn't have to listen to Kimmy prattle. This day was much too perfect to be ruined by cryptic comments.

Under her bright orange tee and cutoffs, Harper wore a purple bikini. A straw cowboy hat helped protect her cheeks that freckled no matter how much block she applied.

In the backseat, Bella was singing a song from *The Wizard of Oz*, adding her own lyrics. After watching the movie on TV one Sunday afternoon, the classic film had quickly become a favorite. Thank goodness the little girl's taste had expanded beyond Ninja warriors.

Settling back, Harper enjoyed the ride. "I've always loved the palm trees on this boulevard."

"Me too." In cutoffs and a blue T-shirt, Cameron looked like he was about eighteen. Those biceps? A shame that his oxford cloth shirts hid so much.

"Did you come to the beach a lot when you were growing up?" Oak Street Beach had been a thirty-minute drive from their house in Chicago. Her mom and dad had taken the family to the lake on warm weekends.

"Lord no. I hit the beaches with college friends. They were my introduction to the coast." His rueful chuckle indicated some serious partying.

"So you didn't grow up around here?"

His lips twisted. "I most definitely did not."

Now, that was a surprise. During her student days, the college students from Savannah told jokes about the upper crust who hadn't been thrilled when the movie *Midnight in the Garden of Good and Evil* brought hordes of tourists. Publicity wasn't what Savannah wanted at the time. And yet, tourism became their major industry, along with their harbor.

Bella continued singing about the wizard while they passed billboards advertising dolphin boat tours. Sunlight glanced off the water stretching on either side, edged by marshes. Low country homes with wide porches could be seen along the shoreline of the inlets. Piers stretched through the tall grass until they reached the water that rose and fell with the tides.

"I love it here." Harper sighed with satisfaction.

Camera looked over. "You mean Tybee Island or Savannah?"

"Both."

"So you came here for the school and stayed because..."

Doggone it, was he fishing? "That's right. I stayed." No way was she going into the boy who was the drawing card.

Boy. Is that how she thought of Billy?

Cameron wasn't giving up. "And you stayed because...you have friends here?"

She chewed on her lower lip. Maybe talking about her past would free her. "Yes. I was living with someone. He decided I wasn't his happily-ever-after."

Cameron appeared to mull that over. "The guy must have been out of his ever-loving mind," he finally said.

"Thank you, but California movie companies don't hire crazy people."

He laughed. "Are you kidding me? Lots of crazies out in California."

That made her smile.

Before long, beach shops appeared along the highway and traffic slowed. Surfboards and inner tubes were stacked near doors. Bright colored clothing fluttered from racks dragged outside to lure tourists. Opening her window, Harper could smell the ocean. The main road turned right but Cameron took a left to where a trim lighthouse rose above the cottages. "I like this beach near North Beach Grill. Less commercial than the public area farther down."

"Works for me." She knew from her college experience that the beach could get pretty crowded, especially on weekends. The restaurants down at that end were always jammed, and lines snaked from crowded public restrooms.

"Are we there, Daddy, are we?" Pulling at the restraints of her car seat, Bella thumped her feet against the seat.

"We sure are, darlin'." Gravel crunched beneath the tires as Cameron pulled into a parking lot. Only took them a few minutes to unload. Since the public beach hadn't opened yet, Cameron had thrown some chairs into the back of the SUV. She was helping dig them out just when a bright red convertible pulled up.

Chapter 18

"Yoo, hoo!" Kimmy had arrived. Huge dark glasses peered out from under a red hat anchored by a flowing scarf. Stepping out of her low-slung convertible, she looked like a model in sand-colored slacks and red windbreaker. Hips swaying, Kimmy maneuvered toward them on red platform heels not meant for sand.

"Isn't this fun to be at the beach together?" After a hug and kiss for Cameron, she turned to Bella. "Got a kiss for Kimmy?"

Lower lip thrust out, Bella pulled Harper toward the wooden boardwalk.

"Well, now." Kimmy straightened. "Hello, Harper."

A gust of wind caught the brim of her wide hat and Kimmy struggled to keep it on. Harper swallowed a giggle. "Hello, Kimmy. Don't you look….red." Really? That was the best she could do?

"Well, I never…" Kimmy looked from Harper to Cameron.

"Ah, I mean, you look so nice in …all that red."

Cameron tamped a surprised smile down fast. One glance from Kimmy and that was gone. A quick wave and Harper took off, a couple chairs under her arm and Bella trotting along beside her. Up ahead children in shorts and bathing suits played in the shallow water while parents stretched in chairs, skin pale as the sand. Felt like spring break.

"Can I go in the water?" Bella asked Cameron when he arrived. Chairs hung from one strong shoulder and he was dragging the cooler. Kimmy followed, stepping carefully, like this might be quicksand.

"In a second, okay?" Cameron dropped the equipment and began setting up.

"Mercy me, child, you'll catch your death in that water." Kimmy shivered and looked out over as if it were the enemy.

"No, I won't." Bella's lower lip came out.

"Let's just get set up, okay, Bella?" Harper and Cameron reached for the same chair. Fingers touched. Electricity shot up her arm. Cameron swept her with a startled blue glance before turning to the water. Lazy breakers hit a broad sandbar before rolling to shore. Oh, so slowly, he ran one hand up his arm. Harper shivered.

As if he'd touched her.

As if she'd liked it.

"But it's way too cold for this water, Harper." Kimmy broke that mood fast. "You're not from these parts, but everybody in Savannah knows you cannot go in the water in early April. You simply cannot."

Harper couldn't resist. "In Chicago, a group called the Polar Bears plunges into Lake Michigan every year on January first. It's a ritual."

Kimmy gasped. "I declare, I have *never* heard of anything so outlandish."

Harper didn't miss the upward tweak of Cameron's lips. "Kimmy, Tybee Island has its own Polar Plunge."

"Barbaric." His girlfriend's face turned pink.

Bella had shed her pink shoes and socks. "I want to go in the water." Her bare toes curled up from the cool, hard-packed sand.

The kid had moxie. Harper kicked off her flip flops.

Pulling her jacket around her, Kimmy screwed her face up. "Cameron, this is entirely up to you, but letting the child go in the water...well, I just cannot imagine."

He was having trouble setting up one of the chairs and Harper turned to help him. In close proximity, the two of them were almost comical, like basketball players trying not to foul. "Well, now, I don't see how a little water could hurt her. There. We're set. Thank you, Harper." Cameron snapped the chair's frame into place.

Kimmy dusted sand from her slacks with short, quick swipes. "Fine. Up to you."

Cameron stared out at the horizon, looking for all the world like a man counting to ten. Pulling sunblock from her bag, Harper motioned to Bella and began smoothing lotion on the little girl's face, legs and any other surface that showed, including that button nose. Then she coated her own "Irish skin," as her mother always described it. Looking up, she caught Cameron watching her. A shiver spilled through her, and she waved the bottle in his direction. "Want some?"

"Yes. No. But thanks. Think I'll just watch...I mean, rest." Sliding his sunglasses into place, he sank into the chair next to his girlfriend.

Kimmy was already pulling folders from a black tote bag that looked way too expensive for the beach. "If you don't mind, sweetheart, I'm so behind."

Tossing her hat onto a towel, Harper held one hand out to Bella. "Come on. Let's explore."

With a wild whoop, they were off. Cawing wildly, a group of sea gulls scattered in front of them and took to the skies. Glancing back over one shoulder, Harper wondered why Kimmy had bothered to drive over. A beautiful day with the guy she was dating and the woman was going to work? As if to prove her point, Kimmy began furiously scribbling on a yellow pad. Harper pitied her staff.

The brisk breeze molded Harper's shirt to her body. Tugging the claw clip from her hair, she let it fall free. Felt like the breeze had fingers and she shook her head with delight. The two of them splashed along close to shore and then stopped.

Bella stared down at her feet to where they disappeared into the water. "Are there fish down there?"

Harper came to a stop and so did Bella. "If we stand real still and look close, we might see some minnows."

Pants rolled up, Bella gave her feet serious consideration. "I see them, Harper!"

"Don't move. Sometimes they nibble on your toes."

"Yuck!" Bella kicked a foot out and a cloud of sand billowed up in the water.

"No, wait and you'll see. They tickle more than anything." The sand settled in the water and sure enough, the minnows returned, darting around their feet.

Bella's delight slowly settled into a frown. "Where is the mom for the babies?"

Harper thought fast. "Fish don't need their mother, honey, just their brothers and sisters. They swim around together all day long."

"I wish I had brothers and sisters." Bella's whispery voice was almost carried away on the breeze. But not before it lampooned Harper's heart.

"Maybe you will someday." Kimmy and babies? Hard to imagine. The water was getting cold. "Want to look for stones and shells?"

"Sure." They scrambled back to the dry sand. When Harper looked back to the chairs, Cameron lifted a hand. She waved, wishing he'd come with them. Kimmy was still hard at work.

The beach was littered with smooth white and gray stones. "Look." She held one up for Bella. "The water wears down all the rough edges."

Bella turned the stone over in her hand and smiled. "Can we keep some?"

"You bet." Yanking out her T-shirt, Harper made a hammock. As they walked, they added to the collection. Easy to find stones but the shells were often jagged pieces. When they found a caramel-colored shell that wasn't broken, they cheered.

"How will I know what's mine?" Bella considered the pile in Harper's shirt tail.

The girl who had everything wanted these stones. "You can have them all, Bella."

"Cool." She scooped one from the heap and turned it over in

her hand.

Stones would just be more stuff to drag around the next time Harper moved. She fought the sudden wave of melancholy.

Really? Was this about Bella? Or Bella's father?

Glancing back, Harper noticed Cameron still faced their direction. Probably checking on Bella. He raised a hand and Harper waved back. A shiver defied the heat reflecting from the sand and chased up her spine.

Bella darted about on the sand, quick and light-footed like the seagulls. The little girl's excitement pulled Harper from her funk. She wouldn't think about the future today. This job was proof that you could never know what lay ahead. One thing for sure, Bella needed more times like this—carefree fun when she could just be a kid.

When she was growing up, Harper remembered chasing fireflies with her brothers and McKenna in the backyard or making tents out of old sheets and playing camp. The seven of them made up most of their games, and they never lacked for ideas. Being the youngest, Harper had a lot of role models. Watching Bella feeling her way, Harper realized how important that was.

Time passed quickly. Before long the sun had passed midpoint. Took them a while to walk back. When Cameron and Kimmy finally came into sight, they seemed to be having an animated conversation. Kimmy was frowning.

Tybee took Cameron back to college, when life had been a hell of a lot simpler. Today he could close his eyes and forget work. But

Kimmy wanted to talk. Their conversation was more a syncing of their calendars. Bella and Harper came running toward them and Kimmy's voice blurred into background noise. That tiny bikini bottom and the flat stomach below Harper's T-shirt? He needed the cool breeze whisking in from the ocean. Kimmy was dressed more for an Alaskan cruise than the beach.

Harper held the front tail of her shirt tight against her stomach while Bella poked around in the sand. From time to time, she'd hold something up for discussion before handing it over. Obviously, Harper was keeper of the catch, whatever that was.

"My goodness." In the chair next to his, Kimmy adjusted the huge sunglasses that he used to find mysterious. "They will catch their death of cold."

"I think it's too warm for that, Kimmy." Sometimes Kimmy reminded him of his mother. She worried a lot and Kimmy took issue with his new nanny about every little thing.

"I'm hungry, Daddy," Bella exclaimed when they'd drawn close.

"Well then, I think we should eat."

Kimmy jumped up. "Sure wish I could join you, darlin', but I should get back to the station. Get ready for tomorrow."

"You certainly are dedicated to that job, Kimmy." Or was it the high profile that went with her job that drove Kimmy? Cameron stood and stretched, flexing his shoulders, sun warm on his back. Harper had dumped her shirt out onto her towel and was helping Bella organize stones and shells by color. "Be right back, girls. I'm just going to walk Kimmy to her car."

Squinting against the sun, Harper glanced up. "Bye, Kimmy."

"Could I have a kiss, Bella?" Kimmy stood waiting.

"Bella?" Cameron turned toward his little girl.

"I'm busy."

He did not want to take this on right now. "Bella?"

With a sigh that probably carried clear to Hilton Head, Bella leapt up and jabbed a kiss on Kimmy's cheek. They'd have a little talk about that later.

Of course Kimmy had to fret about Bella's attitude as he walked her to the car. Only one way to quiet her. Quick and dry, his lips had all the finesse of a revolver with a silencer. She pulled away, dipping her glasses to reveal a frown. "What was that?"

He cracked open her car door. "Let's talk later." Cameron wanted to think about this and he didn't want to act like a heel. That kiss had been uncalled for and left him uncomfortable.

Lips set, Kimmy climbed in. Gravel spun as she pulled out of the parking lot.

By the time he returned to their beach chairs, Harper had cracked open the cooler. Bella's container of cereal sat on top of the ice in the upper tray.

"Eating out here might be a problem." She pointed to the plastic container just as a breeze kicked up, causing mini sand squalls. If Bella bit down and her lunch crunched, she'd have a fit. He didn't need that today.

"I've got a better idea. Let's pack up."

"But I don't want to go home." Bella crossed her arms.

"We're not going home, Pipsqueak. How about eating here in a beach restaurant?"

"Cool." Bella's eyes sparkled like gumdrops. Lately, every new thing had become "cool" for his little girl.

Cameron glanced over to Harper, who was folding up the towels. "How about it? The North Beach Grill is just across the parking lot. Good burgers and tasty low country food."

"Sounds great. Haven't been there in a while." Before she glanced away, he caught the wistful look in her eyes. Had he meandered into one of her memories? Harper might play the gutsy girl who could dance for her supper, but sometimes she had this sad side. Cameron folded up the beach chairs and lugged them back to the car. Wasn't his habit to pry into the private life of a nanny.

Of course, none of the other nannies had stayed this long. And he hadn't felt curious about any of them.

Harper helped Bella into her shoes and socks. Hoisting the cooler onto one shoulder, Cameron led the way back to the SUV. Once they'd stowed everything away, except for Bella's supper, they took off for the restaurant.

The North Beach Grill was dim and cool when they pushed through the screen door. Years ago, Cameron had hoisted a few beers here. One glance at Harper told him she might have done the same. She seemed to know the place. The young waiter brought a booster seat for Bella. Sand gritted on the floor underfoot. The windows had been levered open, and the breeze carried the smell of the water.

While Harper set up Bella's meal, his daughter's eyes circled the room, not missing a trick. When the waiter came, Cameron ordered the jerked chicken sandwich and Harper decided on the grilled fish. They both got sides of red beans and rice.

"And what would your little girl like?" the waiter asked Harper, pen poised over the pad.

"Oh, she's not..." Harper began.

"We have a special meal for her," Cameron broke in. For some reason, explaining Harper's position in the family annoyed him just as much as explaining Bella's strange eating habits. Harper cracked open the Tupperware and handed Bella a spoon.

"What were you collecting on the beach?" Cameron asked after the waiter had brought their drinks.

"Shells and stones." Bella paused from shoveling in the cereal.

Now he remembered why they didn't eat out more often. Cameron could hardly bear to watch her. Frustration compressed his chest with the weight of a sand dune. They had to find a way to help her.

They? Something warm and tingly stirred inside.

But back to the shells. "Got plans for those?"

Bella looked to Harper.

"Oh, we can put them in pretty jars or we can make a Christmas wreath out of them. I've done that before. But Christmas is a long way off."

When her eyes lifted and flitted away, his gut clenched. Cameron had seen that evasiveness before—right before a nanny gave notice.

"You're creative, Harper." Navigating back to the role of employer and employee was a struggle. "Your sketches for the

Winston Hill House have been really helpful. When we get to that point, I hope you'll help choose some wall colors and fabrics. I like to show the restored houses fully furnished. Makes for a quicker sale."

"Of course. Sounds great." Excitement sparked in her eyes.

"Harper, are we gonna make cool Christmas stuff together with our shells?' Bella had her own agenda.

Her answer was slow in coming. "We'll see."

In his family "we'll see" had always meant "no."

Harper was sucking on her straw, lips forming a full bow. His chest and a few other muscles tightened. He had to look away.

"Daddy? Can I have some brothers and sisters like the fish?"

He choked on his pop.

Harper held out her hands, palms up. "Just checking out the minnows today. Lots of brothers and sisters there."

"Not minnows. Baby fish," Bella emphasized

"Right. Baby fish." Grabbing a napkin, Harper whisked the trail of cereal from Bella's chin.

Thank God the food arrived. Bella's questions were a minefield. *Cameron has enough disturbing thoughts in his head today.* By the time they chucked their napkins onto their empty plates, a serious food coma was settling over them. On the ride home, Bella fell asleep. Harper's head bobbed. "Why don't you take a nap?"

She pushed herself up. "No I'm fine. Besides, I don't want to miss this drive."

Always amazed him how she could be content with small things. So different from Tammy...or Kimmy. Harper hadn't gotten all the sand off her legs and they glistened. Were her cheeks sunburned or was she blushing when she glanced down?

"I am so sorry. I'm going to make a mess in your car."

"Doesn't matter, Harper. Let's just call it a souvenir of a great day."

Her smile warmed him in so many ways. Downright disturbing.

His phone went off and the name "Kimmy" came up. He hit the key that sent the call to voicemail.

Chapter 19

In the dream a woman called Cameron's name. Body hot and driven by need, he stumbled into a room where curtains blew wild. The swirling vortex of cool air brought little relief. He charged forward.

Up ahead, a woman waited. Exhausted but throbbingly hard, he sank into her. Felt her arms close around him, welcome and right. She trembled when he kissed her, opened so he could please her, shivered when he trailed his lips over her burning skin. Everywhere she touched, her palms brought coolness, relief. And she wasn't shy, her legs tightening around him.

When he drove his hands into hair that smelled like wisteria, his fingers snagged and came away with the dry ropes of a December vine. Her laughter floated on the air like wind chimes. "Make a wish," she whispered, opening one palm. In her hand gleamed white stones. Closing his eyes he ran his fingers over their smooth surface before tossing them into the sky, so carefree.

When he turned she sank into his arms again, hair a welcome weight on his shoulders. His hands traced her soft skin and supple body.

He had to have her.

But the woman began to disappear, form and features fading.

Damn. Cameron shook himself awake. Coiling upright in a damp bed, he shuddered. What in Sam Hill was that? Then he felt around. Embarrassment brought a hot flush. Hadn't happened to him since fifth grade.

And he didn't need to wonder why. Flopping back, Cameron threw both arms over his eyes. He never remembered his dreams. This one? Unforgettable.

After the day at Tybee, Harper became more determined than ever to help Bella. Seeing her sitting in the restaurant with her gruel, as Cameron called it, just about broke her heart. Harper had grown up with a passel of hungry eaters who'd squabbled over every last piece of bread. The Kirkpatricks didn't just belong to the clean-the-plate club—they were more a clean-the-table group. The smell of meatballs, turkey soup, or applesauce had wafted from the kitchen when she walked in from school.

Those simple recipes in mind, she got to work one afternoon after bringing Bella home from school. Although Bella had promptly plunked herself in front of the TV, the second Harper started to peel apples, Bella was there. She hated to miss anything. "Whatcha doing?"

"Making applesauce." Opening the drawer where Connie kept her spices, Harper pulled out the container of cinnamon. "Want to help?"

"Sure." Bella look so darn cute in her lavender dinosaur top and dark purple pants. Harper had picked up ribbon barrettes in pink and yellow. Bella liked to plaster her hair back with three or four so a rainbow of colors bobbed when she shook her head.

Hauling one of the chairs over to the stove, Harper positioned it next to her and Bella clambered up. Taking the slices of peeled apple, Harper dropped them into the pan that held a little water and stirred, gradually sprinkling sugar over the top. Her little helper's eyes were glued to the action. "Should we add some cinnamon?"

"Ah, huh. Sure." Bella nodded.

Harper handed her the metal container. "Just sprinkle a little okay?"

"Okay." Biting her lip in concentration, Bella gave a shake and a heavy poof rose from the pan, causing a coughing fit. Harper grabbed a glass of water. One sip later they were both giggling. Just another kitchen adventure.

The applesauce began to bubble. "Doesn't that smell good?"

"Ah, huh."

Harper brought the stirring spoon to her lips and blew on it gently. Bella's eyes were glued to every move. Her lips parted when Harper sampled the spicy, warm mixture. "Oh, yum," she said for Bella's benefit.

"Is it good?" Bella sniffed the fragrant air.

"Sure is. Want to try it?" Breath catching, Harper held out the spoon.

Bella backed away so fast she nearly tumbled off the chair. Harper grabbed her, fighting her own disappointment. When she got back to work, Bella stayed at her elbow. How this scene took Harper back to her mother's sunny kitchen in Oak Park.

The back door opened. "What's that I smell?" Cameron draped his suit jacket over a chair and came to stand behind them. "Sure smells good."

"We're making applesauce," Bella said proudly.

"You don't say. You two ladies cooking together? Sounds dangerous to me." Cameron rested a hand on each of their shoulders. Harper grasped her spoon tighter.

"Time to turn off the heat." She flicked the burner off, missing the weight when he dropped his hands to pull off his tie.

Connie had precooked some ribs, and Cameron was going to throw them on the grill. The housekeeper bustled into the kitchen. "Are you two making a mess in here?" But she was smiling.

"I do believe I'll test your recipe." Cameron had circled back to peer into the pan, so close Harper could see his thick sandy eyelashes, the day's bristle on his cheeks.

Her palms tingled. "Right, I'll get a bowl."

Cameron sat down and motioned to Bella. "Want to sit on my lap?"

"Sure, Daddy." She climbed up.

Taking a small bowl from the cupboard, Harper filled it halfway and set it in front of Cameron with a spoon. The smell of warm apples filled the kitchen, so thick she could almost chew it. Suddenly she wished she'd cut thinner slices. Maybe the recipe called for more sugar? Already tasting, Cameron let out a low moan that rippled through Harper's own tummy and lower. "You are a great cook," he told Bella.

"Harper too." Bella poked one finger in her direction.

"Harper too."

Running her hands over her apron, Harper basked in the glow of a grin. Ridiculous.

"Daddy, can I feed you?"

Not missing a beat, Cameron handed his daughter the spoon. "Here you go, darlin'."

"Now you have to be careful. Don't make a mess." Bella tucked a paper napkin into Cameron's open neck shirt.

"I'll be very good." His ramrod posture enforced his words.

"Open up now, Daddy." Dropping her voice, she added, "You're my little boy, okay?"

"Whatever you say, sweetheart."

Had Harper ever seen him so playful? Dipping the spoon into the applesauce, Bella began to feed her father. Connie turned back to the stove, but Harper was riveted. When some applesauce spilled from the spoon, Bella scolded him. "Now you have to hold still. I can't be here all day, you know."

"I'll be good," Cameron promised, enjoying the game.

"You behave now, you hear?"

"Yes, Ma'am."

At first Cameron seemed amused by Bella's comments, but when they continued, his smile disappeared. A chill entered the room. Harper's mind spun while she watched the interaction. How old had Bella been when Tammy died?

"Now it's your turn. Can I feed you?" Cameron's quick question seemed to take Bella by surprise. Nodding, she handed him the spoon. Like a little bird, she opened her mouth and the pleased smile after she swallowed was a sight to behold. Cameron looked like he was holding his breath and Harper was right there with him.

But Bella's smile pinched with sudden concern. "Do I have a mess on my face?"

"Not at all, darlin'. Not at all."

She ran one hand over her cheeks.

"Bella, you're fine, sweetheart. But I'm hungry," Cameron teased. "Feed me again, okay? We'll take turns."

She got back to business, but Cameron caught Harper's eye over Bella's head as the feeding continued. Where had Bella's worry come from? The two of them took turns, one spoonful for her and then one for Daddy, as if they did this every night. When Connie left the room, Harper saw the housekeeper dab at her eyes.

The feeding game raised some serious questions in Harper's mind. But this wasn't the time to ask them.

After that, she launched herself into cooking like a crazed foodie, poring over magazines and searching the Internet. If Connie felt she was getting underfoot in the kitchen, she never said anything. The cooking became therapy. Harper wasn't about to start with a five-course dinner but julienned vegetables? She could handle that without slicing her fingers off, especially if she handled the mandolin with a towel. Tapioca? She could whip egg whites and was rewarded when Bella licked the spoon. Every recipe marked a step forward.

Harper's schedule settled into a new routine. On the days when she took Bella to school, she'd come right home instead of stopping for coffee somewhere and whiling away an hour or two. Now she had a purpose. In addition to her culinary efforts, Cameron's comments had started her sketching again at her work table. The satisfaction she'd once found in creating returned.

Some Friday evenings, she'd meet Adam for drinks. "So how's Mr. Baby Blues," he asked one night as she sipped her cucumber martini.

"Same." But she dropped her eyes.

"Fess up now, girl."

Harper would not get flustered. She simply would not. "I'm, ah, doing some work for Cameron."

Eyes dancing, Adam cocked his head to one side. "Oh really? Cam-er-on?" And he drew the name out in a ridiculous smoky tone.

"Oh, come on. I do not sound like that." She gave her drink a brisk stir with her swizzle stick.

"Ah, hah." Plucking the tiny onion from his drink, Adam munched with pleased contentment. "And Billy? Are we still lusting for the idiot?"

Billy? Amazement sliced through her like a meat cleaver. How long had it been since she'd thought of her ex-boyfriend? "No. Ah, no. Haven't heard a thing. Don't expect to."

The post office was forwarding her mail from their old apartment. Not long ago she'd shuffle through the pile, hoping for some word. Now she tossed the lot into the trash without a second thought. Flyers, advertisements.

All just history. Like Billy.

In the past she'd even called her former boyfriend's cell, figuring in the time difference and knowing he turned his cell off at night. She just wanted to hear his voice.

How lame. She couldn't believe she'd actually done that.

Adam hugged her before she left the bar that night. "I do believe you are cured, lady. Exorcised." They both laughed but as she walked to her car, a new calm settled over her. Her friend had a point.

April was well underway. The rhododendrons were replaced by purple and yellow pansies. Harper often took her sketchbook outside on warm afternoons, keeping her inhaler close. Cameron was calling her in more frequently on his jobs. She told herself she'd be a fool to look for other work right now. Sure, one part of her wanted to get on with her life. But Bella was eating more than applesauce now. The feeding experiment had become routine. Harper loved to see the hopeful glow in Cameron's eyes when he sat down with Bella. Everything seemed to be running smoothly.

"Well, I declare. What a picture." Cameron caught her by surprise one afternoon as he slowly mounted the back steps to the porch. No matter how warm or mussed, the man always looked like he'd stepped from a gentleman's magazine. Bella sat coloring at a table next to her while Harper sketched.

"Just felt so cooped up inside." Flustered, Harper tucked her pencils back into the case.

He leaned against the sturdy handrail. "No need to stop. You're just so...well, a picture." His eyes brushed her like a promising spring breeze.

The attention made her blush. That made two of them.

"But why come all the way down here? Use the second story porch right outside my office."

"Oh, I couldn't." The thought of invading his space shocked her.

"Told you, I won't bite," he said so softly that Bella didn't hear.

One Friday when Connie was off, Harper tried a sea bass recipe with a lot of ginger. Usually Cameron met Kimmy for dinner on Fridays, but today, Harper heard him tell Bella he'd be home for dinner. On a whim, Harper had gotten the good china out and asked Bella to help set out the place mats. That night, Harper proudly served the sea bass she'd browned in the pan, scattering basil over it along with sliced bok choy. After she'd transferred the fish to the oven, she wilted some kale in the oil that remained in the pan.

The crowning touch was her mother's sugar burned carrots, a recipe her Grandma Nora had made all the time. Bella had helped peel the carrots, tip of her tongue caught in the corner of her mouth. Then Harper sliced the peeled carrots and fried them in butter, sprinkling sugar over them so they burned. Bella was all eyes. But that didn't mean she'd eat what was cooking in the pan.

"These taste so good, Bella, so soft and sweet." Harper nibbled one from the pan after cooling it. "Want one?"

Bella shook her head. The consistency might be a huge step for her.

By that time, Cameron had arrived home and stood sipping his wine in the doorway. Although Harper didn't know much about wine, tonight's Riesling tasted pretty good. Her glass sat next to her on the stove. "My word, Harper. However did you learn all this?"

She flushed with pleasure, giving the carrots a quick flip. "Connie's been teaching me and I remember some tricks from my mother, although she rarely gave up the stove. Not even McKenna got a turn with Mom's double ovens. How about yours?"

"Sometimes, I guess." His eyes shuttered. Cameron never discussed his family, and she wouldn't ask. In all probability, his mother employed a cook and never lifted a finger around the house.

In a brave moment, Harper had whipped up pots of chocolate mousse from an online recipe. She'd found glass snifters in the dining room, which made the dessert look even more impressive.

Cameron Bennett appreciated quality, and Harper found herself wanting to meet those expectations.

"Smells delicious, Harper." Cameron pulled her chair out for her as they sat down to eat. Such a southern gentleman. Bella sat across from her, the plastic cereal bowl in front of her on the bamboo mats Harper had found.

A few bites of the sea bass and carrots and Cameron turned to her. She didn't know whether to be insulted or pleased at the astonishment lifting his brows. "Harper, I believe you have outdone yourself. "

She smiled. In her mind, his accolades went on to include "You are beautiful, talented and sexy as all get out."

Her thoughts brought a hot flush to her cheeks.

"Everything all right?" He dropped one hand over hers on the table. Heat crackled through her.

House afire over here. "Fine. Everything's, ah, fine."

His eyes fell to their hands and then rose, cauldrons of molten blue. One furtive glance at Bella and he lifted his hand to resume eating. Tucking her left hand in her lap, Harper ate while her mind spun. This meal had taken so much time, time she'd never spent cooking for Billy.

Made her feel pretty good.

Harper almost didn't hear the landline pierce the quiet spring air. Connie wasn't home so she started to get up.

"Stay right there." Tossing his napkin aside, Cameron marched into the kitchen. "Probably another marketing research person. I'll be damned if I'm going to eat this wonderful meal listening to that phone. People should know enough not to call during the dinner hour."

But apparently the call was not from a marketer because Cameron didn't say anything for a long time. And he did not hang up. Harper put her fork down. Even Bella had stopped eating.

"I understand," Cameron finally said in a terse voice. "Of course I'm coming, Lily."

His sister was calling? Bad manners to eavesdrop but Harper leaned toward the doorway.

"Yes. As soon as possible." Then he hesitated. "Well, I'll have to think about that. But possibly, yes."

Something in Cameron's tone tied a knot in Harper's chest. His footsteps lagged as he returned to the dining room. "I'm afraid I must excuse myself, ladies. Something's come up."

"No mousse?"

"Sorry but not tonight." He met her eyes. "Let's talk later."

"Of course."

Whatever the call concerned, it wasn't good.

Chapter 20

When Cameron left the room after the call from his sister, he took Harper's appetite with him. What had happened? The evening dragged and it seemed like forever until she put Bella to bed. Crickets were singing in the myrtle in the courtyard when she found Cameron on the porch. Long legs stretched onto one of the hassocks, he was smoking what looked like a cigar. The tip glowed red in the darkness. He stabbed it out quickly, using a brass ashtray she'd never seen before. One swipe and it disappeared under the chair.

Soft light from the kitchen fell over the porch. She took the chair next to his. "What's up?"

He stared past her into the darkness. "My father passed away unexpectedly, Harper. I have to go home tomorrow."

"I see." But she'd never heard him mention a father. "I'm so sorry."

"We didn't see eye to eye but he was my father."

"And Bella will go with you?"

"And you, if you don't mind." Usually so self contained, he rubbed one hand across his forehead.

"Of course. Can I help in any other way?" She resisted the urge to hug him.

"I don't think so. I don't know."

Losing a parent—Harper couldn't go there. Her family was such a tight unit.

The silence became oppressive, and she soon excused herself. Upstairs, Harper poked her head into Bella's room. She was fast asleep, one hand curled up next to her cheek. She left the door open leading to the third floor.

Once in her room Harper dug through her closet. What should she wear to a southern funeral? She pictured women in black high-necked gowns and wide-brimmed hats. Her closet sure couldn't measure up to that. A pair of black pants and a purple top would have to do for now. A black jean jacket and a shawl in case it turned cool. She threw her usual scarves into a duffel bag, along with some other accessories. But long after the mansion had settled down, she peeked through her window and saw the light from Cameron's office blanketing the garden.

Letting the sheer drop back into place, she flopped down on her bed, staring up at the ceiling. How she could offer comfort to a man who always had things well in hand?

Right now he didn't. She felt that clear to her bones.

The drive to Hazel Hurst the following day was quiet. Cameron turned on some smooth jazz and mellow saxophone filled the SUV. Harper hadn't slept well. Not even the soothing music could put her to sleep now. She was going to meet Cameron's family.

Harper had packed a "surprise bag" for the trip, just like her mom used to do. Sticker books and magnetic paper dolls kept Bella busy in the back. While her charge played, questions spun through Harper's mind, but the set angle of Cameron's chin kept her from asking them. What had happened to the laid-back guy from the beach? For sure, he was missing in action.

From time to time, Bella's little feet thumped the back of Cameron's seat. He didn't say anything. Just stared blankly over the wheel. Her father and brothers always wore jeans to travel but Cameron was dressed in pale gray suit pants, a blue shirt open at the neck. Maybe funerals were different. He knew what his family expected.

But if Harper had her reservations about quizzing Cameron today, Bella sure didn't. "Daddy, where we going?"

"To visit your grandmother."

Glancing over her shoulder, Harper saw Bella turn that idea over in her mind. "What's her name?" She fit a starfish sticker into her book.

"Esther, but you can just call her Grandma. Aunt Lily will be there too, along with some uncles. You know Aunt Lily. She's visited us."

Bella's face screwed up. "Yeah. I guess."

Leaning over, Harper whispered, "Kind of a lot to throw at her at once."

"Yes, of course you're right." His mood stayed in low gear.

Thank goodness Bella went back to her sticker book.

The ride wasn't that long. Once they got off the highway, the road narrowed to two lanes. Farm fields opened on either side, along with scruffy stands of pine. Kudzu, a vine that grew wild in the South, blanketed some of the fields.

"Damned weed," Cameron muttered at one point. "Kills just about everything."

"So I hear. Looks like they need Jack around here."

Cameron managed a dry chortle. "Very few people here can afford a Jack."

Tension ratcheted up in the car when Cameron turned off the asphalt-covered county highway onto hard-packed dirt. The music switched to something with a deep bass, and Cameron's elegant hands began beating time on the steering wheel. Misgivings churned in her stomach. For a second, she was sorry she'd come, but no way would she let Bella face this alone.

Whatever *this* was.

After bouncing along for at least a mile, they came to a spot where the roads parted. Nailed to a post were names on arrows pointing to one of three trails. Never hesitating, Cameron took a right. The arrow was labeled "Blodgett" in bold black letters. They bumped along. Cameron cut his speed, cursing under his breath and causing Bella to call out, "Daddy, that's naughty."

"Sorry, darlin'." Gritting his teeth, he worked the wheel to avoid potholes that didn't look new. At times, the traffic path veered off into the tall grass and then returned to the road. The first warning posted on a cedar tree advised, "No trespassing." The rough piece of board farther down, "Trespassers will be shot on sight," sent a chill down her spine.

She jerked her head in Cameron's direction.

"No need for alarm, Harper. We are not trespassing. I grew up here."

Just another chapter in the mystery that was Cameron Bennett.

Finally, they reached a clearing where a low country home sprawled. The white clapboard needed painting, and the roof had been patched. Despite these improvements, one strong wind could probably take the structure down.

"God dammit," Cameron muttered. "They were supposed to paint the place months ago."

"Daddy?" Bella's frustration at her father's language was almost comical.

"You'll have to forgive me, sweetheart. Daddy gets upset sometimes."

An assortment of pickup trucks and vehicles crowded the house. The yard could easily be mistaken for a junkyard on the south side of Chicago. Harper didn't blink and hardly breathed. She'd sure pegged this one wrong. Bella had fallen silent. A pack of ragtag yapping mutts charged the car. Harper made sure their doors were locked.

"Don't worry," Cameron told Bella. "These hounds won't attack us."

"Good to know," Harper muttered, clutching the door handle but not opening it. Cameron leapt out and, with a sharp whistle, transformed the snarls to wagging tails. Then he opened the back door, unsnapped Bella's safety belt and hoisted her into his arms. She twined her arms around his neck, eyes on the dogs. When Harper slipped from the car, her stacked black-heeled sandals sank into the loamy dirt. A woman had come onto the porch, and the screen door slammed shut behind her.

Lily crossed her arms over a navy blouse, the ruffled collar in style ten years ago. "So, you've come."

"Did you think I wouldn't?" Setting Bella on her feet, Cameron took her hand. "Harper, you remember Lily, my sister. Harper is Bella's nanny. You met her once before."

"Of course. Nanny?"

Oh, my. Lily looked skeptical. Harper had extended her hand but she curled it back into the handle of her peony purse. What had she gotten herself into? Two young men had slouched out the front door after Lily, and now they stood regarding Cameron. The family resemblance was startling. Dressed in work jeans and well-washed T-shirts, they sure were related to Cameron but had none of his style.

"My brothers -- Fred and Henry Blodgett." Their hands were rough from work when she shook them, the familiar blue eyes honest and curious.

Lily stepped aside, and Harper followed Cameron through the door. The small room was filled with the rich smell of food laid out on a side table. An older woman in a plain black dress sat rocking in front of a fireplace stained with years of soot. If she'd worn makeup and had her hair styled, she would have been beautiful. She'd definitely given Cameron her ice blue eyes, and she rose to her feet with grace. Bella clutched her daddy's pant leg like a life preserver.

"Mama." When Cameron opened his arms, his mother entered them reluctantly. She looked tired.

Then she pushed back. "Glad to see you, son."

His face paled. "Did you think I wouldn't come to my own father's funeral?"

Lily beckoned to Harper. Taking Bella's hand, Harper followed Lily into the kitchen, Cameron's brothers trailing behind them. Time to escape the family reunion that felt more than awkward.

Henry squatted until he was eye level with Bella. "So you're Cameron's little girl? Aren't you a sweetheart?"

Bella obviously didn't know this family, and she buried her face between Harper's knees.

"I guess Cameron doesn't get home often?" Harper asked, looking to Lily.

Henry rose and shook his head. "So many fireworks when Cameron came around the old man. I think he just gave up trying."

Lily shook her head. "But the checks kept coming. Money to fix the house or pay the heating bill. He was always good about that, but Mama had to keep it secret."

Henry elbowed Fred. "Told Daddy her canning business was doing real good."

"Daddy always knew, Henry." Reaching out, Lily ran one hand over Bella's wiry dark hair. "Will wonders never cease? Aren't you a beautiful thing?" Kindness softened her tone. Peering up, Bella gave her aunt a shy smile.

Standing in the middle of a kitchen with a potbellied stove in the corner, Harper fought a crazy giggle. She'd come home with Cameron expecting to find a mansion like the one in Savannah and a gentrified family that had raised a man above reproach.

If these were the Blodgetts, then who the heck was Cameron Bennett?

Harper hadn't been to many funerals. The service for Homer Blodgett provided a rugged initiation, one she'd carry with her for a long time. While the plain pine box sat at the front of the church, hymns rang out in a small, white frame church. From "Onward Christian Soldiers" to "Amazing Grace," voices lifted, welcoming their brother home. Maybe Harper was just tired but the ceremony brought tears to her eyes.

As she lay in the twin bed the night before, Harper had felt lonely, glad to have Bella for company in the next bed. Blustery winds rattled the window panes. Having Cameron in the next room was some comfort. Was he wide awake, grieving the loss of his father? Somehow she doubted that. His mother slept at the end of the hall and they all shared a bathroom. Some kind of creature pattered above in the attic. At first Harper had been relieved when Cameron insisted that the dogs stay on the first floor. Now she wanted to call Moose, Jervis, and Molly upstairs.

"Are you all right with this?" Cameron had asked when his mother had mentioned the sleeping arrangements. "We're pretty far away from any hotel. Things are simple here but clean."

"Not a problem. This is fine." She intended to sleep in her socks and long pajamas. Cameron's face was drawn, and his eyes were bloodshot. The stilted conversation over a supper of collard greens, salt pork and grits had taken its toll. She would have agreed to almost anything that would ease his strained expression. In her reserved way, Esther Blodgett was fascinated with Bella but the grandmother's comments when the bowl of cereal was produced were not kind. Bella spent most of the evening on her father's lap.

As she stood in church next to Cameron with Bella between them, Harper knew all the words to the hymns. "A Catholic thing," she whispered when Cameron turned to her in surprise. "The hymns are the same, you know."

"You are a veritable fount of information."

He'd grinned, as if they shared a secret. That bonding moment felt totally inappropriate and she stowed her smile for later. She wondered if Cameron had asked Kimmy to come with him and she'd refused. Maybe she couldn't get away from her TV show. Harper had a hard time picturing the fashion plate in the small church where no one wore a suit and the dated sport coats probably served well for both weddings and funerals.

"Following the internment, y'all are invited to join the family at their home," the Reverend Deacon offered at the end of the service. No address needed to be given. Going to the front of the church, Cameron joined his brothers and male cousins as they hoisted the casket and led the congregation through the back door.

"What are they doing?" asked Bella.

Harper had to think about that. "Wishing your grandfather well."

"Is my grandfather in that box?"

"Yes." Harper broke into a sweat.

"Is he ever coming out?"

"He's in heaven, Bella. People are happy in heaven." The

questions stopped when Harper took Bella's hand and followed the others out of the pew and through the door.

Homer Blodgett was laid to rest in the adjoining cemetery. Crows cawed from huge willow trees that had just come into bloom, weeping branches of white splendor. The Reverend Deacon opened his Bible, and Esther Blodgett took her place to one side of the elevated casket. Although she clutched a handkerchief, she hadn't shed a tear, at least not that Harper could see.

Breeze lifting his blond hair, Cameron stood with Harper and Bella, facing his mother, brothers and sister over the plain casket that smelled of fresh cut pine.

"My father never went to church a day in his life without complaining," Cameron muttered.

At one point, Cameron swept Bella up into his arms and whispered something in her ear that made the little girl smile. After the minister said a few words, they filed past with the traditional words of farewell. Some left a flower. Others scattered earth. Only Lily wept, leaning on her husband's arm.

By the time they returned to the Blodgett home, the field surrounding the white structure was even more crammed with battered cars and trucks. The sun caught Cameron's black SUV, a shiny contrast. The house itself was fairly bursting with the crew of women who'd come from the church "lickety-split," as they later told her, to set out the feast. The tantalizing smell of food lifted the gloom that had followed the mourners. Hunger rumbled in Harper's stomach. After they trooped through the front door, careful to wipe their shoes on the metal boot rail out front, conversations were helping chase away the memory of that plain pine coffin.

The long buffet table in the front room held a sumptuous spread. Pan fried chicken was heaped on steaming platters alongside ample bowls of pork and beans. A rich mix of succotash stew and crisp hush puppies filled the air. Casseroles needed no identification for this group who heaped plates high with sweet potatoes, butter beans, black eyed peas, turnips greens, and fried green tomatoes no doubt plucked from someone's cellar. Baskets of biscuits were set out with honey and preserves. For now, the guests merely glanced at the berry cobblers and shoofly pie. Dessert could wait. Apparently there was an unspoken order to this meal.

"Harper?"

She looked down into Bella's terrified eyes.

"Don't worry. I've got your cereal with me." Her heart caught when she saw the girl swallow hard with relief. This would not be a good day for any eating experiments.

Cameron stooped, taking his daughter's chin in one hand. "We got you covered, sweetheart." Overnight, her employer had gone back to what Harper now saw were his roots. She stood in awe that he could be such a contrast to this scene and yet fit in so well.

Carrying heavy plates, they all spilled out the front and back doors to tables set up under the trees. Once she had Bella settled with her cereal next to Cameron, she went back inside. Both family and guests seemed to part while she added a chicken breast, some peas, and a few hush puppies to her plate.

"That's all?" Cameron raised a brow when she took the seat across from him.

"I'm saving room for the shoofly pie."

He smiled.

Although Lily stopped to chat with Cameron, the men seem to give him a wide berth. Bella was getting restless. Spying a rope swing hanging from one of the huge maples, Harper pushed her half eaten meal aside and took Bella's hand. "How about a swing?"

Bella nodded. Dressed in her dainty blue dress and patent leather shoes, she looked so sweet. Harper's heart fairly broke that Bella hadn't even sampled the hush puppies that were so delicious, especially with the honey butter. But she wasn't quite to that point yet and the group of strangers had thrown her. Together, they romped toward the swings.

"Higher, higher!" Hands clutching the rope, Bella made her demands with a giddy smile, and Harper complied. How well she remembered the swing in her own backyard in Oak Park.

Breaking away from what looked like a serious conversation with his sister, Cameron ambled over. "Looks like you found my favorite spot in the whole place." He'd taken his jacket off and hung it on a bush. Had he ever looked more handsome, shirtsleeves rolled up and top button open? Leaning against the tree, he glanced up. "This old tree is way older than I am."

"Did you come here a lot, Daddy?" Bella called out, swooping toward them. "Is this your swing?"

His smile held memories. "Sure is, darlin'. It was about the only toy we had here growing up. Well, this and our slingshots and marbles. Simple things."

To Bella's delight, her father took over the pushing. He had a special trick of spinning the tire that got her giggling.

"Thanks for coming with me," he said when Bella was out of earshot.

"Doesn't sound as if you come home much." The words sounded more like an accusation, and she wanted to pull them back.

He hadn't missed the tone. "I was not welcome here, Harper. My father was a heavy drinker and a bully. After we got older, he toned it down but I never forgot his fits of rage. When I refused to follow in my father's footsteps and work the farm, he called me ungrateful. I left for school on a scholarship, concepts my father could not understand. My marriage to Tammy infuriated him. In his mind I was supposed to marry Lucinda Wilkins down the road. He had big plans to bring our properties together."

"And your mother?"

"She did what she could. My father looked the other way when my brothers put her on the bus to come to Savannah. She and my wife never got along." He measured Harper with one look, like he wondered how much more she could stand. "She seemed to enjoy Bella. Maybe you noticed that my mother's not the kind to sing lullabies."

Sadness carved a hole in Harper's heart. "Isn't some grandmothering better than none? Wouldn't the Goodwins fill that role for Bella? They seemed like nice people."

He didn't look convinced. "It's complicated."

"So you said." She pushed back the hair that had fallen out of the purple scarf binding her forehead. "Things are never the way you think they are."

A grin tweaked his cheek. "You wouldn't be talking about anyone in particular, would you?"

She smiled. "Nope. No one in particular."

Shoulders working in the most distracting way, Cameron kept pushing the swing, his eyes on Bella. "You're a hard one to read, Harper Kirkpatrick."

She erupted into laughter. "Me? I overheard your brothers talking about your sharp eye with a gun. How you wrestled wild boars to the ground."

"You up for a little target practice later?"

She crossed her eyes. "Sorry, but in Oak Park, we do very little target practice. "

"I'm sure if you did, you'd be an expert shot."

"Not really but I appreciate your confidence." She wasn't going to tell him about all her unfinished projects. "Easily distracted," her high school teachers had told her mother.

"So what's the biggest surprise for you?" His question jerked her attention back. "Coming here. What surprised you the most?"

How she wished she didn't blush so easily.

"Harper, you'd suck at poker."

"I imagine I would." How could she find words that wouldn't hurt his feelings? "Ready for dessert?"

A breeze teased curls into her hair and she brushed them from her eyes. When she turned, Cameron's eyes had become caldrons. She felt the heat burn to the bottoms of her shoes.

"Oh, I'd like dessert all right," he whispered.

Harper couldn't get a darn word out. Instead she stopped the swing. "Well, then, er, we should go inside."

Lips curved into a mischievous smile, Cameron lifted his daughter into his arms. Together they walked toward the house, tall grass swishing around them. Bella buried her face in her daddy's shoulder. The teasing glint in his eyes had vanished. Harper was relieved to slip inside the crowded house where chatter dissipated the riotous feelings having a hey day inside her. Grabbing a plate, she stared blindly at the delicacies arranged on the table. None of them would fill this hunger.

A woman in a black hat with lots of netting cozied up to Cameron. "Why, Cameron, we never see enough for you. And you brought your girlfriend?"

Chapter 21

Girlfriend? Harper stared at the woman.

Two plates in one hand, Cameron was scooping up banana pudding as if Bella were really going to eat it. "Mavis Parker, I'd like you to meet Harper Kirkpatrick from Chicago. Harper is Bella's nanny."

Harper's world readjusted. Nanny. Of course.

"So very pleased to meet you, Harper." Curiosity sharpened the woman's glance.

Lily stopped Cameron with a hand on his arm. He gestured toward the door. "Harper, why don't you take Bella outside and eat? I'll be right there."

"Sure thing. Come on, Bella. Let's go sit with your grandmother." Was that a flash of concern in Cameron's eyes when Harper took the plate of banana pudding from him? She made a bee line for the door and the family table under the trees. Bella trailed behind.

"Come sit with us, child." Esther motioned to the seat next to her.

Bella sat down and Harper sat on her other side. When Harper put the plate of banana pudding in front of Bella, the little girl swept it aside. "I'm hungry. I want cereal."

"Cereal? But it's dinner time." Picking up her knife and fork, Esther plopped a piece of chicken onto a clean plate and cut it into bits. Then she nudged the plate in Bella's direction. "Eat, girl. No need to go hungry at this table."

The Blodgett boys kept eating but they hadn't missed the drama. Tears brimmed in Bella's eyes. Harper's heart pounded in her ears. So this was the sensitivity that had shaped Cameron?

"I'll get more food, honey." She wasn't about to use the word "cereal." Harper sprinted for the kitchen where she'd left the box. The hurt in Bella's eyes made her trip on her way up the worn wooden steps. Shins burning, she hurried inside.

"What's up?" Cameron asked when she passed him talking to Lily.

"Nothing." Their conversation looked serious. She wasn't going to bother him.

When she returned with the bowl of cereal, Bella picked up her spoon and, still sniffling, began to eat. Harper couldn't stomach the peach pie, and she hoped whoever brought it didn't see her cover it with her napkin. Her throat closed every time she glanced over at the stern-faced woman watching her granddaughter like a bird of prey.

People were stopping at the table to pay their final respects, but Esther's attention focused on Bella. "Well, I never."

Harper sucked in a breath of relief when Cameron took the seat next to her. Lily also joined the table. Cameron caught his mother staring at Bella. "What is it, Mama?"

"A grown girl eating like that."

Cameron's brothers exchanged a look with Lily. They'd obviously heard this tone before.

Cameron's features sharpened. "You know, Mama, I'm not in the habit of badgering my child about what she eats or does not eat. I have never rubbed mashed potatoes in her hair or made her sit in front of a plate of black-eyed peas until midnight because she didn't care for the taste."

Never blinking, Esther persisted, "I would think you could afford to give her more than cereal for her meals."

"This is not about what I can or cannot afford." Cameron bit his words off as if they were beef jerky. "It's more about what my child prefers."

Even the far tables had fallen silent.

Harper wanted the ground to open and swallow her. And she wanted to take Bella with her.

"Cameron, why don't you tell us about the latest houses you're working with." Lily's voice came high and thin. "I do love to hear you talk about your business."

Esther cast one more needled glance at her granddaughter before shifting her attention to her sons, the ones who might listen to her without challenge. Bella finished eating and pushed her bowl away. The sad expression in her eyes frustrated Harper no end.

Why couldn't she fix this? She was pretending to be something she wasn't, plain and simple. The cheerful, fun loving nanny. Maybe Bella would be one more project she just couldn't finish.

Glancing at his watch, Cameron got up from the table. "Speaking of my business, I have to get back to the city."

Lily's face fell. She didn't want her brother to leave, but the afternoon sun was slanting to the west. Cameron had had enough. Harper began packing up Bella's things.

"I'll just take her to the restroom, Cameron." Relieved to be away from that table, Harper chattered mindlessly as she trooped toward the house with Bella. When they reached the porch, Lily motioned to Bella from the corner.

"Want to see something?" she asked her niece.

Bella cocked her head with her usual caution. "Like what?"

"Like puppies."

Harper watched Bella's resistance melt and followed her around the corner. A bunch of squirming brown and white mongrels romped and played in a pen while the dog called Molly stood watch.

"Will you just look at this?" Stooping, Harper held out a hand and puppies tumbled toward her. "How old are they, Lily?"

"Six weeks. Time to find good homes for them. You look like a dog lover."

Harper shook her head. "The way I move around, I couldn't have a dog."

"I want a puppy," Bella piped up, fluttering one hand at the darling creatures. "Can I, Harper? Come here, puppies."

The balls of fur tripped over each other, trying to reach Bella. But the tiniest one sat back, probably used to being last.

"I like the little one." Bella reached out and Lily swooped up the puppy. The runt of the litter gave an excited yelp before licking the dickens out of Bella. Harper had never heard the little girl giggle like that.

"This is the only girl in the litter," Lily told them. "I'm afraid the boys have made her shy with their roughhousing."

"Aw. Can I keep her?" Bella gazed up at Harper.

"Guess we'll have to see what your dad says." Harper had no clue, but she secretly hoped Cameron would relent. Bella and the puppy were so taken with each other.

They found him stowing their luggage into the back of the SUV. He did a double take. "What you got there, Pipsqueak?"

Harper held her breath. Could he see how much this meant to Bella? Trepidation darkened Bella's eyes. "A puppy. Can I keep her, Daddy? Please?"

Hands on hips, Cameron sighed. "You'll have to take him out, walk him. All that stuff."

Harper smiled. She'd never seen Cameron weaken like this.

"Not 'him,' Daddy. She's a girl. Oh, I will. I promise." Bella tightened her hold on the puppy. "Thank you, Daddy. Oh, thank you!"

"What are you going to call her?"

"Pipsqueak," Bella whispered.

Cameron laughed. "Sounds perfect."

Before they even pulled out of the long rutted drive, Bella was asleep in the backseat, the snoozing puppy curled up in her arms.

"I appreciate your coming with me." Cameron settled back like a load of tension had been left at that farmhouse.

"I wanted to be there for Bella." Was it ridiculous to feel that Cameron had needed her just as much? "Do you go back home often?"

"Not unless I have to. Way too many bad memories." He had the steering wheel in a strangle hold.

Harper thought back to the raucous Sunday afternoons with her brothers and McKenna when they'd watch NASCAR races or root for the Chicago Bears. Pretty relaxed compared to the tense interaction of the Blodgetts.

"When did you change your name, if you don't mind my asking?"

"When I realized how the world works."

She pivoted to face him. His hardened profile squeezed all the air from her lungs. Searching her purse, Harper took a couple draws from her inhaler. "And how does the world work?"

"I think you know, Harper. You're the girl who worked for Rizzo. Maybe it's different in Chicago, but I don't think so. I didn't want to scrub out a living on that dirt poor farm. Even if it took me forever to pay off my student loan, I was not going back."

"But the people seemed nice."

"You never met my father."

"Was he like your mother?" She pictured a joyless, unrelenting couple.

Cameron's lips tightened. Evening was falling, and their headlights threw two pools of light onto the highway. "You know how you flit around the house, singing your little songs and dancing? My mother cooked and cleaned, trying to live up to my old man's expectations. Hardly a southern belle, my dear. We all missed his expectations by a mile and the boys especially did not escape the belt.''

Harper shivered. She could hardly imagine.

"My parents *made* it hard. My father was mean to Mama and mean to us. If the okra was undercooked and still sitting on our plates at the end of the meal, he rubbed it in our hair. Nothing she could do about it. I don't ever want my little girl to know that kind of anger.''

The air had whooshed from her lungs, and Harper had to spend some quality time with her inhaler. Cameron may not think differently, but he'd carried the scars of his upbringing into that mansion on Victory Drive. He snapped on his playlist, and Billy Holiday filled the dark vehicle with songs that brought an ache to her heart.

Or had Cameron's story done that?

Purple and yellow crocus sprang up in small clusters in the garden, a welcome relief after the dour sadness of the Blodgett funeral. Unfortunately, pollen spun through the air with every breeze.

"I'm keeping Bella inside for now,'' Harper told Cameron. "The pollen is wicked. She doesn't seem to be bothered by it—not at bothered as I am—but I don't want to take chances.''

Harper was the one rubbing her eyes and reaching for her inhaler every two seconds. Bella was busy with Pipsqueak, and thank goodness the puppy didn't seem to aggravate her breathing problem. If anything, the spells lessened. Bella slept with the puppy, even though the little dog had more than one accident. The large house seemed to confuse her. More than once, Harper had found the puppy alone and shivering in one of the rooms. After that, Harper kept Pipsqueak at her side when Bella was in school.

"The dog needs to be trained," Cameron said when Harper mentioned the incident one Sunday.

"She's just a baby."

"Lily could have trained her before she handed her off." Newspaper in hand, Cameron sat in his library wing chair. Since the funeral, he'd been withdrawn and preoccupied. Kimmy hadn't come to Sunday dinner last weekend, and Harper sure didn't miss her.

"I think Pipsqueak is a good addition to this house," she told Cameron.

"Whatever you think, Harper. You're in charge."

"That's a scary thought."

His smile widened. "Sometimes I quite agree."

Blushing, she grabbed the entertainment section and took it to the back porch where she could watch Bella toss a ball to Pipsqueak in the yard.

The following week, Connie called in an army of backup help for a thorough spring cleaning. Draperies were taken down and carted to the cleaners. Furniture was waxed until it gleamed, and every window became a shining mirror. Tarnish was banished from the heirloom silver, which Cameron grudgingly admitted had been purchased from an antique shop downtown. At Harper's insistence, all the cleaning was accomplished without using any aerosol products that could worsen breathing problems.

On a Friday that promised to be especially busy in the house,

Harper took Bella to the Marine Education Center on Skidaway, one of the islands that extended into the ocean on the eastern edge of Savannah. The nature trail through the woods was pleasant and Bella was excited beyond belief to see dolphins rising from the canal, grey backs shiny in the sunlight. The inside exhibits featured sea horses, jellyfish and even an alligator. The touch tank fascinated Bella. Harper lifted her to see the horseshoe and hermit crabs better.

"Do they live in the sand? How do they breathe?"

Harper was stymied. "Wish I had an answer, Bella."

The soft pat on Harper's hand came as a compete surprise. "You don't always have to have the answer, Harper."

"Now, that deserves a hug."

Wrapping her arms around Bella, Harper realized this little girl had stolen her heart. The more she felt for Bella, the more difficult the job became. Caring so much for Bella wouldn't end well. She'd had enough heartbreak, thank you very much.

Cameron continued his feeding sessions with Bella. One day after Bella had skipped out of the kitchen with Pipsqueak Harper decided to pose the question. "Cameron, did your wife ever, well, complain when she fed Bella? I'm just wondering where Bella's concern comes from."

His sigh could have been heard down on the river. "Not that I ever saw. But I've wondered the same thing, Harper." His eyes met hers. "Tammy wasn't exactly happy with the role of mother. And she hated my family. Wanted nothing to do with them. If Bella was just being a baby, her mama might have thought it was the Blodgett country ways coming out in her."

By this time, his face had flushed an angry red and dampness rimmed his eyes. "Oh, Cameron," she said softly, wanting to comfort him so badly and not knowing how.

Jumping up, he tucked the chair in with an abrupt scrape. "That was then. I think Bella's making progress, don't you." His eyes begged her to say yes.

"She is. With your patience."

"And yours." His words hung in the air. Silence settled. Their eyes seemed to be doing all the talking. Thank goodness Connie bustled into the room and Harper escaped, her heart beating so fast, she was sure the whole neighborhood could hear.

After that being around Cameron became incredibly difficult. If he entered a room, Harper exited. He took her breath away, literally. She wondered what a doctor would say. "Yes, you have hot employer syndrome, Ms. Kirkpatrick." Trying not to make it obvious, she struggled with her feelings. Then it hit her.

She didn't know when or how but she'd fallen in love with Cameron Bennett. And this felt so different than anything she'd ever experienced. Good grief, they hadn't even kissed—the very thought made her weak. She loved him. Her feelings terrified her.

When Harper and Bella got home from the Marine Education Center one day, Connie was bustling around the kitchen, Pipsqueak yapping at her heels. The housekeeper had bought low country shrimp and was stirring up a hot sauce with plenty of horseradish, just the way Cameron liked it. "He won't make it home for dinner. So busy with that Winston Hill project. Do you think maybe you can take this over? Bella will be fine with me."

Fifteen minutes later, Harper was on Drayton headed for the Victorian section of town. She was eager to see how the work was progressing. This was the project they'd talked about weeks ago, and he'd taken her sketches with him. The plans might be rolled up in a forgotten tube somewhere. Still, excitement bubbled in her chest. The cooler of shrimp and sauce sat on the seat next to her. Finally, she would see Cameron at work. She sure hoped he wouldn't be there alone.

Chapter 22

Harper drove through the district of homes with high gables,
elegant porticoes and porches with lots of spindle work. Many
needed work. The city had been working to reclaim historical
treasures in this area just south of downtown Savannah. Harper
was all for it. She'd been involved in some of the efforts when she
was in school. Now her tires bobbled over the cobblestone streets
as she circled the block, trying to find a parking space. She passed
Cameron's black Bentley twice. Not hard to pick out the house
with scaffolding in place and paint cans on the porch. Finally, she
succeeded in easing the SUV into a tight parking space. Grabbing
the small cooler, she jumped out and circled around to the back of
the house.

Hammers rang out and Willie Nelson crooned about Georgia
from a jambox. She pushed open the back screen door and it
whapped shut behind her.

"Hi there. Can I help you?" A good-looking guy in a yellow
hard hat was positioning a kitchen cabinet against a wall.

She held up the cooler. "Cameron Bennett?"

"Figures." He jabbed a thumb toward the front.

After stepping over some two by fours and skirting a table saw,
she walked through what would be the dining room into a front

hall. Her footsteps rang on the plank floors. Still, no Cameron. Looking around, she tried not to breathe in the sawdust already tickling the back of her throat.

In front of the parlor bay windows sat a work table strewn with sketches. No mistaking Cameron's handwriting. Her throat thickened when she recognized her own drawings mixed with his. Coming closer, she read, "Harper suggests moss green fabrics with warm taupe undertones."

Holy cripes. He'd taken her seriously.

The cooler thumped to the floor. All her life she'd wanted to be more than the coddled youngest in her family. She skimmed her fingertips over Cameron's notes on the pages. Drats, was she tearing up? The last thing she wanted was for Cameron to see her crying. In the back hallway, she found a door marked with a handwritten sign that said "bathroom" in bold red letters. Slipping inside and closing the door with a bang, she was horrified when the door knob clattered to the floor. She heard a metallic thump on the other side as well. Perfect. The rod had fallen through.

Slipping one finger through the empty hole where the knob had been, she tugged. Nearly tore a nail off and the darn door didn't budge. She gave the door a good kick that did absolutely no good. The guy in the kitchen had switched stations, turned up the volume and was singing along. She thumped on the door with both hands. "Help! I'm stuck in here!"

The only response was a roll of the drums.

Harper took a deep breath. The sun might be setting, but the heat in this bathroom had been building all day. Thank goodness she was only wearing a T-shirt and her cut-offs. She started to pick at her lime nail polish. At some point, one of the guys would have to use this room, right? She slid to the floor, drowsy in the heat.

When she woke up, the sawing and hammering had quieted. No music playing. For a second, she panicked. Then footsteps on the stairs above jolted her upright. Heck, she'd know that stride anywhere. "Cameron? I'm in the bathroom!"

When the door banged open, she looked up, wiping her eyes.

He held out the red and white cooler that almost matched the sweat-soaked bandanna around his head. His pale jeans looked soft, cupping lean muscled legs. "This yours?"

"Yes." She choked out the word.

Cameron set down the cooler, along with a can of pop.

"Hey, you okay?" When he ran his hands up her bare arms, shivers used Harper's body as a dance floor.

"Ye-es."

"You sure as hell are not." Tugging the gray T-shirt from his jeans, Cameron dabbed at her eyes. One look at those toned abs and her heart began hammering against her ribs. Under his trim suits was the body of a Greek god. Her absurd physical response slammed her like a piece of pipe, smack across her stomach.

"Level with me. Have you been crying?" he persisted.

"Yes. No." She tried to push some stray hair back up into her barrette, but a lock caught in her green hoops. "I got trapped."

"Happens to all of us at one time or another." With a slow smile, he worked to slip her hair free. One finger did a sweep of her cheek.

"It does?" She let her cheek fall into his hand.

"You bet. Lord, your skin is so soft," he murmured. Fumbling, he reached down for the pop. "Here, take a sip."

"Root beer. My favorite."

"I know."

Grabbing the can, she pressed the cool metal to one flushed cheek and managed a whispered, "Thank you," before taking a sip.

"You look like you could stand something stronger than root beer," he murmured.

Oh, she needed *way* more than the pop.

And that was a bad, bad thought that could get any girl into trouble.

He was in deep shit.

"This'll do nicely, Cameron. Thank you." Sweat beaded Harper's nose as she popped open the can, holding it to a figure that took Cameron's mind on a wild ride. Her torn Tybee Island T-shirt made her look outrageously sexy. Whatever had been bothering her, Cameron wanted to fold her into his arms and tell her that everything would be all right.

But this was a woman who didn't take help kindly. Catwoman? That night she left him wondering if she really liked to wield that whip. He'd never been into that but this was a girl who could make a man think twice. "This reminds me of that first night," he murmured.

"Not my finest moment." When Harper chewed on her lower lip, his mouth got as dry as sawdust.

"I thought you were…great."

"Really? No." She dropped her gaze, and he heard her swallow. "You're doing a great job here. I, ah, saw the drawings."

Cameron pulled his mind from thoughts that made his jeans tighten. "Think we can work together on this project? We'd, ah, make a good team."

"Maybe." Taking a couple deep gulps of pop, she finally came up for air. "Yum, this is so good."

"Yum. Right." Need awakened in his gut, a beast teased from a long nap.

"Oh, I'm sorry. Want a sip?" She held out the can.

He grabbed the can. His hearty glug, glug was embarrassingly loud. Cameron didn't give a rip. Heart like a jack hammer, he wiped his mouth with the back of his hand and handed the can back. Trying not to stare at the rapid rise and fall of her chest that jumbled the letters of Tybee Island, he lifted his gaze. Her hazel eyes had turned to taupe, a color he'd like for his favorite office armchair.

Must be the heat.

Might be *his* heat.

Desire rampaged through his body like high tide spilling into the Savannah marsh.

Her lips parted. "Cameron?" A delicate frown brought her brows together.

Taking the pop can, he set it on the sink and drew her into his arms. "Come here, little girl."

At first, Harper jerked tight. Then her body released, every damn curve settling against his body. He kissed her damp forehead and she sighed. For just a second, uncertainty riddled him. After all, she was his employee. Harper's slow smile deepened her eyes to cat-tail brown. Maybe *that* was the color for the damned chair.

"Aren't there rules about this?" she whispered.

His lips trailed the edge of her chin. One shoulder bumped up, and he eased it down, burying his lips in the soft hollow of her neck. She smelled like citrus and his tongue flicked out. Tasted like it too. "Never pay much mind to rules."

"In the mood to break some, are you?"

He left her neck unwillingly and considered those full lips. "Hell, yes."

"Gonna enjoy it?"

"Absolutely."

"Oh, I hope so. Me too." And she sighed.

Her body felt warm, like she'd been baking in the sun at Tybee. The memory of her tiny bathing suit that day stoked his heat. Cameron tightened his grip until he could feel every mind-bending curve that had kept him awake at night since that Sunday.

She jerked away, and cool air cut an unwelcome swath between them. "Wait a minute. What about Kimmy?"

"We both decided it would never work. I think she's relieved."

"Are you?" Harper's arms tightened around his neck.

"What?"

Harper ripped something from her hair. Curls spilled to her shoulders in liquid caramel waves. "Any regrets after you called it quits?"

"Wouldn't be here if that were the case."

Harper raked her fingers through her hair and pursed her lips. He was toast.

Didn't matter that it must be ninety-five in here. Didn't matter that they were stuck together like super glue. When he kissed her, Harper sighed through slightly parted lips.

He liked the sigh. Liked the kisses that got longer, hotter. Wetter. Their tongues did some exploring, the kind that doesn't need a map.

Finally she pulled back. "Going home to Hazel Hurst with you explained so much."

"Let's not over analyze." The skin under her chin was so soft.

"You're right. I can do that, you know."

"Yes, I know. Enough is enough." He jerked her waist closer. Crap, she hitched one leg over his thigh, rocking her body slowly against a part of him that sprang to life.

He was going to bust a gut...or something in that vicinity. "You enjoying that?"

"Yep. Sorry." She clenched her jaw and leaned back, like she was trying for a good angle.

Cameron groaned. "Nothing to be sorry about." He dropped kisses on her long damp neck until she shivered. Giggled when he whispered that he wanted to lick her like a popsicle. Then he silenced her moans with his lips.

Craziness made his head spin. Felt like he was about to plunge into water so deep he might never surface. The only other time that came close was when he'd persuaded Tammy to elope.

Caution nipped at the edges of his mind.

"This is probably a bad idea." Panting, he came up for air.

"Absolutely." She yanked the sweatband from his hair.

"I can't help myself. Don't want to." He rested her on the sink and cursed these damn jeans.

Harper threw her head back, blotting her neck with his scarf.

"You have to stop teasing."

"Then stop moaning."

"Not gonna happen."

God she was hot. Cameron took her lips like he owned them. His entire body burned. He was working up a serious sweat and was glad his workers had left. Lips and hands went everywhere, like their bodies were Braille and they were reading each other for the first time.

Had he been treating Harper like a girl when she was really a woman? The thought hammered him, knocking him breathless. Chest heaving, Harper stilled in his arms.

Harper Kirkpatrick was all woman.

And he wanted her.

Wanted her so bad, he started to shudder from holding back.

"Hey, you okay?" She swiped back his matted hair with fingers that left tingling tracks.

"More than okay." He cupped her breasts through the soft fabric, flicked his thumbs across their peaks before trailing fingers down her rib cage, wanting to memorize each ridge. Her hips kept undulating until he seriously wondered if the guys had gotten around to hooking up the shower in this room. The heat had pumped up his blood pressure for sure, but to leave would be to lose this. Couldn't risk it.

"I need some water." He turned on one of the spigots behind her, relieved when water spurted out on a burst of air pockets.

She laughed, her teeth flashing. "Getting overheated, Mr. Bennett?"

"Burning up, Ms. Kirkpatrick." Cameron's eyes never left her face as he scooped and dribbled cool water down her cheeks and throat. With an impatient moan, she yanked down the neckline of her tee. His breath caught as he watched it funnel into the deep valley between her breasts. Harper reached behind her and let the water run over her hands. Then she pressed them wet and cool on his cheeks.

"Haven't been this naughty in a while." But her eyes looked kind of sad.

Cameron nudged her to one side and ducked his head under the faucet. She laughed when he came up sputtering. He felt like he was seventeen again, down at the creek with Lucinda Wilkins, wondering how far he could go. "This brings back some memories."

Harper's laughter died. She looked at her wet clothes with surprise, like she didn't know how this had happened. "I shouldn't be doing this."

He drew back. "You mean because you work for me?"

Shaking her head, she ran one wet hand through her long hair. "That and I was, well, in love with someone. Wasn't that long ago, and we shouldn't...I mean I shouldn't..." Stuttering, she handed him his scarf.

Shock knifed him. "Who? That Adam guy you meet for lunch?"

"Heck no, Adam's just a friend. But there was, well, someone. It's over but…" The confusion in Harper's eyes shook him up plenty.

Setting her on her feet, he wetted the kerchief under the faucet until it was sopping. Then he knotted it around his forehead, wishing it were a block of ice.

One sip of that warm soda and her eyes turned moody.

Cameron blinked. If that's how it was, painful as it would be to be around Harper while she dreamed about someone else, he could not lose another nanny. Especially not this one. Bella adored her.

And so did he. The realization sliced him like a x-acto knife.

Reaching down, she grabbed the small cooler and shoved it at him. "Almost forgot your supper. Connie will kill me."

"That'll happen. Forgetting, I mean."

"But it shouldn't." Her eyes clung.

"Only one thing I'm hungry for right now and it's not shrimp." His mother would tell him he was being stubborn again.

Looking troubled, she turned to leave.

He grabbed her hand. "Share it with me?" He couldn't let her go, not like this.

She hesitated.

"I hate to eat alone." He slipped his fingers through hers.

"All right." She studied their hands.

"We can have a picnic on the back porch."

Harper leaned away and then swayed back toward him. "Sounds

nice."

He snagged a couple of cold beers from the refrigerator and led her outside. The original back porch still stood, although it would be replaced in a couple of weeks. The men had dragged a picnic table up here. Cracking open the cooler, he grabbed the plates Connie had set on top of the container of shrimp. Harper opened the plastic tub of sauce, and they both dug in, shelling the shrimp before dipping them into the sauce.

Food was a safe topic. "Connie makes a mean sauce. Can you feel it hit the back of your throat?"

Harper just nodded, looking like she was a million miles away. He was consuming two shrimp for her one. He felt famished. Insatiable. They ate in silence, the only sound the crackling of the shells as they tore them off. Didn't matter how many. Nothing touched his hunger.

"Your breathing's okay?" he asked, loving the way the moonlight accented Harper's fine features.

"Yep. Besides, I have my inhaler." She shrugged, taking another shrimp.

When a drop of hot sauce appeared in the corner of her lips, he swiped it with one thumb. She lifted her eyes and smiled. "Thank you."

"Just taking care of you."

The pulse throbbed at the base of her throat. "Yeah. Right."

Their look was long and steady. He fought the urge to sweep the food from the table and take her right there.

But he didn't want it like that. She looked confused. Troubled.

Cameron cleared his throat. "Now about the Winston Hill project…" He felt like a fireman talking a victim off a ledge.

Somehow, he had to get Harper back in her comfort zone.

Chapter 23

What had she done? Harper threw herself up the back stairs of the house. She could hear Cameron pulling the Bentley into the garage behind her as she ripped open the kitchen door.

Connie looked up from loading the dishwasher. "Everything okay? Did Mr. Bennett get his dinner? You don't look so good."

Gripping one of the kitchen chairs, Harper sucked in a breath. "Must be something I ate."

"What? I just bought that shrimp today."

Harper raised one hand. "No, it wasn't the shrimp. Could you put Bella to bed tonight?"

Connie nodded, but her eyes held a question.

In the TV room, Ninja warriors roared. Harper stuck her head in. "Not feeling well, Bella. See you tomorrow, honey."

Bella looked up. "Okay. Sorry you're sick, Harper."

"I'm sure I'll be better soon." *As soon as I have my head examined.*

Harper heard the back door open as she sprinted up the stairs. She didn't breathe again until she threw herself onto her bed. The springs squeaked as she rolled over onto her back. What the heck? Jumping up, she yanked open her lingerie drawer and shoved one hand under the panties. After pulling out the framed picture, she settled into the rocker.

She'd felt so out of control tonight with Cameron. Cripes, she had to bring up Billy to stop the train about to mow her down. Harper tossed Billy's picture onto the bed. She loved Cameron. But memories so obviously had interfered tonight. She didn't want half of him. She wanted the whole Cameron Bennett. Lord knows she was being stubborn and McKenna would probably tell her that. But if she couldn't have him, heart and soul, if he couldn't get beyond memories of his dead wife, well then, what future did they have?

But Harper had never felt this way before. Cameron pulled on her body and her mind in so many ways. Like she wanted to live inside him. The thought terrified her. She was just beginning to get a grip on her life and she could endanger everything. Give a piece of herself away and risk losing a job she liked? And just when she was really enjoying the extra curricular work they were doing together on Winston Hill House.

Oh, this was extra-curricular all right.

She didn't want to feel like a hook-up. Her chest knotted when she remembered Cameron's hesitation. Could a man ever get over losing a wife he truly loved? Harper had sure been ready to take it further. Starved for physical comfort, she'd acted like a trollop. Harper touched her throbbing lips, reaching for the feelings that had driven her crazy.

Took her a long time to get to sleep that night. Crazy dreams shook her awake, hot and sweaty. In her dreams she was reaching, blinded by some light but always searching. Her hands came up empty. When she dragged herself to the window, she saw the light from Cameron's office below. Looked like he was working late.

Harper tried to relax into April, her favorite season in Savannah. The trees and bushes had turned to early summer green. Pollen-filled tulips made her eyes itch and her nose run. Still, she liked them.

Harper liked a lot of things that were bad for her.

Usually she felt so carefree in April. Everything seemed possible. Not this year. Since the episode at the Winston Hill House, she stayed away from Cameron. Not easy but necessary. As the days passed, thoughts of leaving ran through her mind. She'd even pulled her duffel bag out of the closet one night.

"That would be cowardly," McKenna told her when Harper called her sister in desperation. "And you are not a coward, Harper."

Harper had fallen back onto her bed with a sigh. "I know you're right. But I am jumping out of my skin."

The throaty chuckle from her sister made Harper squirm. "Maybe they call that love, baby sister."

In her heart, Harper knew that was true.

"Isn't your birthday coming up?"

"Right. Bella's too."

"Perfect. Why don't you wait until then. See how you feel. Better to leave because you're headed for something else, not because you're panicked and bailing. You have to work through this."

"But he's my employer."

"Yes, he is and the two of you should talk about that."

Her sister was right. After ending the call, Harper tucked the duffel bag back into the closet. Going home to Oak Park would be more a retreat than a jubilant return and that sucked.

One evening she was making a meatloaf with fierce punches and jabs when she glanced up to find Cameron in the doorway. Eyes on the bowl, he looked startled. One swipe of those baby blues, the shadow of a grin and he disappeared. Her hands shook so bad she could hardly pick up the recipe card.

Pipsqueak was growing in ungainly spurts and Harper took her on walks while Bella was in school. The puppy tired long before Harper did. She loved cuddling the puppy's squirmy warmth and carried her upstairs for soulful conversations. The mutt would listen with liquid brown eyes and roll over for a tummy rub.

Trollop. Harper wanted the same—from Cameron. A real problem.

The puppy never left Bella's side and even slept in the big queen size bed. Now when Harper picked Bella up from play school, Pipsqueak yipped on the seat next to her.

Harper worked to fill her time and empty her mind. Her thoughts were filled with Cameron Bennett, in all his complexity. And Cameron had become her body's obsession. Every time she saw a sink, she blushed remembering how she'd balanced on the edge of one at Winston House while Cameron's lips teased and tormented her. She'd relived that evening a hundred times and the mental pictures still stole her breath, like an August day in Savannah. The other picture etched deep was the sight of him at his father's grave. Life hadn't dealt Cameron Bennett a fair hand, that's for sure. And after being raised under harsh circumstances, he'd lost the wife he adored.

Meanwhile, Bella had begun to eat, and she was sampling way more than cotton candy or applesauce. The feeding sessions between Cameron and Bella led to sliced peaches, then pears. Chopped up spaghetti eventually was replaced by pizza. Feeding Pipsqueak had helped Bella turn another corner. Harper could hear her tell the puppy that she had to eat or "or you won't grow up to be a strong dog." The earlier hectoring tone had been replaced by loving concern.

Still, nothing was the same. She had to face up to that. Being around Cameron had gotten so hard. The job she loved more than anything had become unbearably awkward. Leaving seemed the only answer. After the conversation with McKenna, she decided to wait until after Bella's birthday party. She tried out her announcement on Adam first.

"You're going home to Chicago? Are you crazy?" Adam's cinnamon spice tea slopped over the side of his teacup. They were seated at Gryphon Tea Room, an early birthday present from Adam.

"This isn't right for me anymore."

"What are you saying? You love Savannah."

Picking at her cucumber finger sandwich, Harper searched for the words. Her gaze traveled around the historic apothecary shop that housed the Gryphon. Sure, she loved the history of this city, but she couldn't turn a corner without bumping into memories.

Before it was Billy and now, Cameron. Every time she passed the Telfair Academy, she could feel Cameron's arms around her, his chin on her forehead while they barely moved to the music. Still made her heart speed up when she thought of him rocking out to the faster beat. The beat of the drum still resonated in her body.

And Cameron? He resonated in her heart.

"Chicago had its own past. Maybe I belong to that history."

Adam's jaw dropped. "Where you begin isn't necessarily where you end up, Harper. I grew up in Dubuque. Life moves on."

Sometimes Adam made so much sense.

Sometimes Harper didn't want to hear it.

"But my life isn't moving forward here in Savannah. I'm going to miss you." Adam had been a loyal friend. He was the guy who listened to whatever dirt she dished out and made it into stone soup.

Ripping open another packet of sugar, Adam stirred it into his tea. "Is it your job? Is that what you're running from. Or is it Cameron Bennett?"

"I'm not running from anything." Her mind stuttered to a halt. The blue eyes. The unruly dark blond hair that he didn't plaster back with goo anymore. Harper smoothed her hands over the white linen tablecloth. "Maybe my work is finished here. Cameron will understand." The name came out soft, like she didn't want to let it go.

Adam's mouth fell open. "Wait, it *is* Bennett. He's gotten to you."

Taking a scone from the tea caddy, Harper crumbled it in her fingers.

"If I knew you weren't going to eat that scone, I would have grabbed it first."

"Sorry." She whisked the crumbs into a napkin.

"Is Billy Colton involved in this somehow? He hasn't contacted you, has he?"

She groaned. "Lord no. That is so over."

"Good. You can never go back, you know. Things are never the same."

"I see it now. At least this time I finished something, Adam. Bella is eating."

Adam summoned the waiter. "Oh, missy. Don't kid yourself. You definitely have unfinished business."

The bill arrived in one of the quaint antique books Gryphon used for the check. "There's something you're not telling me." Adam slid a credit card in with the bill.

Harper played with one green hoop earring. "Can't talk about. I feel like such a slut."

"That bad?" Adam set the bill aside. "Spill, missy."

So she did. She'd never held anything back from Adam.

"So what did he say to you later?"

"Are you kidding me? I've been avoiding him."

Adam threw up his hands. "Of course. Avoidance is always a good way to settle a situation. This is why you never saw it coming with Billy."

"What do you mean?" Suddenly Harper was hungry. She grabbed the single leftover tuna finger sandwich.

"From what I could see, you and Billy always avoided confrontations. Talking about the need for world peace, this season's color palette, or contemporary theater is easy. The personal discussions are something else entirely." Adam leaned closer. "Being with someone is called a relationship because you relate."

The tuna went down her throat in a painfully dry swallow. Adam was right. She'd always assumed Billy understood her. His comments in their theater class were always so on point. They'd jumped into their relationship lickety split and then held on for dear life. What had they really had in common besides pizza with chipotle spices? She'd sat through more horror films with him when she really preferred foreign movies. Subtitles irritated the heck out of Billy. When they partied on weekends, she wanted to dance. Billy preferred a corner where he could listen to the music and write his own lyrics. The one time she'd taken him home for Thanksgiving, he'd been overwhelmed by her family. Billy only had one brother, Al. "How do you put up with all this?" Billy had asked her on the drive back from Chicago.

Put up with it? She hadn't known what to say. Back at school, Harper and Billy quickly fell into their campus life and Chicago was forgotten.

Had that school existence been realistic? Or was the day-to-day with Cameron and Bella real life?

The SUV was quiet when Harper drove Adam back to his salon. When she entered the kitchen later, still preoccupied, Cameron was there, paper spread out on the table. Lately, he'd changed his style. No more khaki slacks and oxford shirts around the house. Now she found him in jeans and a T-shirt. Sometimes she wished he'd go back to the stiff, unyielding oxford cloth. Her body gave a pitiful jolt now that she knew what lay beneath the soft cotton shirt and jeans.

She wanted it.

"Hey, Harper." When he looked up from the paper, his blue eyes were ringed with dark shadows.

"Could we talk?" She sat down, tugging at her spring green miniskirt.

He put the paper aside. "Sure. Of course." A muscle flexed in his jaw.

Bella wandered in from the TV room, still in her action figure PJs. "Harper, wanna play badminton?"

Harper tore her eyes from Cameron. "Right now?"

"Yeah. I love it when we play together." When she climbed onto Harper's lap, Bella smelled like the puppy. Harper couldn't help but nuzzle her neck. Pipsqueak loped over and Cameron scooped the dog up. "Daddy says I'm having a birthday party. Do you want to come?"

"Wouldn't miss it." When she turned to Cameron with a chuckle, his eyes had melted to Blue Moon ice cream. "The auction item you won in February?"

"Yep, May second is just around the corner."

"Daddy says I can invite anybody I like, and I like you." Bella blinked up at her. Harper's heart turned over.

Cameron cleared his throat. "I told Bella the Goodwins would be coming. Her grandparents."

"You invited them, really?" How amazing.

He looked uncomfortable. "Bella and I had a little talk about grandparents."

"And how they will fit in her life?" she offered gently.

"That remains to be seen."

"And your mother? Will she come to the party too?"

His jaw moved, like he was working a piece of gristle. "She's been invited. We'll see."

Wow. This was huge.

"Lotsa people are coming, Daddy says." Bella clapped her hands with excitement. "I never had a birthday party."

Cameron grinned. "But I sure don't know what to get my little girl."

"I have an idea." Harper's mind had been busy, and this plan had kept her from obsessing about Cameron.

Bella crinkled up her nose. "An idea about a present for me?"

"Sure do. I was thinking we might do something in your room, but it has to be a surprise."

Bella tilted her head. "You could tell me now."

Harper pinched the tip of her nose. "Then it wouldn't be a surprise.

Even Cameron looked intrigued. "Decorating? Good time to start over."

"Starting over, right." Harper couldn't even go there.

Only later, when she was upstairs changing into jeans did Harper remember that she'd sat down with Cameron to talk about that night. Find out where they were.

Now she had more time. More time to find the right words.

Time passed quickly while Harper worked on sketches for Bella's room. She left them on Cameron's drafting table when he was out of the house. Adam's comments about communication came back to her, but old habits die hard.

Bella's room would be a pretty spring green with touches of ninja blue. The blue comforter would have a green girl warrior appliqued on the top, with generous matching shams. No more ruffles or feathery fringe to catch the dust.

Connie helped Harper move Bella to one of the second floor guest rooms so that the birthday room could be a complete surprise. "But I want to see!" Bella had complained, lugging a basket of her shoes over to her temporary room.

"Birthdays should always have at least one surprise," Harper told her, ruffling her hair.

Cameron's workmen strung yellow tape across her bedroom door, which tantalized Bella even more. Pipsqueak gnawed at it, leaving bits of yellow plastic all over the house. Harper had written out invitations for every student in Bella's preschool class. Two days before the birthday, everything was about ready in the bedroom. At Harper's insistence, Cameron had agreed not to look at the room. The men had worked a long day putting the final touches on the paint. A Barbie doll birthday card had arrived from McKenna, and Harper put it on the dresser in Bella's temporary bedroom.

Extraordinary Celebrations, the company providing the party, had come out to the house weeks before to view the garden. Miles and Candace, the owners, discussed logistics with Cameron. What a contrast between this group and Rizzo, part of a past that seemed so long ago.

Harper wanted the day to be special but hesitated to become too involved. This would be the first and last party they'd ever have together. After Miles and Candace left, Harper was able to slip away with the excuse that she had to pick up Bella.

"I'll go with you," Cameron said. "We're done here."

"Oh, no. I, ah, have some errands to run."

Her words snapped his features closed. "Oh, well. If that's the case."

He knew she was avoiding him but Harper couldn't think about that now. The time for talking had passed. Any conversation now might end with her resignation. The party was just around the corner. No way would she spoil that day for Bella.

Once in the SUV, she didn't head straight to school. Instead, she detoured through Daffin Park, locked the car, and sat on the bench where she'd met the Goodwins that day in February. What a child she'd been that day, so unaware of the family complications that made up Cameron's life. She still didn't understand them.

"Reached any conclusions yet?" Adam asked during one of their lunches.

"Decided to delay our heart-to-heart talk until after the birthday party."

"Ah, the story isn't over," Adam had said with a smirk.

"I can't take much more."

"More what? Lusting?"

"Come on." But the heat in her cheeks brought a satisfied smile from Adam. The huge mansion had become too small. Even passing Cameron in the hall felt strained. She tried to tell herself that this all had to do with how generous he'd been with her. He'd given her a chance to succeed, including the work for Winston Hill House. She'd been able to chip away at her credit card bills. All told, she was in much better position than when she started this job.

Relegating her time here to a line on her resume would be difficult but she'd do it.

Cameron began to spend more time away from the house. The joint meals they shared in the dining room? The silence between the two of them felt awkward, even when Bella was telling her father about school. But Harper wouldn't have to tolerate the dinners for long, a thought that brought both relief and sadness.

On the morning of Bella's birthday, Harper heard the little girl calling her. "Harper, wake up! Come on down!" Ripping herself from sleep, she piled blindly down the stairs in her sleep pants and tee. Cameron had the workmen put a huge blue bow on Bella's door. Now the birthday girl was ripping it down while Pipsqueak yipped with excitement.

Still in his track pants and T-shirt, Cameron was rubbing his eyes but stopped when Harper showed up, crossing her arms tight over her chest.

"Gosh, I thought she'd fallen or something."

He grinned and looked away. "Nope. Just the birthday girl. But I'm glad you're here. After all, this gift is from you too. We wouldn't have anything…ah, this, without you."

The early morning warmth of his body reached out for her when he brushed back his sleep-tousled hair. When his eyes circled back to hers, she couldn't look away.

"Can I look now, Daddy?" Bella clamored at his feet.

"You bet."

Shoulders squeezed tight with excitement, Bella pushed open the door. "Oh, wow."

Harper swelled with pride. A castle stood in one corner, made of blueish gray with green touches. Shelves were made of castle bricks, and the door to her closet had magic written all over it, the worn wood neatly braced with metal in the shape of a B. Even the bedside tables were fabricated tree stumps. Lamps were huge mushrooms and the dresser, stacked logs. Oh, to be five again.

Bella looked stunned, running her hands over each piece of wood and throwing herself in the center of the bed. Took two tries but Pipsqueak scrambled up next to her. "Look! I'm a real Ninja princess!"

"That's not all, Bella." Going to the bedside tree trunk, Cameron pressed a button. Bella's mouth fell open when a gazillion stars appeared on her ceiling.

He could be so amazing. "Wow. Pretty impressive, Dad." The man never ceased to amaze Harper. Sure, many of the ideas had been sketched out in her drawings, but she couldn't believe the execution.

With Bella in his arms, he was watching her. "The first work in your portfolio." He was so close she could see the sleepers in his eyes and she stopped herself from brushing them gently away.

"Yes, yes it is. Thank you."

Her portfolio? So he expected her to leave? The crushing disappointment surprised her.

"Anyone want breakfast?" Connie called up. The smell of applesauce and bacon wafted up the stairs.

With a screech, Bella twisted from Cameron's arms. How wonderful that the little girl was finally learning the delight of food.

The look on Cameron's face told her that he might be thinking that same thing. "Thank you," he said when he turned.

"Of course. My pleasure." He was so close, close enough to kiss her. Suddenly aware that she needed a shower in the worst way, Harper dashed for the door and climbed the stairs to her room but the look in Cameron's gaze followed her.

One glance and she melted into a puddle.

She had to get out of this house before leaving became too painful.

Or had she passed that point?

Chapter 24

Harper took Bella to the park so the birthday girl wouldn't see Extraordinary Celebrations setting up for the party. After swinging for a while, they wandered over to the fountain. Harper had picked up a handful of stones from the play area. "Make a wish, birthday girl." She filled Bella's small hands with pebbles. Giggling, Bella closed her eyes and tossed. The stones plunked into the water, and they watched the circles ripple out to the edge of the pond.

Bella pressed one stone into Harper's palm. "Your turn."

Closing her eyes, Harper turned her back to the fountain and tossed. Her wish felt hopeless.

"Can I tell you my wish?" Bella skipped as they returned to the car.

"Then it might not come true. That's the thing about wishes."

Bella climbed up into her carseat and crossed her arms. "Okay. Then I'm not saying nothing."

By the time they returned to the mansion, the trucks were gone. Above the garden wall, balloons bobbed. "Close your eyes, now, Bella." The birthday girl pressed both hands against her eyes. After Harper pulled the car into the garage, she took Bella from the back seat. "Now take my hand. We're going around the front to get you dressed in your party dress."

"I thought you said I didn't have to wear dresses anymore."

"Today is a very special day. I think all your friends from school will come in dresses."

"Then I want to be pretty too."

Once inside, they went straight to Bella's room. The little girl quivered with excitement. Instead of the fussy ruffled dresses Kimmy had favored, Harper had chosen a blue princess dress. Sparkles dotted the full skirt and she'd found a matching crown. The blue Mary Jane shoes also glittered. Bella ran one hand over the full skirt. "Magic. Just like my ceiling."

"Walk over to the window and stand in the sun," Harper said, happy Bella was so delighted. It had taken three trips to Oglethorpe Mall and Hilton Head to find this creation. When Bella spun in the sunlight spilling from the French door, the skirt sent sparkles dancing every which way.

"I'm a princess," Bella whispered.

"You sure are, sweetheart." Pipsqueak agreed, leaping at the points of light that danced across the room.

One glance at her phone told Harper the guests would be arriving soon. Her jeans and T-shirt wouldn't cut it for a birthday celebration. "Bella, want to show Connie your dress? I'll meet you downstairs, okay?"

"Don't take too long." Bella scrambled for the stairs with Pipsqueak bouncing behind her.

Upstairs, Harper slipped into one of her standby outfits—the flowered ruffled skirt and pink top. She pulled her hair high into a ponytail and slipped into her green slides. After dashing some pink gloss on her lips, she headed for the stairs just as the front doorbell rang. When Harper reached the bottom of the stairs, Connie was directing the baker to the back of the house while Bella twirled in the foyer.

"Doesn't she look beautiful?" Connie closed the door.

"This is my princess dress." Bella smoothed one hand over the skirt.

"Let me see, honey." Harper jumped at the sound of Cameron's voice.

Bella looked up to her father. "Do I look pretty, Daddy?"

"More than pretty." Cameron beamed. "You are my angel."

"Everything set outside?" Harper whispered to Cameron while Bella twirled.

"Come and see for yourself." He led them through the mansion to the back.

A cluster of children looked up from where Candace had them corralled at the foot of the stairs. "Happy Birthday, Bella!"

"Oh, my." Clearly shocked, Bella slid her fingers into her mouth. Then she seemed to remember. Big girls did not suck their fingers. With a nervous giggle, she grabbed the rail with both hands and went down the steps.

Balloons were attached in clusters to every bush and tree. In the corner twirled a small merry-go-round with zoo animals bobbing up and down. A netted trampoline stood ready, and a clown was blowing up balloons and fashioning animal hats for the guests. Under the large oak, a small band played the happy birthday song.

"Happy birthday, Bella." Candace greeted her at the foot of the stairs. "I'm Candace, your hostess for today."

Candace was as good as her word. They'd sent invitations to everyone in Bella's playschool class, as well as any neighbors in the area. The service had planned an impressive list of activities.

"That auction prize was the best investment I ever made," Cameron murmured, watching the clown work his magic.

"Sure was."

Then Harper saw them. The Goodwins stood under the archway that led from the street. Mr. Goodwin held a huge package wrapped with a pink bow. They looked terrified.

She heard Cameron's sharp intake of breath. Then he straightened his shoulders and walked toward them. Watching the three of them together, Harper couldn't help but admire Cameron. Any man working out his past with such grace got her vote. He was one handsome hunk in his beige pants and the black mock turtleneck. Cameron Bennett may have been born a roughneck but he'd become a true southern gentleman.

Harper drew closer.

"Hello, Harper." Mrs. Goodwin nodded her silver blonde head. Probably fresh from the hair dresser. Both grandparents were dressed in club casual.

"Want me to take that? I'll put your present near the cake."

Mr. Goodwin looked relieved to surrender Bella's gift.

Bella dashed over. "Come on, Harper. Want to get your face painted with me?" She pointed to the smiling teenager stationed near the fountain.

The older couple's eyes were glued to their granddaughter.

"Bella, can you say hello to your grandparents?"

"Do you remember us, honey?" Mrs. Goodwin asked, looking so uncomfortable Harper wanted to hug her.

Bella cocked her head to one side before a light flickered on in her eyes. Coming closer, she gave them a quick embrace. Shaking the surprise from her eyes, Mrs. Goodwin managed to hug her back, as if she held a prized piece of crystal. Mr. Goodwin unfortunately missed out on this round because Bella darted off to the face painter with a quick wave.

"Why, I think she remembers you, Linda Sue," Mr. Goodwin said with amazement.

"I believe so."

"Let me find you a place to sit." Cameron led the couple to a cluster of wrought-iron furniture under one of the large oaks. Mrs. Goodwin looked around with appreciation. Who knew what issues the three of them had had in the past. Harper was just glad they seemed to be resolving them, for Bella's sake.

The girl was painting an enormous purple and pink butterfly on Bella's cheek. Harper stood next in line. Cameron circled the garden, seemingly delighted by what he saw. The swelling in her throat surprised her. How sorry she would be to leave all this. Her regret had nothing to do with the grandeur of the place and concerned just the people.

While she was turning that thought over in her mind, Lily and Esther Blodgett wandered into the garden. Catching Cameron's eye, Harper nodded to them and he walked toward them.

The butterfly on Harper's left cheek was almost finished. Seeing

her dad welcome his family, Bella pointed. "That's my gamma."
Her matter-of-fact acceptance surprised Harper. Cameron ambled
over with Lily and Esther.

"This is for you." Esther pushed the pink-wrapped gift toward
Bella.

"Heavy," Bella said, looking to her dad, who grabbed it.

"Why don't we sit down?" Cameron ushered them to one of
the benches.

"The birthday present's for you, Bella," Esther explained. "But,
well, it really is your father's too."

Lily wore a secretive smile.

"Why don't you open it?" Harper prodded Bella once they were
all seated. Didn't have to ask her twice. Bella's tiny fingers made
short work of the wrapping paper.

"For heaven's sake," Cameron muttered when he saw the heavy
crockery feeding dish with the alphabet stenciled around the wide
lip.

"We all used it," Lily explained. "All four kids. Cameron was
the only one of us who knew his ABCs by the time he outgrew the
bowl." She gave her brother a hug, and it warmed Harper's heart to
see the siblings together. The Blodgetts weren't the Kirkpatricks
but every family shared a unique history.

Bella tipped her head up to her dad. "Daddy, did you eat from
this dish when you were a little boy? Just like me?"

Cameron nodded. "Sure did. And I had to eat all my food.
Even the lima beans."

He must have seen Harper's expression because he stopped

right there. Bella was making so much progress. No need to mention the lima beans or okra story.

A clown was cooking hamburgers and hot dogs on the grill. The scent curled invitingly through the air, and more than one passerby peered in through the gate.

"Bella, why don't you show your grandmother and aunt where the food is, darlin'?" Cameron nodded toward the buffet table.

"We'd sure like that." Lily held out one hand. Bella hesitated just a second. Then she linked her hand with Lily's and the three of them trooped off across the grass.

"Your girls," Harper murmured. "Quite a trio. Want me to take that dish?"

"Before I break it?" he teased, handing over the childhood treasure. "I can't believe my mother kept this."

"Women can be sentimental." She clutched the heavy crockery to her chest, imagining the towheaded toddler eating from this bowl.

"Yeah, I guess. And I was the youngest, after all. Last child and biggest disappointment."

"How can you say that?" The bowl clanged against the wrought-iron bench when she set it down too fast. Darn thing was heavy. So were his words. "Look at everything you've accomplished."

Disbelief flared in his eyes. "You mean the house and everything that goes with it? Not the kind of thing my people value, Harper. We come from a farm, where the land is the thing that counts. That's how they look at it. Anyway, that doesn't matter. They're not the ones I want to impress."

Harper studied her green slides, flexing her pink-tipped toes and not trusting herself to look at him.

He sank onto the bench with a sigh. "I am plumb tuckered out."

She laughed, nudging the bowl over and settling next to him. "Said like a boy from Hazel Hurst."

"You got it." Linking his hands behind his head, Cameron smiled. When had she seen him this content? She wanted to lay her head on his broad chest, listen to the beat of his heart and never leave.

That thought brought her bolt upright.

"What? Did you get stung by one of those bees? I asked Jack to spray." His quick sweep of her body brought heat to her cheeks.

"Oh, no. I'm fine." She sat back, the wrought iron warm against her back.

One arm behind her, Cameron studied her through the dappled sunlight filtering through the tree overhead. The air felt heavy with unsaid words.

Uneasy, she pulled her attention back to the party. "This sure was the best prize at the Telfair Ball that evening."

"*You* were the prize that night. Reminded me I'm not that old."

"You're not?"

His burst of laughter made her cheeks flame. "I mean, I'm not sure. Just thought you were older."

"Really? You think of me that way? Great." Disappointment darkened his eyes. Reaching over, he tucked a wisp of hair behind her ear. The finger swiping from one hoop earring to her chin didn't seem like an accident. "I'll be thirty next year. Too old?"

Suddenly, things had become way too personal.

"Maybe we should get something to eat," she whispered.

He heaved a tight sigh. "If you say so."

Grabbing the dish, Harper leapt to her feet. "I'll just take this inside so it doesn't break." Her heart hammered against her ribs as she worked her way through the kids to the steps. Five minutes with Cameron and she just about forgot this was a children's birthday party.

She dashed inside the house so fast she nearly tripped. Stowed the dish on the counter and grabbed her breath before returning to the party. When it was time for the cake, Cameron lit the five blue candles. Bella was beside herself when he set it in front of her while everyone sang. Pipsqueak went crazy. All three grandparents sang, and it hit Harper that they'd never shared a birthday with their granddaughter. Chaos and confusion reigned but so did a lot of love. This was how birthdays always were at her house. Cameron glanced around with a look of satisfaction, and she was so happy for him. The opening of the gifts passed in a flurry of paper and laughter. Candace listed each gift on her notepad so that thank you notes could be sent.

After all the birthday guests had drifted through the back gate, Candace and her crew bundled up every burned candle and crumpled napkin and disappeared through the gate. The Goodwins hovered, clearly not eager to leave. With his mother and sister in tow, Cameron approached his in-laws. Not wanting any fireworks,

Harper was close on his tail.

"Thank y'all for coming," he said. "Bella really enjoyed it."

"We enjoyed it too," Lily said. "Right, Mom?"

"Sure did." Esther compressed her lips as if she had more to say, but Lily had her outspoken mother in hand.

"We could order pizza, if you'd like to stay," Cameron offered.

"Oh, good heavens, no," Linda Sue Goodwin piped up. "Don't want to overstay our welcome."

But Cameron didn't leave it there. "You're always welcome. I'm sure Bella would like to see more of you. Me too."

His efforts to heal their rift touched Harper's heart.

"Well, now. That would be real nice," Mr. Goodwin said. "Perhaps another time."

"Of course. Right." Cameron left the door open. Bella had come barreling from the corner of the yard, Pipsqueak hard on her heels. "Bye, Grandma. Grandpa." The words came easier now.

"We have to get on the road, too." Lily looked to her mother for agreement and took car keys from her purse.

"We thank you, son." Esther's words came slowly, almost begrudgingly, but Cameron's face cleared as if he recognized how difficult this was for his mother.

"I hope you'll come again, Mama."

Hands shaking and head down, Cameron's mother fussed with the buttons on her blouse. She didn't reveal her emotions easily.

For while, they played with Bella's gifts, but the birthday girl was exhausted. Harper had no trouble putting her to bed. Connie drifted home and Cameron disappeared upstairs. She heard his door close. But Harper wasn't ready to closet herself in her room just yet. Slipping into her sleep pants and top, she took a cup of decaf onto the back porch and sank onto the rattan loveseat. In her mind, the darkened garden still rang with Bella's birthday joy. Harper stowed happy memories from a day she'd always remember.

Her peace was short-lived. She felt Cameron in the doorway before she saw him.

"Mind if I join you?"

"Of course not."

He sat down with a sigh that reverberated in her chest, extending one arm behind her. "Great party, right?"

"The best. Bella loved it."

"So did I. This couldn't have happened except for you."

"Thank you."

Moonlight etched the planes of his face. Reaching over, he traced her cheek with a soft caress and she shivered. In the soft cotton, her breasts came to life. One touch. That's all it took. He was so very close. She felt so vulnerable. His tentative smile grew and she slid into his arms with amazing familiarity.

"Harper," he breathed kissing her closed eyelids. "I want you."

"I know." She burrowed into him, like she was Pipsqueak. His heart thudded against her cheek. A light beard rasped her forehead. She didn't care. "Oh Cameron." Her arms tightened around his neck with no remorse.

She wanted him. Now.

No turning back.

The kisses began where they'd left off at Winston House, lips open and tongues probing. He felt so good and tasted wonderful. Angling, Harper pushed into him, wanting to feel every angle. When he ran one hand up her body, she fell back and granted him access. No games. Not tonight. Not anymore.

She shivered when he nudged up her loose top, slowly circled one nipple with his tongue and then nipped with his teeth. Was that his groan or hers? She cupped his crazy curls, coaxing him for more. A damp rush told her she'd never felt this turned on. But this was more than sex, more than arousal.

At least, for her.

"Like the outfit," he murmured.

"My PJs." She gasped when he teased the skin under each breast with his tongue.

"Up late, are we?" One hand gentle behind her head, Cameron pulled her closer, dipping one hand under her waistband. His fingers sank into her wet warmth, triggering a tightness. "Maybe you should be in bed."

She tensed and opened, every nerve ending bucking to life. "Good idea."

Cameron took her chin in one hand. His eyes flipped from pilot light to burner blue. "Really?"

With a helpless quiver, she let herself fall limp into the hammock of his desire. Words wouldn't come but a nod did. Sliding her from his lap, Cameron took her hand. They soft-footed it through the house. Every time her mind raised a question, Harper shut it down. She would not overthink this.

She wanted to feel tonight, not think.

Upstairs, all was quiet. In seconds they were in his room and Cameron eased the door shut. Even Pipsqueak must be exhausted from the day.

"Lights?" he asked.

"No. Please. Just you."

With a smoky glance that made her toes curl, he flipped on the overhead fan and pulled her down onto the bed. "Now where were we?"

"You're the man with the blueprints, Mr. Bennett." She edged over on top of him, settling her knees on either side of his hips. His gaze holding hers, he stroked her calves. This wasn't the time to go slow. She might change her mind. With an impatient tug, Harper ripped off her top, dropping it to the floor. Smiling, she ran her hands up his shirt. "Too many clothes."

"My word, let's take our time."

"Let's not." Her fingers plucked at the damn shirt.

"All right then." A couple more clinging kisses and he slid her onto her side. His shirt and slacks disappeared. She felt so restless and way overdue. Like she'd been moving toward this moment since she first saw Cameron at the foot of the stairs that night. Felt like she was coming full circle and she inched his shorts off with great appreciation.

"Pleased, Ms. Kirkpatrick?"

"Test ride time, Mr. Bennett."

He cocked a brow. "Right now?"

"Right now." Call her a trollop, but she could not wait.

He opened the side drawer. She heard the tight snap. Harper welcomed his weight, loved the muscled thigh easing her legs open. With one easy slide, he filled her. Then he paused. In the darkness, his eyes glittered. "Harper?"

"Oh, Cameron. Please."

No words. They might not be the right ones.

She was good at that.

Instead, she gave a twitch of her hips.

Wonderful man that he was, Cameron began a rhythm slow and steady, a pace she could count on. So she climbed, enjoying the buildup. Loving his response, every grunt, every surge. She caressed, she coaxed, brought her nails down his back until she cupped him. He seemed to wait until he felt her tighten and shatter at that exquisite peak.

Oh, my. A southern gentleman in every way.

Then he flexed, grabbed her hips. Harper swallowed his groan with her own.

"Mustn't wake the children," she whispered seconds later, feeling the knot unwind but not the desire.

"Always so... so considerate," he panted, kissing her damp forehead. His body eased away but not his eyes, or his hands. "So bossy. And so sweet."

Words of love pulsed in her mind and pushed against her lips. But she didn't say them. Just shut her mind down.

Cameron filled the night with his lovemaking. Considering his profession, his creativity wasn't a total surprise. They tumbled from the bed to the chair. Stretched out on the floor and arched over the drafting board. His hands were, oh, so talented. Moonlight patterned his taut muscles through the mullioned windows.

Finally, when her thighs ached and her muscles were spent, he spooned his body around hers in bed and yanked the sheet up. Overhead, the palm fan moved in lazy circles. She'd never felt more treasured, never felt such comfort.

But he hadn't said anything. Not really.

Was she kidding herself? Again.

Would this be enough?

Before dawn, she slipped upstairs. Reality waited in her room. Harper ran one hand over her sore throat, where "I love you" was lodged tight.

Chapter 25

Lots of giggling going on upstairs. Cameron smiled just to hear Bella laugh with Pipsqueak yapping in the background. Harper's rich chuckles bubbled down the stairway.

But her silence had slammed him that morning in the kitchen. Harper wouldn't look at him, much less speak to him. Hope shrank to the size of a damn coffee bean. He decided to work but he could hardly stand to look at the drafting board and left for his office. Finally he'd drifted home way past their dinner hour. He wasn't hungry. After splashing some Maker's Mark over ice, Cameron carried his glass into the library.

Leaving his drink on the side table, Cameron walked over to the shelf that held the books he never had time to read. Bella's baby picture drew him, and he picked it up. She'd been such a tiny thing. They had all been so happy then.

But what did they really know at that age? He was in college and Tammy was still a child, spoiled by her parents. He didn't want Bella to ever grow up with that kind of entitlement.

Look how they'd ended up.

When she found Cameron studying his wife's picture, Harper knew she was doing the right thing. Maybe everybody had a picture of a past love tucked in a drawer or on a shelf, but that didn't bode well for a relationship. Staying here promised only heartbreak. Especially after last night. She shouldn't settle, wouldn't settle. Seeing Cameron poring over family pictures snapped her back to reality. But she wanted to leave the house and precious Bella on a good note.

She cleared her throat. "Cameron, could we talk?"

He jerked around, eyes guarded.

Harper's knees weakened, so she eased into a chair. Early evening shadows crept into the room. Eyes wary, Cameron picked up his drink and took a sip with quiet deliberation.

Here they were. Again. She'd changed so much since that interview.

"I'm giving my notice. I think I should do that, don't you?"

Another long sip. His eyes burned steely blue in a pale face she longed to cup in her palm. But he said nothing.

Her hair had fallen from the ponytail, and now she pushed it back. His eyes followed every move. "I just think I should." *Because I love you so darn much.*

"Don't suppose I could change your mind." His lips barely moved.

"No. No, I don't think so."

"Is this because of last night?"

"In a way." Thinking back brought a wave of searing heat. She was glad she was sitting down.

"What if I told you it would never happen again?"

"That isn't possible." Her heart clutched at the satisfaction that swept his features and was gone. Her love for him threatened to swamp her.

But *his* love was what she wanted. The rest would be meaningless without that.

Wouldn't it? Oh, how she was tempted. For a second she hesitated before slipping back into the rut of her decision.

He loosened a ragged sigh. "Can you wait until I find your replacement? That seems only fair," he threw in, almost as an afterthought.

"Yes, of course. How long might that take?"

His laugh held a bitter edge. "Usually not long. The salary is too good, and I suppose I'll have to raise it. Again."

She balled her hands against her stomach, glad she hadn't eaten much that day. "If you're trying to make me feel bad, you're succeeding."

His handsome features settled into that inscrutable expression he wore so well. "Sorry, Harper. I have no reason to make this painful for you. After all, you've done a great job with Bella. I'm grateful."

"Toughest challenge I ever faced." She couldn't help feeling proud. "You were wonderful with Bella and her eating problem. I don't think she would have reacted the same way with me."

"It's just a beginning. There's so much more to do." The bewildered shake of his head almost made her relent. She almost told him that of course she'd stay.

But she just couldn't. She settled before and knew she wanted more. Pushing up from the chair, she couldn't help looking at the family photos on the bookshelf. The three of them had been such a perfect family. "You must really miss her."

Following her eyes, Cameron drew closer and picked up the photo of his beautiful wife cuddling their newborn baby girl. The lump in Harper's throat felt bigger than Bella's entire birthday cake.

"Miss her?" His voice held an empty echo. "She was leaving me for someone else that night. We'd had a rough week with Bella. When the baby finally quieted down, I left Tammy drinking in the kitchen. Figured she'd earned it. But her note made it pretty clear. Someone was waiting. Drunk out of her mind, she ran the stop light at the junction leading to Hilton Head. The truck driver couldn't brake in time. Plowed right into her."

Harper's head hurt from not breathing. "Oh, Cameron. I am so sorry."

He set the photo back down. "I've never admitted that to anyone, although I think her mother suspected. A guy from my fraternity, no less."

"How could she desert beautiful little Bella?" *And you.*

"We were young and Tammy liked the good times. Bella cried a lot and Tammy just couldn't take it. Her parents never forgave me for what happened." Clearing his throat, Cameron looked mystified and almost embarrassed. "Now if you'll excuse me. Long day. Of course I'm happy to provide a reference."

Harper watched him leave, back ramrod straight. Cameron Bennett was a proud man, and she'd just dealt him a low blow. But this time she would look out for herself. This time she would not create a relationship that didn't really exist. She followed him upstairs, feeling so darn weary. Connie was just leaving Bella's room.

"Come and kiss me goodnight!" Bella called out.

Pushing the door wider, Harper went in to give Bella a kiss and hug.

Poor little thing. How Harper ached to give this little girl enough kisses to make up for every night her mother had been gone.

"I love you, Harper," Bella whispered against her neck.

"I love you too, sweetheart." How she longed to say those words to Cameron. Regret followed her up to her room, where she rocked in her chair until long after the lights came on along Victory Drive.

Sleep didn't come that night. McKenna had left a message on her phone. "What's this about you coming back to Chicago? Let's talk. Guess my question would be, is this really what you want?"

Harper had no answer. She didn't return McKenna's call.

Harper was disappointed when Cameron hadn't found another nanny by the time her own birthday rolled around. The job market must have improved. Not every girl would be as desperate as she'd been when Cameron hired her, able to move in and start immediately. Upstairs, she had everything packed and ready in the boxes she'd stowed in the attic four months earlier. The drawers were empty, her drafting board folded up.

The phone rang with her usual ringtone of pealing bells. When she answered, McKenna launched into a belated and raucous version of "Happy Birthday." So amazing that she could still laugh. For the past week, there'd been no grins or giggles. Thank goodness Cameron had decided not to tell Bella until the new nanny had accepted. This time he was interviewing candidates in his office. Probably a good decision. Harper didn't want to see them. Didn't want to think of them sleeping in this room.

"So what's the update?" her sister asked.

"No new nanny yet."

"Hey, you don't sound excited about coming back to Chicago. Are you positive that this is what you want?"

"I'm sure I will be when I get there. Adam has offered to drive me home."

"And you've sent out resumes?"

"Stop being such an older sister!"

"Fine, you can help me get Vanessa ready for *Eye of the Tiger*, that TV show I mentioned."

"Sounds good." Anything to keep her mind off what she was leaving behind.

Finally, they said goodbye. When Harper came downstairs, the mansion felt so empty without Bella and Pipsqueak. Connie had taken them both to the park. "No one should have to work on her birthday," she'd told Harper.

Harper was puttering around in the kitchen, licking the chocolate frosting from the bowl Connie had left on the counter. The smell alone was enough to start her salivating. Connie had made a spectacular three-tier cake, dark chocolate all the way through. If the frosting was any indication, the cake would taste yummy.

When the doorbell rang, Harper dropped the spoon back in the bowl with a clatter and headed for the front of the house.

But Cameron got there first. From his unruly blond curls to his Italian loafers, Cameron looked so handsome. Her heart hurt as she watched him open the door. The thought of a future without him opened an empty pocket where her heart used to be.

When she saw who waited outside, that pocket slammed shut.

"A visitor, Harper." Cameron's voice held a crisp edge.

She inched forward. "Billy?"

His tall profile was dark against the bright Savannah day, but there was no mistaking Billy's ponytail. Was that a bedroll in back of him on the porch? Her former boyfriend wasn't at all shy about walking right in.

"Adam told me where you were. Hey, girl, I'm your birthday present."

She ignored his open arms. Harper's mind was working, but her mouth wasn't.

"You can talk in the library, Harper, if you like." Cameron was looking at Billy as if an alien had dropped from the sky. "I'll be in the kitchen."

"Hey, thanks, dude." Head bobbing, Billy looked around. "Nice digs."

Stepping into the library, Harper waited for Billy to follow but she wasn't about to sit down. Having him in this room felt so wrong. She moved to the center of the red Oriental rug and stood there, feeling awkward.

"Looks like life's been treating you good, babe."

"I'm the nanny, Billy. What are you doing here?"

Billy rocked back on his heels. She could see the sophomore she'd fallen in love with—the rebellious hair, the rakish smile. But these weren't the blue eyes she loved.

"I'm back, Harper." His smile stretched too wide. "Hey, I thought you'd be happy."

"Back in Savannah?"

He shrugged. "Yeah I stopped by our place. Did you know some other couple's living there? I went to Adam's shop, and he told me where you were."

"That's nice, Billy. So you lost your job?"

A red flush flooded his face. "How'd you know?"

"Just a guess. Otherwise you wouldn't have returned."

"I missed Savannah. I mean, you."

Perfect. Harper had rehearsed this scene so often in her mind. The moment didn't feel as good as she'd thought it would. She just felt sorry for him. "It's over, Billy. Really over."

His complexion deepened, but he didn't look surprised. "It is, huh?"

"What we had was fun and felt good for those years, but, well, I've changed." *And you haven't.*

His shoulders slumped. "I'm really sorry, Harper. Guess I made a mess of things."

"You'll figure it out. You always do. Besides, if you hadn't done what you did…"

"You wouldn't have all this, right?" He pivoted on the heel of one battered boot.

"I'm the nanny. I don't *have* anything."

"Yeah, sure. I saw that guy." Billy's sad eyes dialed back to hers. "Saw how he looked at you."

"Bye, Billy."

"Right. Happy Birthday, anyway." He reached for her.

Revolted, she skirted him and made tracks for the front door, wrenching it open.

"See you around?"

"Maybe. Good luck, okay?" Then she did hug him. The guy just looked so sad, so clueless.

After all, she'd loved him. Once.

But he was the boy from her past.

And that love was nothing compared to what she felt for Cameron. She didn't know what the future held. But she wanted to explore it with a man.

One man. And if he didn't love her, well, he'd learn to. She had to believe that. Suddenly, Harper was willing to risk it all to be with him. She'd stay.

When she reached the kitchen, Cameron was standing at the window. Next to him on the counter stood her three-tiered chocolate birthday cake. "He's gone so soon?"

She sidled closer. "Not exactly the birthday present I was hoping for."

Cameron's eyes softened. She wanted to wrap that look around her like a quilt, but she'd settle for his arms. She loved how his lips tucked in at the corners when he smiled. Loved how they felt so soft at the start of a kiss, so darn demanding at the end. And his arms? So secure and comforting when he settled them around her.

"Can you pull your ad for a nanny?" she managed when her head stopped spinning.

"Never placed it."

That made her chuckle. "Oh, aren't you confident?"

"I've always believed in the future."

She touched her forehead to his. "Bella told me she loved me. I can't leave a little girl who loves me."

He pushed back. "What about the *man* who loves you?"

The sudden head rush made her giddy. But he wasn't getting off so easy. "You mean Jack has a crush on me?"

"*I* love you. You're the love of my life, Harper Kirkpatrick. How could you have any doubt?" His eyes turned to blue velvet.

"A girl likes to hear the words, Cameron."

He melted. "Oh, Harper. Sweetheart. I'm a southern boy. You know that. Takes a spell to get around to saying what we feel."

"I need it now."

Cameron's kiss was comfort. And it sure felt like she'd come home.

Took a while to breathe again. "So then, we're moving on from the past?"

"Absolutely."

Harper's eyes swerved to the counter. After all, it was her birthday. "I just came in here for the cake."

"Right, me too. I'm having a private party. Are you the

entertainment? I heard your kicks are spectacular."

"Cake later?"

"My thoughts exactly."

THE END

Her Favorite Mistake

Sometimes you make a mistake. Sometimes he's hard to forget. When Vanessa appears on *Eye of the Tiger*, a popular reality TV show, she isn't prepared to see her Vegas Hunky Hottie again. She desperately needs the Chicago Internet mogul's help, but he's the last man she wants back in her life.

Oh, Alex recognizes her all right. In Vegas four years ago, she'd called herself Vivien Leigh. They'd hit it off. While he was planning breakfast, the long-legged brunette had slipped out. More than a little ticked off when he sees her on the set of the TV show, he becomes Vanessa's mentor to help her ramp up Randall's Whipped Cream Cakes. Revenge can be sweet.

Then he gets to know her. Really know her. No way in hell does he want to be her favorite mistake. But he wasn't counting on her toddler stealing his heart. His skill with sand castles and cinnamon toast takes Vanessa by surprise. Can they create a future out of past mistakes?

Subtle, sexy love scenes. "Her Favorite Mistake" is part of the Windy City Romances series.

Her Favorite Honeymoon

Hard to keep your head on straight in Italy. Even harder to keep your heart. The wedding might be off for Amy Shaw, but the honeymoon? No way will she forfeit a week in Tuscany. Travel Chums pairs her up with Mallory. But Amy expects a woman, and the man from Savannah doesn't expect her surprise. From Rapallo to Venice, can they keep their pact for a platonic tour? So many temptations. So little time. They find lots of excuses to break the rules because there are lots of surprises along the way.

Fresh pesto in La Cinque Terra, peach bellinis in Venice—hard to put it behind, especially when her family shows up to keep them company. Mallory's first wife had misled him. Now he has the chance to observe a woman's family first-hand before he sweeps her off to Venice, just the two of them. Outrageous fun and tempting decisions for the Windy City girl taking .... her favorite honeymoon.

Her Favorite Hot Doc

One feisty midwife. One Hot Doc with a secret. One mission trip to Guatemala where there's no place to hide. McKenna Kirkpatrick presents a challenge for the head of her department when she joins Montclair Specialty Hospital. Ranked a Chicago Hot Doc, Logan Castle has a reason for supporting established protocols while McKenna pushes the envelope. She also likes to push his buttons. Thrown together on a department revamp, Hot Doc soon discovers that McKenna generates her own heat.

Has he ever met a woman this outrageous? Has she ever been this drawn to a colleague's bedside manner? They may have grown up on opposite sides of the L tracks on Chicago's West Side, but Logan's like the chocolates hidden in McKenna's desk, so very hard to resist. When her Hot Doc joins Midwives in Action for a summer mission trip to Guatemala, McKenna wonders if working together in the remote highlands of Central America will resolve their differences... or end the romance for the Windy City girl. *Her Favorite Hot Doc* is the third book in the Windy City Romance series.

About the Author

Barbara Lohr writes contemporary romance, both adult and new adult. A flair for fun and subtly sexy love scenes are her trademark. Her Windy City Romance series launched in 2013, featuring feisty women who take on hunky heroes and life's issues. Barbara lives in the Midwest and the South with her husband and a cat that insists he was Heathcliff in a former life.

For more information on the author and her work, or to sign up for her newsletter, please see:

www.BarbaraLohrAuthor.com

www.facebook.com/Barbaralohrauthor

www.twitter.com/BarbaraJLohr

Acknowledgements

Many thanks to Romance Writers of America and my two local groups, the Ohio Valley RWA and Central Ohio Fiction Writers. The loops and forums of writers who address writing and publishing issues are also invaluable to me. On a more personal level, Sandy Loyd and Marcia James, where would I be without your sage advice and senses of humor? I look forward to enjoying this journey together.

For my daughters, Kelly and Shannon, when we shared Judy Blume and Madeleine L'Engle together, we never saw what lay ahead. Keep those reading lamps on over your beds. I am thrilled to have your creative input. My grandchildren, Bo and Gianna, bring me such joy and will probably appear in quite a few of Mama B's novels. To my husband Ted, words aren't adequate to thank you for your love and support, especially when my computer crashes and you have to provide tech support. May we have many more wonderful years together that include trips to Leopold's for ice cream.